"Wwas still trying to make sense of seeing Angela's eyes in Christine. He didn't see them now, but still there was something incredibly familiar about her that went beyond a slight resemblance. Whatever it was, it gnawed at him.

He watched her standing tall, with shoulder-length blonde hair with reddish highlights and a body with soft curves and shoulders that swayed and danced, as if her favorite song was playing in her head. Every time she moved Dan felt as if he were being hypnotized. When she laid her eyes on him, they pulled him in. They were a powerful and alluring green that no artist could ever duplicate. Every time she blinked, they recharged with an electric sparkle that seemed to shoot right through him. When she smiled, he smiled. There was no avoiding it.

Angela's eyes were brown. Damn, what made me think of that?

"What are you looking at?" she asked. "It looks like you're looking right through me. Answer me. How's the coffee?"

"I'm sorry, I don't mean to stare," Dan replied nervously. "The coffee? It's the best ever." No matter how hard he tried, it was impossible to behave normally staring at a woman who looked so much like his late wife.

The Diner

by

Dean Michael Zadak

This is a work of fiction. Names, characters, places, and incidents are either the product of the author's imagination or are used fictitiously, and any resemblance to actual persons living or dead, business establishments, events, or locales, is entirely coincidental.

The Diner

COPYRIGHT © 2016 by Dean Michael Zadak

All rights reserved. No part of this book may be used or reproduced in any manner whatsoever without written permission of the author or The Wild Rose Press, Inc. except in the case of brief quotations embodied in critical articles or reviews.
Contact Information: info@thewildrosepress.com

Cover Art by *Debbie Taylor*

The Wild Rose Press, Inc.
PO Box 708
Adams Basin, NY 14410-0708
Visit us at www.thewildrosepress.com

Publishing History
First Black Rose Edition, 2016
Print ISBN 978-1-5092-0901-9
Digital ISBN 978-1-5092-0902-6

Published in the United States of America

Dedication

To my dad.
Every day I am touched and inspired by your spirit.

Prologue

"Buck, but what about Dan? After everything he's been through and now losing both parents like this. You should stay behind to help him," Adeline said, as her chest heaved and fell with each weary breath. Her hands shook as she clawed at the clasp on her purse to retrieve a tissue.

"Addy, we talked about this. It's the only way. Dan will see this through to the end. He's stronger than you think, and he's a fighter. He'll take care of everything."

She stared through the passenger side window mouthing words that she knew her husband couldn't hear. Over the last few weeks, she had spent countless hours alone thinking and praying, trying to convince herself that they were doing the right thing. She looked out the window to see the scenery transform from a still life painting into a blur. She was unable to find the courage to look at the speedometer and felt too ashamed to look at her husband given what they were about to do so she took inventory of her purse while trying to think of one last argument that would convince them to turn the truck around.

"And don't worry, there's nothing in your purse of any value," Buck insisted, placing his hand over hers in a vain attempt to quiet her trembling hands, but he couldn't linger there; at this speed he needed both hands on the wheel.

Addy pulled down the visor and flipped the cover on the mirror. Staring back at her was a person she barely recognized. Deep crevasses traversed her face and gone was the adventurous glint in her eyes. Now they said, "I'm tired." As she brushed the wispy gray hair from her face, she caught a glimpse of her skin that hung from bones as brittle as a single pane of glass.

Her arm fell in defeat across her lap. The cancer had won. The doctors said it was only a matter of weeks. Out of the corner of her eye, she caught a glimpse of Buck looking at her more than he was the road which meant they had slightly less than five minutes.

"How can you be sure? He doesn't even know anything about the diner and what it means to our friends or to the town," she said, breathing heavier after every word.

"He'll figure it out. Our boy doesn't have the patience for unanswered questions, and he certainly won't settle for keeping things the same. The diner will drive him crazy. So he'll look around. He'll find what I left him. There can be no more after us."

Addy nodded and dabbed her eyes. She turned to her husband and studied every detail and feature of his face. She had never been a religious person, so she really didn't know where they would be next, but knowing they wouldn't be trapped in Circle Lake, their home town, was comforting. Wherever it was, she wanted the last thing she cast her eyes upon to be the man she loved.

She reached over and folded her small hand around as much of his hand that she could hold. Buck dropped his hand off the wheel for a few seconds as the truck

The Diner

seemed to be glued to the road.

"Only a few more miles. Don't be afraid. We're doing the right thing."

"Why aren't you afraid?"

"I'm done being afraid. If only I had this kind of courage months, even years ago. But... Dan will take care of things. He's stronger than I am."

The next few minutes passed in silence. Everything that needed to be said had been talked through from every angle over tears, wishes, and might have beens.

The traffic light in the distance grew brighter. They were getting close.

"Close your eyes, Addy."

Buck hit the gas.

Addy couldn't. She stared straight ahead with one hand on her purse and the other in the hand of her husband.

Buck saw the huge elm tree in the distance. A quick look left and right. There was no cross traffic to complicate their plans. Speeding up kept the green light on his side, so he pressed the accelerator all the way to the floor.

The pickup truck flew across the payment like it was gliding on the wings of an angel. The motor hummed as the speedometer hit 105mph. Bottoming out slightly as it charged down the off ramp, the truck flew through the intersection and into the grass, never once veering off course. The tree grew larger before them.

Addy felt Buck's grip tighten around her hand. It was painful, but she didn't mind. She felt safer. She looked at her husband. His eyes were closed. Addy turned to see what her husband couldn't. She closed her eyes as a tear fell down her cheek.

She never heard the horrendous sound of crunching metal and smashing glass.

The darkness was replaced with white light.

Chapter 1

Like a pendulum in a grandfather clock, Dan Scheffelin swiveled back and forth on the corner stool at the counter staring blankly at the guests that wandered his parent's diner…his diner. It was the worst place to have a memorial service, but he knew, it was the only place. He thought coming home to the diner where he grew up in should feel more comfortable. Instead he felt uneasy, like he was a guest and not the owner.

Nervous energy got the better of him. He had to move. As he walked between the booths and tables, he felt like a guard walking a prison yard. All conversation seemed to cease as he approached a group of guests. A few sad eyes fell on him, while others secured their grips on their coffee cups. And it seemed that no one was without a cup of coffee. Oddly, nearly every cup was full. Those that weren't were quickly refilled from the carafe on the table. Some drank it black, some with the precision of a chemist, added sugar or stirred cream into it turning it from amber black to a silky, swirling caramel color. They all kept their cups close as if someone was about to snatch them away. Bewildered, Dan shook his head and started back for the relative safety of the counter stool.

On his way, he overheard Rob Sanders whisper, "Poor guy. He's had a brutal few weeks. First his wife gets killed, now his parents."

Dan stopped in his tracks wanting to hear what his dad's old friends had to say next.

"I don't know…it's hard to feel sorry for him. I mean, he's got more money than God," replied John McQueen sitting across from Rob.

"What does that have to do with anything? Don't you get it?"

"I'm just saying. You know, this food isn't bad," John added, stabbing at a healthy helping of beef tips and garlic mashed potatoes that littered his plate, while bits and pieces avoided his napkin and landed on his shirt. "But to be honest, I prefer Buck's grilled cheese. I sure hope he doesn't close this place."

Dan wasn't the only person to hear the comment. A quiet hum fell over the diner. He could feel everyone staring at him. Feeling like an actor who forgot his lines, he looked around the diner for a cue. Nothing. He cleared his throat.

"Thank you for coming, everyone. Let me know if you need anything."

Silence.

Dan fell heavy on the stool. It wasn't only the burden of making all the arrangements but the weight of so many eyes on him that got to him. Death had a way of making people stare just a little longer at the grieving. The eyes that cared most for him were nearly finished shedding the last of the tears for his wife Angela who died only a week before his parents. Now with the news of his parents' death, the tears began again, and his every move was scrutinized. He felt alone after Angela's death, but now he wondered what lonely was really going to feel like. After a deep,

The Diner

cleansing breath he acknowledged everyone in the diner with a nod. It was all he knew to do. Slowly everyone went back to their conversations and their coffee.

With his elbows resting on the counter behind him, Dan took the diner in. It was a far cry from Scheff's, the three-star Michelin-rated restaurant he and Angela had created. From Chicago to Miami, Washington, D.C., and as of last year, New York, and soon, Los Angeles, Scheff's was the perfect restaurant to spot celebrities, socialites, and political power brokers.

I wonder who comes here.

Dan looked out across the diner, and his eyes fell where he bet his dad's did routinely, on the two most frequent guests sitting at their usual table in the far corner. Even though he heard their comments earlier, watching Rob and John provided a much needed break from the depressing madness he had experienced to this point. Rob tugged at his outdated tie, while saying something to John, who apparently had no interest in listening. He was busy picking food off what Dan was certain was his best golf shirt. Rob fidgeted about and then sank deep into the worn, faded vinyl covered booth, massaging his arm against the window that was warmed by the hot July sun. He stared deep into his coffee. Dan wondered what was so interesting at the bottom of the cup. Hopefully it was clean. After a labored sip, Rob lowered the cup and glanced over at the table on his right. Dan recognized his wife, Barbara, sitting with some of the other wives. She was looking back at Rob. Dan marveled at how they held each other's gaze as if they'd never see the other again. Though they were well into their sixties, Dan figured they had plenty of time to keep sharing glances and

7

whatever else people that age share. Feeling better, Dan gave the other diner guests a good looking over; it seemed that no other couple possessed that quality. As a matter of fact, he didn't even see another couple talking to each other.

John McQueen sat back and ran both his hands through his hair, which now had thinned and faded from a broom thick, bright red in his younger days to a yellow, oaky color. Suddenly, John threw his arms into the air and then leaned across the table, inches from Rob's face. Dan half expected it. Though he couldn't hear exactly what they were saying, he knew they were arguing about something. As a kid, Dan recalled how nearly every Saturday morning they would gather to debate anything from fishing to the latest news from the auto assembly plant from which they both retired. Back then, their wives would sit alongside them and consider what book would be read next at book club or who would host the next quilting meeting. When it came to discussing what was going on in town, their conversation never got above a whisper, though Dan never knew why and could care even less. Though he could always tell when his dad was listening. There were times when Dan would be in the middle of making a burger or milkshake, and his dad would unexpectedly send him on his way. "That's enough, Daniel. Go play ball with the guys. It's too nice to be inside." Dan never had a chance to plead his case for staying around a bit longer. He was quickly ushered out the door. And as much as he enjoyed hanging around the diner and working the grill, Dan loved playing baseball and bumming around with his friends. Still he couldn't understand why he couldn't finish cooking the burger

The Diner

or pouring up the shake.

With a nostalgic smile on his face, Dan looked away from the old-timer's grudge match but couldn't find anything worth his interest. Everything looked and felt like a TV rerun and oddly eerie. Rocking side to side on the stool, he kept one leg poised to make a dash into the kitchen. The kitchen was and always had been his oasis away from the craziness in the dining room of any of his restaurants. However, the constant traffic of family friends, expressing their sympathies wouldn't allow for a clean getaway. Words were easy when they talked about his parents; somehow his parents dying in an auto accident outside of town was easier to talk about. Only a few could come up with meaningful condolences about the loss of his wife. No one really knew Angela, only what they had read about her in the papers. Most offered up, "And your poor wife…we couldn't believe what they were saying." The "they" was the TV and tabloid journalists. Family and friends found it difficult to process a death that was that highly publicized.

Each time he thought the last of the sympathies was expressed, another wave of his parents' friends lined up. Dan didn't recognize many of them. They always walked away before he could ask their name.

"Your dear parents, we miss them so. If you don't mind me asking, what are you going to do with the diner? You can't close it. No, you mustn't close it. And the coffee. You must keep serving this wonderful coffee. Oh, there are other places for coffee, of course, but it's just not the same. You know what we mean, don't you, Dan?" asked more than one person, in more than one way.

Dan wanted to scream, "I've lost my wife and my parents inside two weeks. Do you think I give a shit about where you get your coffee? Make your own damn coffee!" Instead, he nodded and said, "Everything will be fine."

He also couldn't understand why the fate of the diner was so important to the people of Circle Lake. Sure, it was the only place in town to eat. As a matter of fact, it was the only restaurant within twenty miles in either direction. Over time, a few restaurants had tried to make a go of it, but none could survive beyond six months. He recalled that the last attempt was three years ago. The place never opened. For some reason the owner gave up after the arduous licensing process, which struck Dan as ridiculous. He never once had an issue securing permits and licenses for any of his restaurants.

Another outburst from Rob and John grabbed his attention. Grateful for the distraction, Dan knew what would quiet the old-timers down. The timing was perfect with no guest approaching; Dan made a break for the kitchen. As he burst through the swinging kitchen doors, he stopped for a minute and stared at the desk stationed off to the side, out of the way of the mainstream kitchen traffic. His dad called the space his office. Instead of file cabinets and a credenza sitting behind the desk, there was heavy gauge wire shelving stocked with canned goods, spices, and paper products. The desk was a tarnished, gunmetal gray. It looked like it belonged in a factory or warehouse for the shift foreman to work from. Dan remembered how every now and then someone would rush in from the dining room and accidently run into the desk. It never moved.

Rather, they would bounce off it and limp away rubbing their leg. Not seeing his dad sitting there brought a lump to his throat. He'd have to go through the desk soon, since it held all the paperwork necessary to run the diner, but now was not the time.

Before heading to the grill, he surveyed the kitchen. A red concrete floor and white tiled ceiling that had yellowed from years of cooking were home to more stainless steel shelving and countertops, iron black appliances, and waist-high sinks that were in the same place they had always been. The kitchen could easily be reconfigured to accommodate an automatic dishwasher and modern appliances. He'd change it all too, that is, if he decided it needed to be changed. Besides, everyone knew their way around it, and it worked fine. He was anxious to put it to the test again.

"Is everything as it should be out there, Scheff?" asked Carlos Alvarez, a long time, trusted manager of the Scheff Restaurants. Carlos was there for every one of the Scheff's openings and was quick to volunteer and take care of all the details for Dan's parents' memorial service.

Dan noticed a few of the employees look up awaiting his response. He wondered what they heard. Whenever someone at his restaurant called him "Chef," he always heard "Scheff."

"Oh yeah. Great job by the way," Dan replied referring to the memorial dinner. He made his way behind the kitchen prepping counter and steam tables.

The employees from the diner and those that Carlos brought from Scheff's cleared a path for him.

"Relax everybody. Just keep doing your thing."

Dan looked left and right along the aisle in front of

the grill. Instinctively he reached up and grabbed a spatula hanging with a variety of other utensils. He could have found one blindfolded. Stationed by the grill, he tested the heat by waving his hand over it and decided it was too hot so he turned it down. He reached for the squirt bottle of clarified butter that his dad always kept on the shelf and with two slices of bread in one hand, he sprayed a stream of butter which quickly bubbled up. He threw the bread on the grill as if he were tossing a pair of horseshoes and moved them around like chess pieces to soak up the butter. Reaching behind, he opened a freezer drawer and took out a bag of French fries and put two handfuls into the fryer basket. He then retrieved the cheese, bacon, and tomatoes that were in the next drawer over as they had always been. As a matter of fact, everything in the kitchen was in the same place as it was when he left at age eighteen to study cooking abroad. He'd only been in the kitchen a handful of times in the last fifteen years, and that was only to help out when he visited his parents. His diner muscle memory came back to him in no time. The menu was simple and unchanged since he was a kid. Feeling the heat and the smell of the grill, he recalled the joy in making something so simple taste so good. He wondered if he may have lost that joy.

"Don't press on it," his dad would say. "No one likes a flat grilled cheese. Make it puffy. Make it light. Then they'll order two." And they usually did.

Dan brought the toasty goodness over to the cutting board. Everyone watched him as if he were a surgeon performing open heart surgery. He sliced the sandwich on the diagonal and placed it on a plate. Swirling around with efficiency and grace, he grabbed the basket of fries that were done to a perfect golden brown and dumped them into the warming tray. Again, without looking, he reached up and wrapped his hand around the salt shaker and seasoned the fries.

With the grilled cheese plated up, Dan walked from the kitchen to the dining room. He could feel the entire kitchen staff staring at him, except for Carlos. Carlos was busy counting serving trays.

"I am a chef, you know," Dan said with a smile. "And I still remember how to cook a few things," he added as he backed through the swinging kitchen doors.

"Here you go. I'm sure this is what you've been waiting for," Dan said as he set the plate down in front of a startled John.

"Gees, I just talked him down," Rob said, smiling. "And now you go and spoil him. You're just like your father."

Silence.

"I'm really sorry," Rob said.

"Oh, don't be. I'll take that as a compliment. No one indulged the two of you more than he did."

"We're truly sorry for your loss," Rob chimed. "We loved your parents. We love this place. And of course, we're so sorry to hear about Angela."

"This is great," John said, with a bunch of fries in his mouth. "Better than Bucks."

"Geezus, John," Rob exclaimed.

"Well, it is. I'm just sayin'. Dan, you're not gonna sell the diner, are ya? We need this place," John interrupted. "Whatever you do, don't sell it to Gardner," he carried on as his mouth continued to ignore any cues from his brain.

Rob rolled his eyes and looked up at the ceiling.

13

"Sorry. I have yet to find a way to put a muzzle on my old friend here. But please, whatever you do, don't sell this place to Gardner. That will never work."

"What?" Dan asked, caught completely off guard as his back stiffened. He hadn't thought of Ernest Gardner for years. When he was younger, all his dad's friends treated him as one of their own, patting him on the head and asking him about his day. Not Gardner, he gave him the creeps. All the kids were afraid of him. His dad must have known that because he would always rush Dan out of the diner anytime Gardner was expected to be in. Dan was grateful; however, the panic in his dad's voice always troubled him. As an adult, Gardner's name rarely came up, and it was always a whispering conversation between his parents. As soon as Dan showed the slightest bit of interest, the conversation ended as abruptly as it had started.

Before he could press John further, a brilliant flash of light above the entrance caught his eye, but it was nothing compared to the blanket of silence that fell over the dining room.

Chapter 2

Standing in an ethereal silhouette of light that was streaming in from the front door was a stately man. Dan figured he was roughly the same age as the other guests, probably in his mid-sixties. Age looked to be the only similarity. He was wearing a finely tailored suit with his gray hair cut perfectly, not a hair out of place. Even from a distance, Dan could make out the impeccably manicured hands as the light bounced off each finger tip. Below a razor-sharp crease in his pants, his shoes shone with equal brilliance. No one approached or came within ten feet of him as he surveyed the diner. On his right was a woman dressed so elegantly that she easily stood out from the rest of the ladies in the diner, who wore the best thing they could find at the local department store that matched their scuffed pumps and flats. Dan guessed that she was roughly the same age as the man. He admired how she carried her advanced years so beautifully. She wore makeup, but it wasn't painted on. It softened her face and made her glow somehow. Her brown hair accepted its graying accents perfectly. When most women would have had their hair colored, she wore her gray hair like a crown.

Though she was next to the man, she wasn't standing close to him. Instead, she was holding the hand of a young woman, probably in her mid-thirties.

At first glance, she looked hauntingly familiar to Dan, but he couldn't place her. Her face was expressionless as she looked around the diner.

"Dammit, he's here," John spit out. "Is that the new waitress with them?"

Dan didn't hear a word John said. He was immediately consumed with the memory of his dad chasing him from the diner before Gardner arrived.

Can't run away now, Dad. I have to face him.

"Dan, is there something bothering you?" Rob asked.

"Huh. No, sorry. Enjoy the sandwich. Talk to you guys later," Dan said, without looking at them. His eyes were now locked on the three new guests.

Before Dan could make it all the way over to greet the couple, a woman grabbed his arm. Dan didn't recognize her.

"Excuse me, Dan. I didn't mean to eavesdrop, but what did you say you were going to do with the diner?"

A dozen or so people turned their head to listen in, while the others looked at the young lady with the Gardners.

"I didn't say. Thank you for coming. Now if you'll excuse me."

"But, Dan, we need to know. We deserve to know," the woman cried out.

"I'm sure you'll find everything will be to your liking. Again, thank you for coming. If you'll excuse me, I must greet my new guests," Dan replied, confused by the woman's outburst. Shaking it off as best he could, he walked toward the entrance.

"Mr. Gardner, isn't it?" Dan said, extending his hand. "Thank you for coming."

The Diner

"Think nothing of it, Daniel. We're sorry for your loss. And please, call me Ernest. I don't believe you've met my wife, Dorothy. And of course this is Christine Connor, she started here a few days ago. Your father asked me to help him find a waitress to help out around here. I think for today we'll have her greet the guests, don't you?" Gardner said more than asked. "Dorothy, why don't you escort Christine near the entrance, perhaps behind the cash register? That will work out perfectly."

Dorothy feigned a smile and led Christine to her station.

"Sure. That's fine. I'm sure my father had his reasons," Dan replied, blinking his eyes and shaking his head. If his dad felt the diner needed more help, then so be it. Having his own restaurants, he knew how hard it was to keep a good staff.

"Indeed he did. I'm sure Miss Christine will become a welcome permanent fixture here. Again, we are sorry for your loss. Everyone in town feels it. It's not what we expected or needed, I assure you. If only your father had...I'm sorry, I digress. One more thing, you need not answer anyone's questions regarding our diner. Are we clear, Daniel?"

"It's Dan," Dan replied, shaking the cold from his hands that lingered from the handshake with Gardner. Hearing "Daniel" cut him to the bone. The only people he tolerated calling him Daniel were his parents and Angela, because they always said it with love. When anyone else said it, it made him feel like he was being reprimanded. Dan turned back to face Gardner. "And Mr. Gardner, anyone can ask anything they want of me. It doesn't mean I have to answer."

17

"I see. Now I'm sure you have other guests to attend to, so we'll let you be. We'll talk soon." Before joining Dorothy and Christine, Gardner went about greeting each guest as if they were there to see him.

That son of a bitch...he's walking around here like he owns the place.

Feeling dismissed, Dan decided to check on his father's friends. At least they made him feel welcome and at home.

"How are you two doing?" Dan asked.

"We're good. Especially him," Rob said pointing to John who was devouring the grilled cheese sandwich and French fries. "And don't worry about us, just keep your eye on him," Rob continued, nodding in the direction of Gardner.

"Yeah. Thanks, Danny. That was delicious," John said, looking at Gardner who was now talking with Christine and Dorothy. "Gees, you know what? That new girl looks like Angela."

"Geezus, John," Rob exclaimed, as he turned to look at Christine.

Dan looked around to see the heads of the guests turn like falling dominos toward the front of the diner. They were looking at Christine sitting behind the register collecting sympathy cards and then directing the guests to the buffet. The guests' eyes seemed to linger longer on her than Dan thought they should. It was as if they were studying her, cocking their head from one side to the other as if they were trying to remember her name. Every couple walked away whispering. Then one or both would look back at Christine and smile.

Christine glanced over at Dan with a warm smile.

The Diner

They stood looking at each other for longer than it takes to say "Hi." Self-consciousness got the better of them. Dan didn't know what to make of it. She winked at him and smiled. An eerie chill ran up his spine. In that split second, Christine looked like his late wife with her shoulder-length blonde hair and soft eyes that often said more than any words could. Roughly the same height at five feet seven, Christine was more softly shaped while Angela had a taut, runner's body. Still, from behind, they could easily be mistaken for the other. From the front, the differences were only slightly more pronounced. Angela had glamorous beauty. She was always extremely well put together, her hair looking like she just left the salon, with impeccable makeup, manicured nails, and jewelry to accent even her lounge wear. She could afford that type of treatment. Dan was certain Christine couldn't, otherwise she wouldn't be working here. Her hair wasn't styled; it was simply cut and brushed. Her face wasn't masked in makeup. And her hands looked soft, with nails worn and dull.

"Hey, Danny. John didn't mean anything," Rob said.

"I'm good, guys. Don't worry. I got this."

"I wish your father had," John muttered, as Rob stared him down.

"What was that?" Dan asked.

"Ignore him," Rob said. "We'd just like to see this place stay open, that's all."

After a head nod and a deep sigh, Dan walked back to the counter stool, occasionally glancing over at Christine, who was busy attending to the guests that were coming and going. Dan tried to distract his mind from the lingering effects of all the talk of death with

19

the mourners by losing himself in the diner. The place looked like it was trapped in a time warp. Many of the new nostalgic diners sported bright, colorful lights, white porcelain tiles, and chrome fixtures, while his diner suffered from tired furnishings, dull lighting and walls in desperate need for a fresh coat of paint. The dark, pinewood chairs were covered in scratches and dried food and would need to be replaced. The chairs were staggered around wood-grained Formica tables, many of which were badly chipped and repaired with duct tape, the same duct tape used to repair the high traffic areas of the carpet.

How no one has tripped and killed themselves is a miracle. There is no way that could be cleaned properly. I should have replaced the carpet for them long ago.

Looking at the white walls, which had faded into an unappetizing yellow, Dan contemplated what color he'd repaint them. Nearly every inch of the walls was covered with photos, pictures, and framed newspapers that, in a way, chronicled the history of the diner and Circle Lake. It occurred to Dan that he had never really looked at them, he only saw them.

Despite being home to so many memories, Dan's restaurant instincts told him that the whole place needed a makeover; it needed to be refreshed. That was if and when he did anything with the place. Still it looked better than half the places he was use to seeing in any city. The place was worn but clean, a credit to the employees. The pride in their work was obvious.

"You have a nice place here, Buck," he said under his breath. "I miss you."

Dan spun around and stared at the wall behind the

counter which was lined with cups, coffeemakers, a soft drink dispenser, condiments, and other service items. His attention turned back to the two coffeemakers that looked like something out of a Depression era movie. The chrome and polished brass reflected every ounce of light in the place causing a halo effect around them.

We'll keep those.

As a kid he had a blast working behind the counter. He'd make ice cream floats for him and his friends. He even invented a few new flavor concoctions to the delight of his mother. She would tell him that he made the best ice cream drinks, but his dad never allowed them on the menu. Didn't matter, he got to enjoy them. Dan was about to jump behind the counter and recreate one when Mae Walden, a very close friend of his mother, walked over with her husband and touched Dan on the shoulder. Dan nearly fell off the stool.

"I'm so sorry to startle you, dear. I had to tell you that we'll miss Addy and Buck. Such good people and good, good friends. This must be so difficult on you. Us too, we hardly ever attend a…I can't remember the last…anyway," Mae stammered, paused and then swabbed a tear with a tissue pulled from her purse.

"Attend what? Remember what?"

"Nothing, sweetie. It's so sad…you know. I was wondering. No. Now is not the time."

"Thank you," Dan replied. He was pleasantly surprised to see that Mae had a companion now. The man looked vaguely familiar, and Dan wondered if he was someone from town. Dan didn't remember when exactly, but some time ago her husband Milt had suffered a heart attack and then come down with pneumonia. As he recalled, it was the pneumonia that killed him.

Milt and his dad were best friends. He had worked over at the auto assembly plant as a foreman from the day it opened. Milt even tried to convince Buck to come work at the plant, but Buck was happy working for himself. Not Milt, he always worked for someone else. If he wasn't taking orders from someone at the plant, he was taking them at home. Mae constantly bossed him around. As a result, Milt hung out at the diner religiously, not in the dining room, but in the kitchen tinkering with the appliances. He was the one who kept all the ovens, stoves, and refrigerators working for so long.

"I'm sorry," Dan said extending his hand out to the gentleman, "we haven't had a chance to meet."

"What are you talking about, Dan? This is Milt, my husband. You remember Milt," Mae said, turning her gaze toward her husband who stood there seemingly uninterested in anything. "Milt?" she said, taking him by the hand.

"Hey there, Danny boy," Milt said, coming to life. It was as if Mae threw a switch and turned him on. "You still got that Mustang? Remember how that transmission gave us fits? We rebuilt her three times, but then she cruised. Great car. Be happy to tune her up if she needs it. Gees, we had it humming, didn't we? I'll come by and check on it. What a shame bout your parents. So what are you doing now?"

"Honey, you know that Dan has a restaurant in the city," she said as her eyes locked onto Milt with a penetrating stare. "He forgets things from time to time," she said turning back to Dan. "We'll be leaving soon, so if we don't see you later, please let us know if you

The Diner

need anything. And I trust you'll do the right thing about keeping the diner open. Come along, Milt. We need to pick up our dry cleaning."

Before they turned and walked away, Milt's face went blank as if every thought had been vacuumed from his head.

Dan stood stunned. As a kid, Dan was afraid of Mae. Not only did she order Milt around, but she ordered everyone.

"I trust you'll do the right thing with the diner." *She hasn't changed a bit.*

Seeing Milt, a shell of his former self, saddened him. He was certain Milt had died. Yet, Milt was the only one who helped him work on his '67 Mustang. They had to rebuild the transmission three times; no one else knew that, not even his father. Dan recalled how Mae had made a big stink about Milt spending so much time on the car, complaining that he worked on cars all day long, "Why would you want to work on them in your spare time?"

As Dan was reflecting on his memories of Milt, the door to the diner flew open. An elderly gentleman burst in and stopped abruptly and looked around. Dan was certain he was looking for someone and assumed it was him. Dan walked over, but the man shuffled past him and headed directly toward Ernest Gardner who was sitting at the booth nearest the entrance.

"I'm not doing it," the man said sharply. "It's not what Helen or I want."

The diner turned silent as everyone turned to witness the exchange.

"Mr. Harper, we've been through this. The arrangements have all been made."

"You can't do this," the man said as he pounded his fist on the table.

"Oh but I can," Gardner replied as he gripped the man's forearm.

"Is there a problem?" Dan said, seeing the look of pure terror on the man's face as he grimaced in pain. Dan looked down at Gardner whose face looked distorted. For a moment, Gardner's flesh was ashen gray, but the color quickly returned. Dan decided it had to be a result of the outdated fluorescent lighting.

"This is none of your concern, Daniel. Lloyd Harper and I recently entered into a business arrangement. Isn't that right, Mr. Harper?" Gardner replied.

"Uh-huh," Lloyd Harper said pulling his arm free. "Sorry to hear about your parents, Dan. Maybe they had the right idea all along.

Lloyd Harper bounced off the bench seat and then stumbled out the door.

"Ignore him, Daniel. He's been through a lot. Despite what you witnessed, I am helping Mr. Harper through this difficult time. I can do the same for you."

"Thank you, but I'm fine," Dan replied, ready to return his stool. He would have except that Gardner was no longer looking at him. He was looking around him. Dan turned around to see Dorothy slowly releasing Christine's hand.

Dorothy turned toward Dan with black hollow eyes that sent shivers coursing through his entire body. She smiled, but it wasn't one filled with warmth. It was cold, and with purpose.

He looked at Christine.

Her head turned slowly toward him as Dorothy

The Diner

backed away. Christine's eyes were shut. When she opened them, his knees buckled as he stared into the eyes of his dead wife.

Chapter 3

"This has to stop. Death is not an option. Apparently, I have not made that point clear enough. Buck and Addy will be the last. Look at what their decision has led to. Now Lloyd Harper...can you believe it? Lloyd Harper is standing up to me. To me, Ernest Gardner..."

"You must channel your inner strength, not this human portrayal of fear and anger," Dorothy replied.

"I am not afraid," Gardner replied. After a deep sigh, he sat back in the booth and continued. "Yes, I am angry. I will send another message."

"No more death."

"No more death, my dear," Gardner replied as he looked around the diner and settled on Christine who was busy working behind the cash register. "It appears that your efforts are beginning to take effect."

"It's more than effort, Ernest," Dorothy replied sternly. "I was not expecting to handle a fourth client. It has always been three or less."

"Yes. Yes. However, this was unavoidable and of course, necessary. I promise you that the others will not tax you too much."

"See to it and peacefully. Don't forget. The more energy I expend, the less I have for you."

"Understood. We will be successful. Just look at her. Proof once again that the network I have created delivers the perfect specimens."

"She is special. Time will tell if she is perfect."

"Time is a luxury we don't have," Gardner said, pounding his fist on the table. "There is too much at stake. If my business is to continue to grow, I can't afford her to be anything less than perfect. You must succeed."

Dorothy didn't respond. Instead, the white from her eyes disappeared as her pupils grew turning her eyes completely obsidian black. Her shoulders shuddered as her head waved subtly back and forth.

Gardner did his best to swallow.

"My dear Dorothy. I am sorry for my outburst. Please before anyone notices. I cannot handle more pain."

Dorothy shoulders relaxed as her eyes returned to normal.

"Pour the coffee, Ernest," she said, as she looked over at Christine.

Chapter 4

Dan's face fell into his hands. Sweat was streaming from every pore. He did his best to convince himself that he was just tired and what he saw was all in his imagination. Still his hands remained glued to his face as his heart nearly beat through his chest. If he didn't pull himself together now, he feared he might never be able to. After a deep breath, he brushed the hair from his face, hopped up on the stool, and spun around to face the back of the diner.

"When you get that look on your face, I always know it means you could use a cup of coffee."

"Huh?"

What is she talking about, "When I get what look on my face?"

"Yeah, that would be great," Dan replied, doing the best to hide the anxiety in his voice and looking up to see Christine with her back to him fixing a cup of coffee.

"You know I make the best coffee out of anyone here," she said, smiling. "That's what brings them here."

"Is that right?" Dan replied, twisting back around to see if Gardner was still watching him. He wasn't. Instead, he was involved in a deep conversation with his wife.

"Well?" she pressed.

The Diner

"Well, what?" Dan said, thrown off guard. He was still trying to make sense of seeing Angela's eyes in Christine. He didn't see them now, but still there was something incredibly familiar about her that went beyond a slight resemblance. Whatever it was, it gnawed at him.

He watched her standing tall, with shoulder-length blonde hair with reddish highlights and a body with soft curves and shoulders that swayed and danced, as if her favorite song was playing in her head. Every time she moved Dan felt as if he were being hypnotized. When she laid her eyes on him, they pulled him in. They were a powerful and alluring green that no artist could ever duplicate. Every time she blinked, they recharged with an electric sparkle that seemed to shoot right through him. When she smiled, he smiled. There was no avoiding it.

Angela's eyes were brown. Damn, what made me think of that?

"What are you looking at?" she asked. "It looks like you're looking right through me. Answer me. How's the coffee?"

"I'm sorry, I don't mean to stare," Dan replied nervously. "The coffee? It's the best ever." No matter how hard he tried, it was impossible to behave normally staring at a woman who looked so much like his late wife. There were differences too. Angela had an athletic body, mainly as a result of the Hollywood trainers that punished her into top photographic condition. It wouldn't do for her to look tired and out of shape. She was the face of the Scheffelin restaurant empire. Christine didn't have a runner's body; she had a woman's body. A working woman's body. A mom's body.

A nice body.

"No, it's not. It's just coffee, though don't say that to anyone around here. They'll argue the point to death. I mean, I've only been here a few days, but they do love the coffee," she said with both elbows on the counter, leaning in and stretching her back giving Dan a full dose of green eyes.

"The back is the first to go when you're standing on your feet all day," Dan said feeling the need to say something while he closed his eyes and stretched. He could no longer look straight into her eyes, afraid he'd never be able to look away.

"I'm not kidding, this is the best coffee I've ever had. Better than anything I serve in any of my restaurants. You're right, this must be why everyone comes here and why no other restaurant can make it around here," he teased back.

"Truthfully I didn't even make it. Oh well, I guess I better start cleaning up," she said, reaching for a bus tray.

"Hang on. Wait until everyone leaves. And thanks for staying to help," he said with a smile. "And what's a guy gotta do to get a refill?"

Christine topped off his cup. "Oh wait, you take cream."

How does she know that?

"I need to ask you. Have we have ever met before? Have you ever been to any of my restaurants? You look familiar," Dan asked, as curiosity got the better of him.

"I know what you mean. I feel like I've met you before too. Weird, right? I've only been to the city once. And I was six at the time. My aunt took me there

The Diner

to see a play. I've barely been out of Richfield. I still
live there with my parents and my four-year-old son,
Charlie. He's why I'm here, though it takes me awhile
to get here, but so what."

"What do you mean, 'He's why you're here'?"

"I can't live with my folks forever. I'm not
married. And I intend to show Charlie just how
awesome his mom is. This job is my start."

"But why here? I mean, how did you end up here?
Gees, that didn't come out right. And hey, it's none of
my business. You're here."

"Believe me; I'm happy to be here. I'm just glad
that the people keep coming back and drinking the
coffee. This place is always busy. It's crazy that there's
not another restaurant around for miles, but thankfully
it's here. I mean, I applied at a bunch of places in
Richfield. I never even applied here. I never thought to.
To be honest, I was getting really discouraged. No one
was interested in me. Then the Monday before last I got
a call to show up here for work. I remember it like it
was yesterday."

Dan shuddered.

The day after Angela's service.

"Yeah, I'm glad it all worked out for you," Dan
replied still a bit shocked at the timing.

The air hung around them for what felt like hours,
but it was only seconds. Feeling like the room was
closing in and having run out of things to say, Dan
turned around toward the dining room to see Dorothy
Gardner whispering to her husband. Gardner nodded,
winked, and then smiled at Dan. He then took his wife
by the arm and started walking over.

"Well, we'll be going." Gardner's booming voice

31

shook Dan. He saw Christine quiver as well.

"I'm sure we'll be talking about our diner and how you'll be doing the right thing for these people and this town. Maybe even tomorrow," Earnest Gardner said, as Dorothy quickly huddled next to Christine, wrapping her hands around Christine's. "Again, we're both sorry for the loss of your parents. Is everything in order, Dorothy?"

Dorothy didn't say a word; she finished speaking to Christine and slowly released her hand. Christine said nothing. She looked straight out through the diner windows. Gardner took his wife's hand.

Shaking his head, Dan closed his eyes tightly doing his best not to jump all over what Gardner had said. He felt like the words had punched him hard in the face. Calling it "our diner" and "you'll be doing the right thing" echoed in his head. When he finally erased the words from his mind, he looked up to see the Gardners walking toward the door.

A quick burst of light flashed when they stepped through the doorway. It was the same flash of light he'd seen earlier when Milt and Mae walked out. He thought it had to be a faulty ballast in the fluorescent ceiling light fixture, figuring the opening and closing of the door shook it loose. He looked over at Christine, who was now tracing Gardner's steps all way past the windows of the diner.

"Wow. I don't know what to think about that guy," Dan stated. "Christine, is there something wrong?"

With her eyes still staring off into the distance, she replied, "That's the guy that called me and told me to show up for work."

Chapter 5

The last of the guests left around 4:00 p.m. Outside, a few of them loitered and stared through the windows straight into the diner as if they had left something behind. With twice the staff, the diner was cleaned in no time. Dan helped out where he could, but he was moving too slow and getting in everyone's way. Unlike working the grill, the muscle memory of cleaning and closing the diner wasn't as sharp. He was distracted by too many memories and the eerie and oppressive feeling left behind by Ernest and Dorothy Gardner.

And why would Gardner call Christine to work here?

He couldn't dislodge the question from his mind. He didn't ask Christine any more about it, concluding that she had told him all she knew. And the last thing she needed was to be peppered by a bunch of questions, of that he was certain.

With the diner closed for the evening, the staff started milling about the counter as Dan took his place on what was becoming his favorite stool. Seconds later the Scheff's restaurant team came out to join them led by Carlos.

"Well crew, is everything as it should be? Cleaned and put away?" Carlos asked of the Scheff's team.

They all nodded in unison.

We're good here, Scheff," Carlos said to Dan. "Where are we tomorrow?"

Dan looked at Carlos and then at the eyes of the diner employees. They were the saddest scared seven faces that he had ever seen. In addition to Ray, the former military cook who was hired to give Buck a break now and then, there was Evelyn who would celebrate thirty years at the diner later this summer provided it stayed open. The other waitresses were Rosie Bitner and Molly Winkler. They both had more than fifteen years of service. As it was, they were now splitting shifts and tips with Christine, but it was still better than no job at all. Both of them were in their sixties and as Dan saw it, they had to work, since their husbands no longer did. Standing with his hands jammed in his front pockets was James, an eighteen-year-old who worked part-time in the kitchen. Buck said he could be a good cook someday if someone took the time to train him. Finally, there was Mindy, the sixteen-year-old bus girl. She wanted to work. She was saving for a car.

"Ray, see you tomorrow morning?" Evelyn asked. "I'm tired and need to get off my feet. Dan, I'm sorry for your loss, dear."

"Just a minute, Ev," Ray replied.

Dan looked back at Ray and then to the others. He knew, without the diner, they had nothing to go to tomorrow.

"Scheff, what are you thinking?" asked Carlos.

"Huh? Yeah," Dan said, coming around slowly.

"Tomorrow? What's the plan?" Carlos asked.

Out of the corner of his eye, Dan saw a few people loitering about outside. He turned his attention back to the inside of the diner. It was where his whole cooking life had started. Though lately at thirty-nine, he felt like his life was over. But now sitting in the restaurant his family created and spent most of their waking hours in, he felt like he was on the verge of a new beginning.

"You know what; I'm going to hang back here for awhile," he said.

There was more than just the pull of the diner nagging at him. Something was going on with the town, the people, and the diner he grew up in. No one wanted the diner closed, they protected the coffee like it was gold, and Gardner walked around like he owned the town and the diner. "We'll be talking about our diner…" *Our diner. No fucking way. Who the hell do you think you are?*

"The team from Scheff's head back. I'll call Stein," Dan said, referring to Scott Stein, the general manager of all the Scheff's Restaurants. "Carlos, how do you feel about running a diner?"

Carlos had been with Dan since the very first Scheff's restaurant opened. Dan relied on Carlos explicitly. Carlos smiled and nodded. He never spoke much.

"Of course. We will be opening tomorrow. What time did you say, Ray?" Carlos asked.

"I didn't," Ray replied and by the expression on his face and relaxed shoulders, he was relieved.

"Scheff, we'll see you when you get here. Everyone else, follow me into the kitchen and we'll work out a schedule," Carlos commanded.

Dan walked over to hold open the diner door and thank the Scheff's team as they left. He waited for the ceiling light to flash, but nothing happened. As he walked outside, he felt like he was walking into a press conference. A handful of people from town were milling about.

"Don't worry, folks. The diner will be open tomorrow," Dan stated above the murmur of the crowd.

Walking back in, Dan glanced at the ceiling as the door closed. No flash.

Huh. That's weird.

Inside, the staff stood still for a moment as Carlos walked into the kitchen. All eyes were on Dan.

"Relax," Dan said, seeing the tension on all their faces. He smiled. "Everything will work out fine. You heard him. If you want to work tomorrow, then you better get in there. He's in charge now."

Christine was the last to enter the kitchen. She stopped and looked at Dan.

"Is there something else bothering you?" she asked. "Would you like more coffee?"

"No. I'm good."

She stared at him with unfamiliar, familiar green eyes. He couldn't see anything else but her eyes.

"What are you thinking?" she asked.

"Nothing. Why, what are you thinking?"

"I have this Tom Waits' song in my head. He said it best. 'Life is so different than it is in your dreams.' Seems so true, right now. I wonder with all you've accomplished, what are your dreams like?"

"I don't know. No one ever asked me before."

"They must be about being famous and opening restaurants around the world," she replied and walked into the kitchen.

He knew one thing; he never had dreams like that. Every dream he ever had felt empty right now.

The Diner

Swiveling around on the stool he was finally alone in the dining room. It was the first time ever. It was quiet.

A diner should never be quiet.

He got up to straighten a few chairs and inspect the place, not because he had to, but it was something his father always did before he closed up. That chore was now his. Everything was perfect, every salt and pepper shaker filled. And every table was polished clean and complete with menus and a full supply of napkins.

Gees, these tables are ugly. I'll have to order new ones.

Someone outside caught his attention. It was Milt Walden, with his face and hands pressed against the window. Dan went outside to see what he wanted.

"Something I can do for you, Milt?" Dan asked, admiring how desolate but still homey the town felt in the early evening.

Milt ignored him. He continued to stare into the restaurant. Dan looked in and saw nothing.

"What do you see, Milt?"

"It's not me in there. I gotta go. It's not me in there." He looked back at Dan.

Dan could see that it clearly wasn't Milt, at least not the Milt Walden he remembered as a kid.

"What do you mean?"

Milt didn't stay to answer. He turned briskly around and broke into a light jog and ran around the corner and out of sight.

This town needs another restaurant just for the nuts to go to.

Before going back inside, Dan looked through the window to see what might have caught Milt's attention, but all he saw was memories.

Chapter 6

Looking out of the front door of the diner, Dan noticed how the small town of Circle Lake did its best to stretch out of sight to his right and left. There wasn't much to it. It was clear that when night fell, it fell hard on this town. "They say New York is the city that never sleeps; well this town turns in just as the sun sets," he said to no one. He had his hand on the lock. The sign in the door already said Closed. All it would take was two full turns and the diner would be done for the evening. Turning it was hard. Not because it was rusted or old, which it was, but it felt like lately all he had been doing was shutting and locking the doors on his life. With the loss of Angela and his parents, he had experienced too many closures. He had openings, if you count the restaurants he opened. But it was more than that. He felt like his life was void of any new beginnings.

"It's just a lock on the door," he said to himself.

Voices from the kitchen caught his attention. They were happy and relieved voices which brought a smile to his face. Done looking for more metaphors and symbols, Dan turned the lock shut.

"We'll open again tomorrow."

He flipped the lights off and dashed into the kitchen as most of the staff was parading out through the back door.

"See you tomorrow, Daniel," Christine said.

The Diner

Once again, hearing "Daniel" cut right through him—not in pain, but right to his heart. He felt the love.

It can't be.

He wanted her to repeat it thinking her voice sounded different.

I must be hearing things.

He rubbed his eyes.

"Are you going to be all right on your own?" Christine asked, her eyes smiling at Dan, knocking him off balance again.

"Yeah, I'll be fine," he replied, after a heavy sigh. "Do you need a ride? I can…"

"No, thanks. I have my own car. And Carlos was sweet enough to put me on in the afternoon so I can take care of Charlie in the morning. This just might work out."

"I hope it does," he said, barely above a whisper, as Christine walked toward the door.

She stopped just before taking a step outside. "G'night, Daniel," she said, with a hint of laughter.

Dan didn't respond. The words wouldn't come out. He could barely breathe. The familiarity of her voice, the way she said "G'night, Daniel." He replayed her voice in his head. If he could have mustered the energy to form the words, what would have come was, "G'night, Angela." Somehow he caught himself.

The diner door closed shut with a bang. He was alone. He raced over to lock the door. Tears had fallen before but never this hard. With his back to the door, he slid down to the floor and let it all out. The loss of his family flowed. Except for him in the diner, nothing was locked inside anymore.

Dan could hear the last car pull away through the

thin metal door. It brought him around, but he was in no hurry to get up. The only place to go was home. Not his home, but his parents' house. Heading back to the city was an option, but not a good one. He and Angela owned a $1.5 million dollar condo on the Chicago lakefront. They'd talked of buying a house, but with their hectic schedules and not having kids, they never felt the urgency to make the move. Angela always said, "We have more important things to do. Besides, our place is beautiful." And it was too, having been featured in a Chicago architecture and design magazine, another Angela public relations coup. Still it was a condo. Not a home. Dan needed and now wanted to go home, to his childhood home.

He pulled himself up and took another look around the kitchen. Catching a glimpse of himself in the glass door of the refrigerator shook him. He barely recognized himself.

"My god, I look like I've aged in dog years."

His typically short light brown hair was now shaggy and looked like it had been combed with an electric toothbrush. Ever since he worked in a kitchen, he had kept his hair neat, like a Marine, high and tight, so he wouldn't have to wear a hat or hair net. In addition to looking tired, his deep brown eyes looked like they had lost their color. So did his skin. It was the middle of summer, but he looked like he'd been stationed at the North Pole for the past three months. Besides that, his skin looked wrinkled and tired. Gone was one of "Chicago's most eligible, successful, and gorgeous bachelors" of some ten years ago. Now he was just successful. And though not ready to admit or believe it, he was eligible. He straightened up. Brushed

The Diner

the hair from his forehead and slapped his face a couple of times to bring some color to it.

"This is going to take some time. I guess I have plenty of that."

No longer disgusted by the image in the refrigerator door, only disappointed, he decided that it was time to take charge of his life and make a change.

"Maybe it's time to unlock the door…and time to quit talking to myself."

With one last look around the tired, old kitchen, he put his hand on the light switch.

"We just might fix you up too."

He locked the door behind him and walked a little taller, straight to his car. The darkening but brilliant orange red sky to the west caught his attention. He couldn't remember the last time he saw a sunset. Appreciating it for a second or two felt rejuvenating. A genuine smile, not like the one he'd been wearing for the past few months, appeared. As he turned back to his car he nearly walked smack into a man. So as not to knock him over, Dan took a large sidestep but twisted his ankle on a crack in the sidewalk. He righted himself before crashing to the ground.

Once he straightened up, chills immediately ran up and down his body as he looked closely at the man in front of him. He was elderly, probably about the same age as his father, seventy or so. His body was thin. His hair was sparse and gray. However, he wasn't feeble. He could tell by the well defined muscles in the man's arms and hands. If he wanted to, Dan was certain the guy could lift his car over his head. He stood there bearing a warm, inviting grin. Dan thought at any moment that the man's big arms would wrap around

41

him and offer the hug of his life. However the man didn't move as if his feet were bolted to the ground.

"Geezus, Milt, it's you. What are you doing back here? I thought you and Mae had left."

"How are ya, kid?"

Dan studied him closer. It wasn't the same Milt he saw inside or outside the diner.

The smile. The eyes. But most of all it was his powerful hands that could do or fix anything. And "kid." He always called Dan "kid."

"Milt, what happened earlier…you know, outside the diner? It was weird…," Dan said, rubbing an unexpected chill from his arms.

"Gees, kid, you look tired. A little out of shape too. Don't worry; you'll warm up in a minute."

"What? How did you know? Tomorrow, I'm going to…"

"Just havin' fun with ya," Milt interrupted. "Hey, I'm sorry about your folks. I want you to know that. And Angela. So sad…still, be careful. What I mean is…we'll talk more soon," he said nervously, looking around like he was afraid of being watched.

Dan followed his eyes, unsure what he was looking for. He thought Milt must have been on the lookout for Mae.

"Listen, kid, I gotta go," Milt continued.

Dan could hear the urgency in his voice.

"What do you mean…be careful. Huh? Why don't you come back tomorrow by yourself and we'll get caught up," Dan pleaded, hoping for the chance to talk to a friendly face.

"Can't do it."

"Why?"

The Diner

Milt grew considerably more anxious. Dan was getting scared for him. He wanted to reach out to him, but for some reason, couldn't. His arms felt like they were chained to his side. Milt began to look out of focus.

"Let me ask you, did you see anyone in there alone?" Milt asked pointing at the diner. "I mean, did you see anyone in there without their spouse? Think about it. We'll talk soon. I'll find you."

Milt raised his hand and knocked the car keys from Dan's hand. Dan reached down to pick them up. Just as quick, he dropped them again. They were frozen to the touch as if he had just taken them out of a liquid nitrogen bath.

"What the hell? Wait. When?"

Dan looked around in every direction, but Milt was nowhere in sight.

"Guess he really had to run. Some things never change."

He picked up the keys as a car passing by the front of the diner caught his attention. There were three people in it. Dan was certain the person in the rear seat was staring back at him. He couldn't tell if it was the Waldens with another person or not.

He pressed the button on his key and all the windows of the black 745i BMW rolled down in unison. Waves of heat came steaming out, which made him look down at his keys again.

How could they have been that cold?

He looked at his arms, realizing the chill was gone as Milt had said. Chalking it all up to a long day, he got in his car and thought about what Milt had asked him. Though he wasn't able to recall the entire guest list,

Dan couldn't remember seeing anyone expressing their sympathies to him alone, except for Milt, only minutes ago.

"None of the guest were alone."

Chapter 7

Trying to give his mind a rest, Dan drove through town slowly trying to find the memory that each building held. He recalled how downtown Circle Lake once provided all the comforts and necessities for the weekend vacationers from the city and suburbs looking for a relaxing day out on the lake. Not today though. The Circle Lake Savings & Loan, the Five and Dime, drug store, and a variety of other small office buildings and store fronts were all closed. Though far from a ghost town, there was still a dry cleaners, insurance agency, a liquor store, barber shop, a nail salon, and of course, Scheff's Diner, his diner. With so many businesses closed, some might say the town was dying. Dan didn't feel that. He didn't feel it bustling with life either. The town was dormant. Something was holding it back.

Or someone.

"You've never been held back in your entire life," his dad would always say.

In Dan's opinion, "held back" meant staying in town and working at the auto assembly plant. That wasn't going to be Dan's path. He loved to cook, and it was only logical that he pursue a formal food education. Showing promise in the diner at an early age, he continually experimented with dishes and recipes, but no matter how good they tasted, his dad never let one leave the kitchen.

"They know our food. It's good food. And they never forget it. It's etched in their mind. We can't change!" Buck would preach that the diner served up memories.

He pressed the point while all Dan wanted was his father to acknowledge what he had created. Buck never relented. And Dan could never understand what Buck was trying to teach him.

"It's about memories."

"It's about the food," Dan would mutter to himself, while feeling deflated.

Rather than continue to argue with his father, Dan looked to his mother to bridge the gap. By placing her gentle hand on Buck's arm while the other fell on Dan's shoulder, the tension between him and his dad quickly dissipated. Still, Dan wanted to know what memories had to do with the food they served, so when the chance presented itself, he'd bring the subject up again. However Buck never revealed anything more than stressing how to make everything on the diner menu the best it could be.

"Maybe you'll have a better chance of changing things from out there than in this diner," Buck told him.

Without a satisfying answer, he chose to put the diner and anything else having to do with Circle Lake in the rear view mirror. He enrolled in the Chicago Art Institute Culinary School while working at Gems, a popular restaurant in Chicago. Shortly after graduation he was off to New York followed by three years in Paris. Although an accomplished chef, he still had the childhood urge to prove something to his old man. He did that with Scheff's.

"Of course it works, because it's fantastic food and a wonderful restaurant. A restaurant is not a diner. It works for you, Daniel, because you work for it. And, like your mother and me, you're preparing something you hope your clientele will come back for and hopefully tell their friends about. But what are you serving? If you're serving a memory, then you have something. That's what our diner does. Remember that," Buck said to him. It was the last real conversation they had on the restaurant business and that was over a year ago.

Having toiled with enough memories for the day, Dan hit the gas and passed through the rest of the town in a matter of minutes.

"Amazing," Dan muttered to himself. He couldn't believe how outside of town nothing, other than the trees, had changed.

It makes it easier to go home.

His parents owned a five bedroom, two and a half bath, Victorian house right on Circle Lake. The lake was small, only ten square miles, but with inviting public beaches. With plenty of shoreline, fewer than fifty homes dotted it. Neighbors were neighbors, but not necessarily neighborly. The biggest stretch of the land was owned by Ernest Gardner. About one quarter of the shoreline served as the southeast edge of his horse farm.

The Scheffelin house was passed down to Buck from his dad, and his grandfather before that. The original house was only two bedrooms but grew into the proud Victorian it was today. Dan didn't know much about the family history. No one talked much about it. He'd ask his dad and mom, but they quickly changed the subject after sharing a look with each other. All that he really knew was the land had been in the family forever and that the Scheffelins always had cooked for the town.

Up until now, Dan never thought much about his ancestors or the importance of the diner to the town. He was always more interested in creating his own restaurant experience. It was clear that Scheff's was something. But was it history? Was it something that would last?

Does it serve memories?

Like most kids, he thought his parents would live forever and then so would the diner. Now the diner's future was up to him. He really didn't think the fate of the diner would matter much. It was just a diner. But it obviously mattered to the people of the town. Worse yet, it was a painful reminder that he was alone.

"I have had enough of being alone," Dan said.

Driving into the parking garage of his condo never felt as warm and inviting as driving down the long tree-lined gravel driveway to the back of his parents' house. He loved this place. There were so many simple childhood memories here. He had played wiffle ball in the vacant lot up the street with friends, dug for worms in the back yard for fishing, and best of all, spent hours on the lake. It was great. The lake was the first thing he checked on whenever he came home, because he knew the house would always be the same. But the lake, it was so moody. He loved it.

Parking outside the detached garage, he looked at his phone, certain someone must have called or texted.

No one.

He was still alone.

The Scheffelins owned four acres of lake front

property. Most of it wooded, while the house stood on a patch of land measuring three hundred feet by five hundred feet. It was perfect. Staring at the backyard, Dan felt like he was seeing it for the first time. Trees stood tall never bowing to their ripe old age with their bumpy roots meandering throughout the backyard which was once a dense forest. Now they shrouded the land from the sun, making the backyard look like it was a few hours later in the day than the front of the house. Like a cold dark alley that opened up to a bustling lighted boulevard, everyone quickly made their way to the sunshine and warmth of the front of the house. The wind blowing through the branches produced a hum that played harmony to the noises and songs of the insects. Pleasantly absent was the sound of people.

Unsettled by the isolation, he jogged to the back door, unlocked it, and quickly closed it behind him. The house was eerily quiet, and absent was the welcoming smell of his mother's home cooking. She always had something on the stove or in the oven, at least she used to, he thought. He quickly made for the front door to get reacquainted with the lake. The mirror sheen to the water told him that everything was calm. He felt better but a little embarrassed by the horror movie scene he created in his mind running from the car to the house.

The first thing he did was open every window. The second thing was get a beer. His dad always had plenty of Miller High Life on hand. Having changed into a pair of shorts and T-shirt, he took the perspiring, unopened beer bottle out to the front porch and sat in his dad's rocking chair. The sound of the twisting bottle cap, the crickets' chirp, and gentle lapping of the waves against the shore told him he was home. The first long pull on the beer was fantastic. It was the best beer he ever tasted. That moment, a hot July night, sitting on the front porch of his parents' house, was the best he had felt in months, maybe longer.

He counted six stairs from the porch to grass. He never knew that before. There were twenty-three tree sections his grandfather had cut to use as stepping stones that led out to the pier. A pale, powder blue, sixteen foot rowboat, turned upside and chained to a tree, was waiting for someone to return it to the water.

As a kid, he'd get up early in the morning and push the boat into the water. After he tied the boat to the dock, he'd go to the garage and grab the seven-horsepower Elgin outboard motor his dad had bought from a customer of the diner. The guy gave it to Buck for practically nothing, said he owed him. Dan never knew what for. It worked perfectly and was light enough that a ten-year-old kid could carry and attach it to the back of a row boat. Just before the sun came up, he'd row about fifty yards from the house before starting the motor so not to wake his parents. Their bedroom was on the first floor and faced the lake. During the summer they always slept with the window open.

When he was older, his folks told him that he woke his mom every time he came bounding down the stairs to have a bowl of cereal before heading out. His dad managed to sleep through it. But the clanging of the oars, fishing poles, and tackle always had his dad tossing and turning. The splash of the oars against the water meant he could fall back to sleep.

Dan surveyed the rest of the yard. A picnic table, a hammock, and a half dozen Adirondack chairs painted in assorted colors littered the front yard that desperately needed to be mowed.

I'll do that tomorrow. But first that boat gets wet.

Everywhere he looked there was memory. He was getting tired of memories. "We serve memories." The words of his father echoed in his head.

"You served the same old thing to the same old people," Dan said to no one, referring to the stale menu of fresh food.

"And many of them came to say 'thank you' today," he'd swear his dad would reply.

Once again he replayed the turnout of guests in his head. As far as he could recall, no one came in alone. What bothered him more were Ernest Gardner and his "our diner" and "I'm sure you'll do the right thing" comments.

With the beer nearly empty and his eyes growing as heavy as the insects feeding off his skin, Dan raised himself from the rocker and went inside. The place looked so big. Empty. It was his house now. A home? He wasn't sure. There was so much to be done. All his parents' personal items like clothes, jewelry, etc., would have to be rummaged through to see what should be kept and what would be donated. But not tonight. With a new beer his hand, he was ready to go upstairs to his room, the room he grew up in, the room he would sleep in. He thought about sleeping in his parent's room, but it wasn't his room.

Too soon for that.

He hit the light and then remembered he had forgot to lock the doors, something his parents rarely did, but a routine living in Chicago. Turning around at the foot of the stairs, he went to lock the back door first and then the lake door. That's what his parents called it, the lake door, not the front door. The act of turning the deadbolts wasn't lost on him.

Locking myself up again. Alone. I should go back to the diner. No one ever goes there alone.

"Dammit. Why doesn't anyone go to the diner alone?"

The Diner

Chapter 8

Despite the emotional exhaustion he had fought over the last few weeks, Dan started to stir as soon as the rays of the sun crept in through the bedroom window triggering his inner child's alarm clock. The sun was up before he could pull his body up out of bed. Sitting on the edge of the bed in a bedroom that had hardly changed in twenty-seven years, he tried to spring up and attack the day like a ten-year-old. It wasn't happening. Next to the digital alarm clock that illuminated a pale yellow 6:15 a.m. was a full, open beer. Maybe one swallow was gone. He had fallen hard and fast asleep. His bones creaked as he wandered around the bedroom looking for his shorts, until he realized he had never taken them off.

He waved his arms like a windmill trying to coax his body to come alive as he slogged down the hallway to the bathroom to brush his teeth. Flipping on the light switch revealed a hairstyle that looked like he had been electrocuted. With his hair sticking straight out in all directions, he backed away from the mirror and took his shirt off. All he could do was stare at himself in disgust.

Geezus, what the hell happened to you?

At six foot one and 205 pounds, Dan knew he could stand to lose about twenty pounds. His body still had definition, but it was a whole lot rounder. Without fear of embarrassment, he flexed his best body builder

53

pose but couldn't hold it. He looked ridiculous. When he first met Angela, his body was Olympic swimmer taut and for good reason. Every day before work, he'd spend forty-five minutes in the gym then thirty minutes in the pool. It was fantastic. He could always feel the stares from the ladies at the health club as he got in and out of the water. But it wasn't his body that caught Angela's attention; it was his eyes. Inviting brown, understanding eyes were how she described them. They seemed to dance with aspirations of a full life and beamed with confidence. Anyone looking into them instantly wanted to strike up a conversation with Dan feeling like they knew him for years. When he and Angela opened their first restaurant, Angela had to take over the hiring chores because Dan's interviews went on too long. The candidates never wanted it to end. Dan loved the idea that someone could be interested in working in his restaurant.

His inviting brown, understanding eyes had their disadvantages however. Since people felt so comfortable around him, it often led to unproductive and often misunderstood relationships with his staff. Angela would often get jealous if he spent too much time talking with a waitress or hostess.

"Don't you see she's coming on to you?" she'd state.

"We were just talking about how the restaurant was doing and what her goals were."

"I bet. I'm going to fire her anyway," she'd say with a wink and walk away.

They would joke about it, tease each other, and when they got home, make love. That was then, he thought. She'd lost her jealous tendencies by the time they opened in New York. She always seemed to be distracted by something.

Looking around the bathroom, he found one of his old Cubs hats hanging on the back of the door. He put the hat on backwards and tossed another glance to the mirror.

Perfect.

With a day's worth of growth on his face and the hat pulled down tight, he looked very "Hollywood," he thought. A haircut was still in order, but that would wait until he took care of a few chores around the house and before heading into the diner.

The morning was already heating up, so he left his shirt off hoping to bring some color to his pasty white skin. Alive was the look he was going for. The key to the boat was where it had always been, hanging on a hook by the back door. He wanted coffee, but that would only slow him up and allow for too many chances to talk himself out of physical activity.

After brushing a few spiders out of the boat, he eased it off the shoreline and into the water. It was amazing how easy it was to move the boat at thirty-nine compared to ten years old. There were oars in the boat and he intended on rowing, but he had to see if the old Elgin outboard motor still worked. Like he had as a kid, he secured the boat and headed to the garage, but not before taking one more look at the lake.

He loved the quiet serenity of the calm water. No angry garbage trucks, taxis, or neighbors to wreck the mood. The small woodlands, in full bloom on either side of the house, blocked the view of the neighboring homes. In the winter, it was different; you could see their houses but never what was going on in or around them. Regardless of the season, it was always quiet.

The backyard was cooler in the shade and a lot buggier than the front yard. He walked right into a spider web. With his arms flailing about, he looked like a baton leader in a marching band as he tried to get the strands of webbing off his face. The encounter brought a much needed smile to his face as he walked toward the garage.

The large three car garage resembled a converted barn. At the north end of the garage was a plot of land, one hundred by two hundred feet. It was the family garden. This was the first year nothing was planted. His dad said he was "giving the soil a rest for a year." Dan stood shaking his head, disappointed that it was overgrown with weeds. He had offered to plant it for them. "When would you have time?" they said. They were right, he didn't have any. Another sad reminder of something else he didn't do any more.

As soon as he raised the middle garage door, he could feel the cool, damp air creep out. The structure faced west, so soon the sun would warm the entire front of the building. The shadow it cast was already retreating as the sun began to heat the large rectangular, concrete entrance. The driveway itself was all gravel and stretched out a quarter of a mile to the main road. He offered to have it paved, thinking it would be easier to clear when the snows came. His parents declined. With his father so adept at moving snow with the plow on the truck, there was no way to convince them to have it covered with asphalt. Dan would have to figure something out before the winter arrived this year.

The first thing he saw was his Mom's Jeep Cherokee. He often wondered why she wanted a SUV.

She said she liked riding up high.

I bet she hadn't driven it in months.

Parked all the way against the far south wall was his 1967 Mustang sitting quietly on blocks and under a dusty gray tarp. Every six months for the last ten years, he'd say, "I have to get that car running." Something else always came up. It had been at least six years since he had the tarp off. The number of memories he discovered wandering around his folks' house was becoming too many to count.

"We serve memories." His dad's voice echoed in his head.

Looking around he found what he was looking for. Under a bunch of old greasy towels was the Elgin outboard motor fastened to a wooden sawhorse. He opened all the garage doors to let in more light. Before even attempting to start the outboard engine, he drained the old gas, cleaned the plugs, and performed as much maintenance on it that he knew to do. After a dozen pulls the engine sputtered, but still didn't start. He was sweating and cursing that he let himself get so out of shape. It was going to be him or the motor. It would start. Dan had no intention of giving up; he never did. Finding some carburetor cleaner on the work bench, he cleaned the engine within an inch of its life. It took longer than expected to reassemble the engine. After a deep breath, he grabbed the pull cord, and ripped it hard, nearly tearing his shoulder from its socket. The engine came to life spitting blue smoke everywhere. He made a few adjustments with the choke and got the engine humming as if it was brand new. He shut it down since it was water cooled and then grabbed a couple of boat cushions and headed back to the boat.

He had intended to row a little longer, but his right arm was aching from the fight with the Elgin, so he stowed the oars. It only took a single pull, and he was motoring around the lake. Like the drive to the house, not much had changed around Circle Lake. Some of the homes had been painted, and few homeowners had redesigned their piers, complete with a new boat. If not for wiping the sweat that ran down his face and feeling the stubble on his face, he would have thought he had gone back in time.

It felt good to be on the lake again. He wondered if any of his friends still lived around the lake. Growing up, his best friends were Mike Miller and Josh Austin. Dan had a different relationship with each of them. As kids, Mike and Dan did everything together from fishing, to movies and working on each other's cars, or just hanging out. Mike lived in the house at the end of the woods on the east side of his parent's house. It was always easier and quicker to get there by boat then it was by bike, car, or hiking through the woods. After high school, they both moved beyond Circle Lake and quickly drifted apart. While Dan pursued a career in food, Mike wasn't sure what he wanted to do, so he took a job at the assembly plant. Dan heard that Mike didn't stay on very long, which didn't surprise him. Mike was too intelligent and ambitious for mundane machinery work, but Dan didn't know what he did next. He couldn't remember the last time he saw Mike. He decided to check out his house later.

Josh and his family lived on the lake too. He and Dan played baseball together. Josh was a great baseball player and was recruited heavily by many colleges. Every summer, the three of them did everything together. They always had a great time, but it seemed like there was always something else on Josh's mind. Dan and Mike each sensed it. Mike ignored it. In contrast, Dan and Josh would have deep conversations but never could arrive at any conclusions.

Motoring around the lake, he checked out their two homes first. They looked relatively the same and certainly lived in, but no one was outside. When he got to the diner, he decided he'd ask around to see if anyone knew who lived there now.

Pointing the boat toward the Circle Lake beach park brought back vivid memories. He recalled when he was younger how the beaches would come alive on the weekends with color and sounds. Carnival-colored beach umbrellas and towels covered the sand. The air was always filled with barbeque smoke, music, and laughter. Dan navigated to get a closer look. Anchoring the boat about twenty-five yards out from the pontoon sunbathing deck that was set out from the beach, he sat and wondered. It was early, but he expected kids would soon be flocking out and playing all kinds of the games, like "king of the mountain," on the floating wood island. At least that's what he'd be doing. Even from a distance, the beach looked relatively the same, only empty. The ball field was still there, but now with a green chain link fence instead of gray. The swing sets and jungle gym were now surrounded by railroad ties and what looked like mulch instead of sand. The beach looked clean while the recreation center, which was built about ten years ago, looked abandoned.

The more he looked around, he wondered about all the people living around the lake. Were the same families still there? Did their kids now own the places?

Any new families? It wasn't that he cared, but in a way, he did. He grew up here when there seemed to be more life. Now it all looked like it was frozen in time. Lifeless. Empty.

With the sun beating on his head, he couldn't brave the heat any longer. He kicked off his flip flops and dove into the water. Refreshing didn't begin to describe it. It was wonderful. After flailing about for a few seconds, he found his stroke which grew stronger with each kick and arm swing. He found the ladder of the pontoon island. It was badly rusted with dangerous edges. He climbed up anyway. The whole deck surface was weathered and splintered.

No wonder no one comes out here anymore. It's a tetanus shot in waiting.

He pushed off and swam back to the boat. Tired, but feeling more alive than he had in years, he made a little bed out of the boat cushions and lay back and stared up at the brilliant blue sky. After about thirty minutes and without any sunscreen, he could feel his skin beginning to bake. The temptation to stay there and fry was powerful. He never wanted to leave the little carefree oasis. He was surprised not to hear any other boats, particularly the way sounds travel across the water. Occasionally, he'd hear a lawn mower, which only served to remind him what he had to do next. However, he didn't feel alone. The feeling of being watched was palpable. It felt like someone had tiptoed across the surface of the water to sneak up on him. Thinking it ludicrous to look around to scc who it might be, he simply lifted his cramped body up to head home and cut the grass. He prayed the motor would start because he had a long row back home. Staggering to the front of the boat, he began to pull up the anchor when about three hundred yards to his right, some movement on the shore caught his eye. It was on Gardner's land, which up until this point, Dan avoided looking at. Even as kid he avoided that corner of the lake. As much as he wanted to fish that part of the lake, it scared him.

Fueling a childhood fear was something he wasn't about to do, so he looked up. It was a man on a horse. Dan thought it might be Gardner, but it could easily be any of his employees. The distance obscured any distinctive facial features, but Dan could still tell he was being watched. It was a man, looking like the statue of Stonewall Jackson. Dan waved but got nothing in return. He stared a few seconds longer. Despite the sweat streaming down his face, the chills running down his body told him it had to be Gardner.

He turned his attention to the motor. With considerable ease, he pulled the cord, and the engine instantly sprang to life. He didn't want to, but the temptation to look back at Gardner's property was too strong. Before turning the boat around, his head came up slowly to see "Stonewall" pulling on the reins and trotting off.

It only took ten minutes to return to home, but in that time he looked back three times. There were now more horses roaming Gardner's land, but no riders.

It took less time to get the old John Deere riding mower started than the Elgin. As soon as he cleaned the spark plug, the mower rumbled into action. It was louder than he remembered. He bounced and shook over the bumpy grass and tree roots. His stomach jiggling from the constant vibration didn't make him feel any better about the shape he was in. Twigs, acorns, and pine cones were flying out from underneath the mower deck and bouncing off the house and trees. Some of them ricocheted and hit him in the chest. Despite the noise and rocky ride, Dan cut the grass in a relaxed trance. Instead of thinking of Angela, his parents, or his restaurants he thought more about his life. He wanted, actually needed, to find out what happened to Mike and Josh.

I wonder what happened to the girls I dated, too. Hmm? What were their names?

He couldn't come up with a single name. Thoughts of Christine seemed to scramble his concentration.

What was it about her?

One more lap and the lawn would be finished. Wishing he had put his shirt on, he picked at the shredded blades of grass and dirt that stuck to his body like glue. The mower was also plastered in lawn and yard shrapnel. Before he showered, the Deere would need to be hosed off first. It was one of his dad's rules.

With the mower still idling in the sun in front of the garage, Dan went to get the hose. As he dragged it from around the garage, the feeling of being watched came over him again.

Movement.

He looked around and saw nothing. With all the trees blowing in the breeze, he figured the shadows were playing tricks on him. He pointed the hose at the tractor but was desperate to turn it on himself. The tractor looked liked it had been freshly painted as the green and yellow colors shined brightly in the sunlight.

"If you're going to do a job, make sure people see that you did it well," his dad said. "What you do is how

The Diner

you'll be remembered."

Dan replayed the words at least a dozen times as he scrubbed the tractor clean. The satisfying feeling of a job well done came over him. It was a feeling he hadn't felt in a long time.

Purpose. That's what's been missing.

Movement.

A four-legged shadow closed in on him.

"Well done!"

Dan looked up to see a man sitting atop a beautiful black horse with a small patch of white on its chest.

"Geezus, you scared the crap out me," Dan said to Ernest Gardner. The horse's breathing was labored meaning that Gardner had the animal going at a full gallop, which puzzled Dan.

Why were you in such a hurry to get here?

"The trail seems to have grown over. No matter, the road worked out just fine for Coach and me. Coach here," Gardner said, patting the powerful neck, "likes to get out. He gets bored on the farm."

"Coach does, does he? I see. Well, is there anything I can do for you?" Dan asked as he began to wrap up the hose.

"Shouldn't you be at the diner?"

"No. But it is open. Carlos is taking care of things."

"Yes, I'm well aware that it's open. There's not a thing in this town that I don't know about. The town is grateful. But you should really be there to make sure no one changes anything."

"Why?"

"Wouldn't do to change things in the only restaurant in town. You know how people get used to a good thing."

63

"I do…that's my business. But we'll see. Change can be good."

"Not for this town."

"I see that. But maybe that's what it needs. Perhaps even another restaurant. You know, give people some options, some choices. It might bring some new revenue to the town too and some new life. God knows this town could stand to have an infusion of life."

"This town has plenty of life. And how would you know? You've been back a day," Gardner said sternly as he wobbled violently in the saddle. His horse never wavered. "As far as another restaurant, the town council won't allow it; you'll keep this one open."

"We'll see. Not sure yet. I need to run the numbers. Running a restaurant isn't just about serving food; there's more to it. As I said, I'll run the numbers. Have a good day, Mr. Gardner."

"I assure you the numbers are fine. You'll do the right thing and keep our diner open," he said leaning as far forward as he could.

The more Dan had thought about it, he had gotten used to the idea of keeping the place open if for no other reason so that the staff could keep their jobs, especially Christine. But now there was no way Gardner was going to tell him what to do. The day he opened his first restaurant was the last day he took orders from another chef or from a maniacal owner. And right now he wasn't about to take orders from anyone, especially a man on a horse.

"Mr. Gardner, there is no our diner. Let me be clear, it's *my* diner. Maybe it was my mistake when I said, 'We'll see.' So correction, I'll see. Right now, I need to finish up here and then go get a haircut."

The Diner

"You'll do the right thing. Remember…"

"Listen, Mr. Gardner, the last thing…," Dan said as the anger rose in his voice. His defiance was clearly incensing Gardner.

"Dammit! The good men and women of this town count on the diner. Your parents had no right doing…" The horse whinnied and bucked. "I'm sorry. My wife is far better at this than I am. Anyway, I'm sure Bob will make time for you in his chair."

"What about my parents? And what do you mean you're wife is better at it? At what? And Bob who? Are you talking about Bob Radke? He still has the barbershop? Gees, I thought he died."

"Again, I apologize for my outburst. You'll be pleased to know that Bob and his wife Carol are doing quite well," Gardner replied, about to pull up on the reins.

"Really!" Dan said, stunned.

Seeing Gardner readying to leave, he wanted to fire one more barb. "I think I'll head out of town and find a salon. I like my hair cut a particular way."

"I think you'll find it best to support the people of this town. Good day, Daniel."

Gardner galloped off leaving a trail of dust in his wake.

Chapter 9

With the tractor clean, Dan turned the hose on himself. The water was cold and invigorating. He managed to wash away more than just the grass and dirt. Gone, but not forgotten, was the lingering anger from the exchange with Gardner. Still he couldn't put his finger on what about Gardner was making him so angry. Someone telling him what to do was nothing new to Dan since he had spent most of his adult life working in restaurants with egotistical chefs and demanding customers, but this was different. Gardner wasn't someone he needed to please. Rather he was someone he had no use for. Nonetheless, there were all sorts of emotions, most of them laced with panic, behind Gardner's demands. And no doubt about it, Gardner was intent on making sure Dan heard them.

Looking like he was baptizing himself, Dan did his best to wash away the remnants of the conversation with Gardner and replace it with something more pleasant. He could hear his mother's voice in his head saying, "Daniel, what are doing out there with that hose? Don't be ridiculous."

Had he walked into the house covered with grass, she'd be quick to say, "Daniel, look at you. You're a mess. Get out of my house."

Angela would have happily chased him around with the hose or pushed him in the lake.

The Diner

He let the cold water from the hose flow over him. It hid his tears.

Needing to warm up, he jogged around the house to see if anything was in need of immediate attention or repair. All was good.

At least nothing at home needs fixing.

He walked out to the pier and surveyed the lake. He was comforted to see that there were at least six boats on the lake.

"It's the middle of summer. There should be so much more going on out there. Where did everybody go? This is crazy."

As soon as he said it, he thought about all the "crazy" he experienced at the diner.

"Is that what you left me with, Dad? Crazy?"

Dan smiled and looked out across the lake one more time, wiped the sweat from his brow and through his hair, and was reminded of the next to-do on his list.

Pulling out onto the main road, he had two choices. He could go right and reignite his anger by driving by Gardner's farm or go left and get another look at his home town. Either way, he'd reach to the town of Wander Lake, which was home to the Honda truck assembly plant and hopefully a decent hair salon. He couldn't shake the idea that Bob Radke was still alive and working in the Circle Lake barbershop. Even so, he wanted a salon cut, not a barbershop cut. Still, it was worth driving past.

"Fuck you, Gardner," Dan said as he turned left.

Entering the town of Circle Lake from home was even less inspiring than leaving it for home. It was just there, like an old pair of shoes, nothing inviting about it, but comfortable. Dan continued driving at a snail's pace while looking left and right absorbing as much of the town as he could, thinking maybe he missed something last night. There was plenty of open green space between the vacant buildings and those still in business. Unfortunately the green space was mostly brown and dry, in desperate need of a landscape makeover. As he drove past the old Circle Lake Savings and Loan, with plywood covering most of the windows, he thought it would be the perfect location for a restaurant with a spectacular view of the lake. It faced west and would offer the perfect view of the evening sunset.

"Sunsets, that's what I'd call it."

Despite the amount of emptiness in town, it was surprisingly busy for a Monday morning. At least a dozen or more people were walking up and down the street. The town had an energy that he hadn't felt before. Most of the cars were clustered around the diner. He snuck a peek inside but saw nothing of interest. It looked busy. He thought about going in for a cup of coffee, but then he'd never get out of there. Just up ahead, he could see activity in Bob's Barbershop. With little to no traffic in town, he slowed the car to a crawl.

"It looks like ol' man Radke. How can that be? Oh well, I'll check in on him later."

Other than seeing people he thought for sure had died, Dan concluded that this was what a typical day looked like in Circle Lake. For a moment he felt like he was beginning to understand his hometown, but that feeling was quickly erased as he came upon the intersection of the highway where his parents died. With no cars behind him, he sat there for a moment wondering how his parents could have died so tragically. Per the authorities' report, the pavement was dry and there were no signs that his dad suffered from any medical condition that would cause him to pass out. The only thing Dan could think of was maybe they were trying to avoid a deer. Still, they should have been able to stop long before they hit the tree. There were no answers.

The tires of the BMW squealed as Dan hit the gas and sped up the ramp to the highway. He couldn't look at the scene anymore. In a matter of minutes he was upon the western exit to Wander Lake. The eastern exit would take him to Richfield. Thoughts of Christine popped immediately in his head, but when he pictured her he saw Angela.

"I need to shut my imagination down," Dan said shaking his head. "Ah, there's what I need."

Stan's Donuts, one of his favorite spots for coffee, was right off the exit. Dan loved Stan's because there was something quaint about the place that set it apart from Starbucks and all the other coffee chains that one might see on nearly every corner. He preferred their mellow coffee and their egg white and turkey sausage flat bread sandwich. He didn't even consider it fast food since it wasn't a restaurant chain; this was the only Stan's he knew of. It was always spotlessly clean and smelled enticingly sweet. Homemade apple fritter sweet.

Six months ago the temptation had been too strong, and he broke down and ordered an apple fritter. He had stayed over at his parents' house when his mom had what she called a bad case of the flu, though as Dan recalled none of the symptoms were flu-like. He had wanted to hang around and open the diner, but his parents insisted that he head home. "Ray is more than capable handling things. Now go," they insisted. Disappointed, hurt, and with nothing much left to do around the house, he headed back to Chicago

Not sure why he ordered the apple fritter, maybe the kid in him was coming out after spending so much time with his parents, but he did and it tasted great. Later that week, he created an apple fritter caramel tart for dessert to be served at Scheff's. He never told Angela about his indulgence. However, she being the health food police suspected he had something sweet and fried after they kissed. Like always, she let it go and smiled and winked. Her suspicions were confirmed when the new dessert was launched to rave reviews.

Dan had never been in Stan's this late in the morning. The first thing he did was do what he did every time he entered a restaurant, even his own, and that was check the time and see how many people were in it. The more people in the place during the non-peak hours, the better it usually was. Stan's was hopping with very few empty seats.

"Hi," said a cute little redhead with an ear to ear smile. "What can we get for you?"

"Hi, Cassie," Dan replied, seeing the nametag on her shirt. He knew that calling a person by their first name usually broke down unnecessary barriers. It seemed to work this time. After he ordered, Cassie went right to work. Another employee came to help, but Cassie was insistent that she had it all under control.

"So you haven't been here before," Cassie said as he she waited for his sandwich to be prepared. "Are you going to the plant? If so, you probably shouldn't be pulling up in a BMW. You know they build Hondas there."

"Thanks. That's funny," Dan said, as his brown eyes lit up prompting Cassie to lean over the counter and into him. "Actually I'm looking to get my hair cut. Where would you recommend I go?'

"Well, you don't look like a quick in and out kind of guy," she replied with a wink. "Soooo, I'd recommend you go to Joshua Austin's. He just opened a place in the Pine Wood shopping center. I and a bunch of my friends go there. It's best place around."

Ignoring the innuendo, Dan paused for a moment. "Joshua Austin? Are you sure? He could be a friend of mine. We went to high school together."

"Could be him. He's from around here. I guess he lived in Philadelphia for some time, then moved back here after his parents died. Here you go," Cassie said, handing Dan his coffee and sandwich.

"Thanks," Dan said and turned to leave, then hesitated. "You said his parents died. Did they die together, at the same time? When?" he asked insistently.

"I'm sorry. I don't know," she said. "All I know is that I'll be here later and have no plans for dinner. And I don't have to be here tomorrow until 10:30 a.m. or so."

Dan never heard her. He was on his way out the door.

His parents are dead too! That is if it's him. Owner of a hair salon?

The last time he had seen Josh was about seven years ago, running into him at the Taste of Chicago, a food festival at Navy Pier on the lakefront. Dan was too busy cooking for the event to talk long. An empty promise of "I'll call you soon" was made by both of them.

He found the Pine Wood Shopping Center easily. Joshua Austin's salon was in a newly constructed four-unit redbrick building near the highway that was also home to a gourmet sandwich shop, a greeting card store, and a wireless phone store. Like any new business trying to attract customers, all of them advertised their special deals in their windows. Joshua Austin's Salon was no different. It was a full service salon with a sign saying "Walk-ins Are Welcome."

Parked only a few feet from the entrance, Dan squinted as his head bobbed and weaved through the glare off the car and store windows trying to see if he could spot Josh inside the salon. What he saw was a reflection of what was behind him rather than anyone in the salon. The metaphor wasn't lost on him. "I get it. I need to look ahead," he said to no one.

"Welcome. Can I help you?" said a lovely twenty-something woman displaying natural beauty that was in sharp contrast to the old battered metal desk she was sitting behind. It looked like it belonged at the head of a 1970 fifth grade classroom.

"Hi. Brandi, is it?" Dan asked seeing the nameplate at the front of the desk. "I need a haircut. Any chance Josh is available?"

"Josh. That's funny. We call him Joshua. He's just finishing up. Do you know him or something?"

"Maybe. I know a Josh Austin."

"Maybe? Well, Austin is Joshua's last name," she said smiling widely. "What's your name? I'll go ask him."

The Diner

"Tell him it's Scheff."

"Like a cook?"

"Sure. If he doesn't recognize the name, then you can hook me up with anyone that's available," Dan said forcing a smile.

"Oh, we'll take care of ya. Don't you worry, Chef."

Unlike a sports bar that took fandom to an obnoxious level with every inch of the walls covered in professional sport team's pictures, jerseys, and equipment, the salon was decorated with subtle tributes to hometown athletics, Little League, Pee Wee Football, and high school athletics. Dan peered in closer to look at the pictures hanging near the desk.

"No kidding. Scheffy is here?"

Hearing his nickname called out and then seeing a picture of Josh Austin in a batting stance from his senior year in high school, Dan knew he'd soon be taking another trip down memory lane with one of his best friends. Then seeing a picture of Josh standing between his parents on graduation day reminded again, there were other things to discuss.

"You bet. Tell him to give me just a few minutes to finish up here."

Dan took the time to read the old newspaper articles and drink in the pictures.

Circle Lake was a good place back then. What has happened to our town, Josh?

Chapter 10

"What's going on, Scheffy?" Joshua said.

"Where do I begin? I know. Should I call you Justin, or do you prefer Mr. Timberlake?" Dan asked sarcastically, not quite ready to jump into the news from the past few weeks.

Wearing a black straw fedora, three-day-old beard growth that looked like it had been spray painted on to maintain a clean edge between beard and skin, tight black jeans, a muscle T-shirt with fading lettering that said "Hell and Hair Raiser," and red Converse gym shoes, Joshua could easily be Justin Timberlake's stand in. He still had a very athletic build that caused Dan to make another silent pledge to start working out again. Though they were both the same age, Dan believed that he looked ten years older.

"Never heard that before, fat ass!" Josh replied with a smile.

"That's me."

They took a step toward each other and embraced.

"Geezus, it's good to see you," they said in unison.

"C'mon over to my chair, and let's see if we can't clean you up," Joshua said, guiding Dan to his chair in the corner.

Dan looked around the shop admiring how Josh combined many of his childhood memories into a brand new salon making it feel welcoming and comfortable rather than clinical and antiseptic.

I need to do the same thing with the diner.

In addition to Joshua, there were two other male stylists and three female. From the pictures on the wall, to the personal memorabilia such as Josh's old jerseys, ball glove, and bat, to the way the other stylists decorated their stations with pictures and trinkets that mattered to them, Dan immediately felt like he knew a little something about everyone that worked there. He was sure it was intended to put customers at ease and feel relaxed, though Dan could feel something was still missing. It was clear that business was good as each of the six styling stations was filled with a handful of customers waiting for an open chair.

"I think I'd rather have her cut my hair," Dan said, pointing to an attractive brunette wearing skin tight yoga pants, black high-heel boots, and a light blue top that hugged her breasts beautifully. Dan didn't know what to look at first. Her hair was perfect. Her skin was perfect. She was perfect.

"I bet you would. But it's not going to happen. Sherry is booked the entire day. Aren't you, girl?"

"I could move things around," she said with a smile and wink that aroused an old, but familiar feeling in Dan.

"I like it here," Dan said barely making it into the chair. Had Joshua not spun it around Dan would have wound up on the floor.

"Easy, cowboy. I'm going to have Jasmine shampoo you, and then we'll get started. And by the way, I'm not really interested in what you want. I'm going to have to work my magic. Geez, what the hell did you do to this head of yours? Don't answer. You'll have to trust me. Got it?"

"I always have."

"That's true. And you've never let me down," Joshua replied.

Dan turned and smiled back at Josh as Jasmine led him to the shampoo sink. Josh, with an ear to ear grin, brought his palms together in the middle of his chest and bowed.

"Do you need a cigarette?" Joshua asked as Dan sauntered back to the chair looking like he had been pleasantly molested by Jasmine. She not only washed his hair, but gave him a much needed stress-relieving shoulder and scalp massage. It felt like he had left his body as the insanity of the past few days had been melted away by her touch. As he walked back from the shampoo with Jasmine on his arm, he noticed Sherry smiling at him. He couldn't determine who was more attractive and sexier. He decided he'd have to come back a few more times before declaring a winner.

"Damn, you always knew how to do things right," Dan said about to sit down, never taking his eyes off Jasmine as she attended to her next client. He held onto the armrest to make sure he landed in the chair and not on the floor.

"You're no slouch yourself. How are the restaurants doing?"

"All good."

Dan felt like he was back in high school. Though seven fully packed years had passed since they saw each other, he was at ease. And by the way Josh kept touching his shoulder he believed Josh was relaxed and happy to reconnect.

"Hey, I'm sorry to hear about Angela. I didn't find

out until it was too late. I was stuck on the east coast and just got back a few days ago. I know that's a piss poor excuse, just know that I'm really sorry," Joshua said again, resting his arms on Dan's shoulder and giving him a brief embrace.

"No worries. I understand," Dan said patting his hands. "Worse yet, I buried my parents last week."

"Shut up! Geezus. What the fuck? What happened?" he asked through the reflection in the mirror.

"I'm surprised you didn't hear about it. None of it makes sense. Somehow they crashed their truck coming off the interstate. You know, by the two trees. Now there's only one. The authorities said they had to be doing over one hundred miles per hour. They crashed right into the elm." As Dan said it, the less he believed it. "It makes absolutely no sense."

"I did hear about the accident, but never the names. How did he keep that quiet?"

"What? Who kept what quiet?"

"Nothing. I'm just babbling. Son of a bitch. My folks died in a car accident too," Joshua said. "What the hell? My parents and your parents dying in a car accident. That's messed up. Angela too. In New York, right? Gees, I'm sorry."

Dan cast a puzzled look at Josh. There was something he wasn't telling him. There were too many questions swirling in his head. Now was not the time to pepper Josh with a bunch of questions, instead he acknowledged Josh's condolences with a wave of his hand. A few minutes had passed as Joshua went about cutting Dan's hair. Dan wasn't really paying attention.

How could we both lose our parents like that?

"What about the house? What are you going do with it?" Joshua asked, breaking the silence.

"I'm going to keep it. I miss the lake."

"I know what you mean. What about the diner?"

"Everyone keeps asking me that. 'What am I going to do with the diner?' "

"Hey, I didn't mean anything by it."

"No, I know. Sorry. For right now, I'm going to live out on the lake. I haven't decided what to do with the diner yet. How 'bout you? I checked out yours and Mike's house from the lake this morning. Where are you at? Married?"

"Doing the same. I'm living at my parents' house too. I mean it's mine now." Josh hesitated for a second and took a deep breath. "My partner is still out in Philly. He gets back here every couple of weeks. He doesn't have a job out here yet. He works at Elaine's in Philly, you know off Market Street, near the Rittenhouse."

"I know it well. It's a great restaurant and club. I never wanted to open a place in Philly though. Angela and I…" Dan fell silent.

In the mirror he watched his expression change as the pain of losing Angela came flooding back. Joshua patted him on the shoulder again.

"He's getting tired of the club scene and would rather just cook. It's so limiting. He's much better than that place."

Joshua had a firm hold on his hair; all Dan could do was nod slightly.

"Damn you, aren't you going to say something like, 'Oh, that kind of partner,' or something?" Joshua asked, with a long clump of hair in his hand and the scissors poised to chop it off.

"What, and have you give me a nice bald spot? What the hell do I care? No offense, but I couldn't really care less if you're gay. You're still Josh Austin, aren't you? I'm sorry, Joshua Austin. The guy who never struck out?"

"Bravo!" said one of the other stylists cutting an elderly lady's hair the next chair over. "I like you."

"Steady, Simon. Dan doesn't play for our team. Though he may be willing to learn," Joshua said with an ear to ear smile.

"Oh, I get it. You did strike out a lot. With the ladies. That's why you're gay. Makes sense now," Dan said, returning the jab with an equally big smile. "Cut my hair that short, and I'll cut off your balls."

Joshua went back to work, smiling bigger than before.

"You know, I know a guy who has a restaurant in Chicago. Called Scheff's, I think…" Dan continued to tease. "And don't give me any crap. Next time he's in town, have him come see me. By the way, what's his name?"

"Trevor."

"Good god, you really are gay."

"That's it. Where are the clippers? We're taking you back to the days when you wore that ugly Marine cut. Even Simon will take a pass on you then, and he hits on everyone."

Their laughter was contagious.

"You did it again," Josh said.

"Did what?"

"What you always do. Remember that time after the Morton West game? We cleaned their clock. I think

I went 4 for 5. You had a home run and a triple. Mike struck out ten or eleven including their best player four times. The guy was huge. Then we ran into some of their players at Dairyland. That big guy gets in Mike's face and starts screaming, 'I'm gonna beat you worse than my father ever put a whoopin' on me.' "

Dan looked in the mirror, watching Josh as he became more animated. Sherry and Simon walked over to listen.

"What happened next?" Sherry asked.

"Dan was Dan. Always talking people off the ledge. Defusing the craziest moments. I don't know how he does it. Anyway, this guy charges at Mike with fists clenched, and Dan steps in front of him and says, 'Hold on! Your dad beats you? That's messed up.' "

" 'Fuck you. Get outta my way!' the guy says."

" 'Are you kidding? Listen to what you just said. Your dad whoops you.' "

" 'Yeah, so what?' "

" 'Why?' Dan asked. 'I mean, I'm just asking. It seems like you'd rather be beating the crap out of him than us.' "

"The guy stopped cold. He didn't know how to react. Dan wasn't backing down, but he wasn't going to fight either. Dan asked again and the kid spilled his guts, nearly coming to tears. We all wound up sitting around one of the picnic tables out back and talked until Dairyland closed. It was always like that. Dan says something or makes a gesture, and the whole mood changes. Like now, he brought my place to life," Josh said and went back to cutting Dan's hair as if nothing happened.

"I don't remember it quite like that. I recall Mike

The Diner

was pissed because I didn't let him fight. He always wanted to throw down."

"That's Mike. Always looking for trouble. So what do you think?" Joshua asked referring to the haircut.

"Damn. You're good."

"You know it."

"Hey, I need to head to the diner. Why don't you come by later for dinner? We can continue to get caught up, plus there are a few things I want to ask you."

"I bet you do. So then it's probably best we talk some place other than the diner." Josh's face was emotionless.

The new sunburned color on Dan's face faded immediately. It was as if Josh's words punched him in the stomach.

"What do you mean?"

"Uhhh," Josh hesitated. "It's like we can't talk here. I'm too busy, like you would be at the diner. You know where my parents' place...my place, is. Why don't you pop over on your way home? I have a single malt Scotch I think you'll like. We can talk more there."

Josh removed the smock which was Dan's clue that indeed, the conversation was over, at least for now.

"Yeah, sure," Dan said, still taken aback. He reached in his pocket for his money clip.

"Put that away. I owe you. Look what you've done to this place," Joshua spinning him around with pride. His salon was alive.

"Well here, give this to Jasmine," Dan said handing him a ten dollar bill.

"You got it. Come by later?"

"Yeah."

81

"See ya, handsome. Next time I'll cut your hair," Sherry said as Dan and Joshua walked toward the front door.

"Relax. It's all good. Right?" Joshua said, as Dan put his hand on the door to push it open.

"Yeah, I'm good," Dan replied as the color began to return to his face. "Hey, what did you mean by, 'Look at what I did to this place'?"

"You did what you always do; you created a moment that somehow turns into a memory. I don't know. I think this time you reminded everyone that it's perfectly fine to be who we are. See you later. Hey, my clients are backing up." Joshua waved and greeted his next client. "Make sure you come by later."

Created a memory. Hear that, Buck?

Dan stood by the door and looked over the salon. It didn't look any different, but admittedly, it felt different. As he walked to his car, he saw a familiar elderly man walking away from him just about to turn the corner.

"Milt?" Dan yelled and ran after him.

Dan checked the sandwich shop, the greeting card store, and wireless store. They were all busy with customers, but none resembled the man he saw.

"Gees, now I'm seeing things. I could use that Scotch now."

Chapter 11

Dan sat in the car collecting himself outside Josh's salon. There was so much noise swirling around in his head from how everyone close to him, and Josh, had died in a car accident, to thinking he saw Milt, and then Josh not wanting to talk at the diner. It was time to head to the diner, but he'd rather head straight out of town and back to Chicago. It seemed that every time he came in contact with someone, all he was left with were questions like "What happened to you or what's happening in my town?" And somehow the answers were buried back at the diner. Then again, maybe his imagination was just getting the better of him.

Shaking his head clear, he started to notice all the new business advertisements hanging on the windows.

At least those days are behind me. Angela knew what she was doing.

Angela was a public relations genius. It was never Dan's intention to create a place that the paparazzi encircled like vultures. Angela had different ideas and pushed the envelope as far as she could—all the way to New York. Dan was satisfied to stay behind the scenes and was always happiest in the kitchen or greeting customers.

The New York Scheff's had an amazing opening. Angela's picture with the latest edgy celebrity appeared in all the gossip papers for months before and after the opening. Hanging with celebrities is what first caught the attention of the folks of Circle Lake. On the wall alongside the diner cash register used to hang a picture of Dan and Angela on either side of Kevin Costner. That was one of the few recent photos that included Dan, so it was the obvious choice to be hung at the diner. He didn't notice it yesterday. It wouldn't be like his parents to take that picture down.

Celebrities, politicians, and the world's top CEOs fought for a reservation for the New York opening. The popular cable and network entertainment shows lined up rows deep to cover it. Angela at thirty-six could have easily stood next to any present day beautiful actress and held her own. That is if all that was required was to simply stand there. She was never one to "just stand there." Producers, directors, and actors begged her to be in their next project, but Angela was smart to say no. She was definitely not an actress, at least not one for the big screen. Her face always managed to find a home in front of the paparazzi cameras alongside the most popular actor, eating, drinking, and dancing. Rumors ran rampant. She was always reported to be the new leading lady or love interest of Hollywood's hottest marquee names. The lifestyle was contagious, and she couldn't let it go. And the "New York never sleeps" image of Angela was all the people of Circle Lake saw, a face on the cover of a tabloid. The last photo they saw of her was when she left Scheff's in New York around 1:30 a.m., with Ryan Billings. He was the latest twenty-something actor destined to replace Johnny Depp as the next do-it-all, quirky actor.

Ryan and Angela had struck up a quick friendship, one that began nine months earlier when he was filming in Chicago. He knew Scheff's was the place to be seen. Angela made every accommodation for him. As she told Dan, "The more he's here, the better for Scheff's." And when he was there, he was never alone. Angela always seemed to be by his side. To promote the premiere of his film, he invited Angela to New York. She told Dan, "He can do the same for Scheff's when we open in L.A., that's why I need to be in New York. You'll see." With Dan where he always was, in the kitchen of one his restaurants, this time Chicago, Angela went to New York. So did the press. As soon as she and Ryan walked out of the theatre, camera lights lit up the place like the Fourth of July.

While Ryan Billings was busy signing autographs, Angela headed for the limo. Apparently, she had had enough of the press for the night. Blinded by the camera flashes, she stumbled while walking in front of the limo. Out of nowhere, a pickup truck hit the rear end of the limo, crushing Angela between it and a taxi. The truck sped off. The police never caught the driver but found the truck abandoned near LaGuardia airport.

Whispers and innuendo always followed Angela wherever she went, and dying while going out with Hollywood's next big star only fueled the fire. There were rumors that someone heard Angela say, "Tell Dan I'm sorry," before she died. The gossip papers ran the headlines, "Tell Dan I'm Sorry!" No one could prove she actually said it. Regularly the paparazzi staked out at Scheff's in every city, but now they began to back off as they worked on their own damage control, being partially to blame for the accident. It was like the Princess Diana tragedy all over again but with only a small corner of the world looking on. The authorities even questioned Dan, saying it was routine. No charges were ever filed. Regardless, the tabloids ran with all kinds of story angles that implicated everyone short of the President of the United States. Dan never paid any attention to any of it. He knew what kind of marriage he and Angela had; at least he thought he knew. The last few years were tough. They never saw each other. Angela always promised, "After New York, things will be different." That was followed by, "After L.A., things will be different." L.A. never happened, but things were different. In less than a few weeks, Dan lost his wife and his parents.

Chapter 12

Before he knew it, Dan was pulling into his dad's, now his, parking space behind the diner. He didn't have time to think anymore about Angela or what Josh had said. As soon as he got in the car, his phone started ringing. First it was his restaurant managers checking in and then Los Angeles promoters looking for an update on the opening. When the answers weren't obvious, Dan addressed all questions and comments in the same way. "I'm taking some time to attend to personal matters. I'll be in back in touch soon."

Rather than walk in the back door and startle the kitchen staff, Dan decided to walk around to the front. He needed a little more air anyway. Leaning against the shadowy side of the building with one foot up against the brick wall and striking a James Dean like pose was Milt Walden.

"Milt, what are you doing out here? Didn't I see you out in Wander Lake?"

"Maybe, kid. I don't know."

"What do you mean, you don't know?"

"Forget about it, kid. It's not important."

"Well, come on in and let's get a cup of coffee or better yet an iced coffee. You know, that's not a bad idea, I should add an iced coffee to the menu."

"Good luck with that," Milt said under his breath.

"What?"

"Nothing. Listen, kid, you're going to see something in there that I'll explain later. At least I'll try to explain. You can't react. You have to play it cool. Got it?"

"What are you talking about?"

"Look at me. Take a good look at me."

"Ok. So?"

"I'm in there, but it's not me," Milt said, pointing his thumb around the corner of the building and into the diner like he was hitch-hiking. "And kid, that picture. It was me. Remember, play it cool."

Totally confused and frustrated, Dan took a few steps around the corner and looked in the diner. There were plenty of people moving and shuffling about, but he couldn't see faces. The sun's glare off the glass was too strong.

"What are you talking about? I don't see…"

Dan looked back toward Milt, but he was gone.

"Milt! What the hell is going on? Picture? What picture? Damn!"

Dan rushed around to the front of the diner. As he placed his hand on the door, he heard the words "Play it cool." Still, no one was around. After a deep breath to steady his nerves, Dan walked in unsure of what he might see. Everything looked normal enough until he saw Christine standing perfectly still and blinking slowly alongside Mrs. Gardner who was sitting on the edge the booth seat, holding Christine's left hand. In Christine's right hand was a coffee carafe. Ernest Gardner sat across from his wife with his back to the front of the restaurant. He turned and gave Dan a wink and smile. Dan's blood quickly began to boil. He wanted to pick the old man up and toss him out of the

The Diner

diner, but he had to "play it cool," so he nodded with indifference.

Dan couldn't tell if Mrs. Gardner was sharing an intimate secret or holding Christine captive. Regardless, she was doing all the talking. Dan was about to break up Dorothy and Christine when he saw Milt and Mae. Since Christine didn't look in distress, he wandered over.

Milt and Mae were sitting on one side of a booth, with Milt next to the window. Another couple was sitting across from them. Mae was chatting with the woman. Milt looked completely uninterested as he sat in silence, staring out the window. He wasn't looking at anything other than everything that was outside the diner.

Dan walked over. He was about to say, "Milt, what were you talking about before?" but it was clear that this wasn't the same Milt. This Milt had no energy or life about him. His face looked withdrawn, while his expression was one of total disinterest. He stared straight out through the window, looking as if nothing, absolutely nothing, was on his mind. Taking more strength than should be necessary, Dan forced a "Hi folks. Is everything all right?"

"It's fine," Mae said. "Dan, these are the Schneiders. Frank and Mary Anne, but we call her Annie. She looks like an Annie, doesn't she? They moved in a few years ago. They own the old Haskell place, you know on the north side of the lake. The Haskells retired down in Florida somewhere. I wonder whatever happened to them. Hmmm."

Dan guessed the Schneiders were roughly the same age as the Waldens. Frank sat across from Milt and was also staring out the window with a blank look on his face. Mae and Annie were engaged in a happy, lively discussion as Dan walked over.

"Nice to meet you. Can I get anyone anything? Milt, how about you? How about a nice iced coffee? I know I could sure use one. Milt?"

Milt remained stoic, seemingly not hearing a single word. Smiling awkwardly, Mae placed her hand on Milt's hand, and he came to life.

"Hey there, Danny. What's going on? Good to see. So sad about your parents, huh? I'm good here, Dan. How's that car of yours? Boy, we had the Mustang running good, didn't we?"

"Sure did," Dan said, hopefully convincingly, pulling his eyes away from Mae's hand. He wanted Milt to say something, anything, so he could study him closer. He resembled the Milt he saw outside, but different, like a Milt mannequin. "So Milt, how about that iced coffee?"

"There's no iced coffee on the menu, dear. Now I'm sure you have more important things to attend to. We'll see you soon." Mae removed her hand, and Milt's smile faded. He returned to the window.

Dan wanted more, but Milt was done. More urgently, he wanted to tell Mae and everyone at the table and the entire diner that it didn't make one bit of difference that iced coffee wasn't on the menu. He owned the place and intended to serve whatever he wanted. And then he wanted to scream, "What the hell is going on in this town?" Nothing came out. He had been dismissed. Feeling twelve years old again, Dan obediently turned around to see Gardner look away and settle back in his seat. He was obviously eavesdropping.

The Diner

Dan couldn't resist, so he headed over to his table. Mrs. Gardner was still holding Christine's hand.

"Hi, folks. How is everything? Christine?

It took a few seconds for Christine to respond. "Yes. Sorry, I need to see about my other tables." She refilled the Gardner's coffee.

"Doesn't she have lovely hands?" Mrs. Gardner asked.

"I wouldn't know. If you'll excuse me, I'm needed in the kitchen," Dan replied, anxious to walk away.

"Maybe you should find out," Mrs. Gardner replied. Mr. Gardner smiled in agreement and nodded.

"Christine, you can see to your other tables. Thank you," Dan said. Christine flashed a warm smile and walked away.

"Again, I'm quite busy, so I'll leave you two alone to finish your coffees."

"Nonsense. Feel free to sit and talk a bit. I'd love to hear about your plans. Certainly, you're not planning any changes to our diner," said Mr. Gardner.

"What do you mean?" Dan said, standing at the side of their table. He had no intention of sitting down. Had he been at Scheff's or with any other guest, he'd gladly have joined them and spoken eye to eye. But not here. Not now. He liked the advantage of towering over the Gardners.

"Well for one, changes to the menu like adding an iced coffee. This diner's menu is just fine the way it is. We all like it. It's what we all know and remember."

"Yes, I'm aware of that...but we'll see." Dan was ready to explode. "Others might like something new. And an iced coffee shouldn't shake anyone up too much."

91

"But then where will it stop? No, it's fine the way it is."

Dan cocked his head from side to side trying to recall Jasmine's magic shampoo touch that had waned much too fast.

"And look over there near the front door. There's a picture missing. That's not a good change," Gardner continued. "It's not what any of us expect to see when we walk in here."

Dan first looked over by the cash register where the picture of Angela, Kevin Costner, and him once hung. Indeed it was gone and now something else hung in its place. He'd check it out later. Dan turned over his shoulder to see the conspicuous blank spot on the wall.

Picture? Milt? What the hell? Play it cool.

"Thanks, Mr. Gardner," Dan said, swallowing the words hard. "I think you and the rest of the folks might like some of the changes I have planned. Good day."

"There will be no changes, Daniel. Furthermore…"

"What my husband is trying to say," Dorothy interrupted, putting her hand over her husband's. Gardner grumbled and then fell silent.

"Some changes are for the better, others may not be. We've been coming here a long time as has everyone here. Changes to the diner don't make sense. However, Dan, you would be advised to embrace everything this diner has to offer." Dorothy threw a head nod toward the diner counter.

Even though Dan was infuriated, he turned to see Christine cleaning up the counter. She smiled warmly and went back to work.

"I do know a thing or two about running a restaurant, so please do not concern yourself with the diner. In the restaurant business, change is inevitable...much like life. Again, thank you for coming," Dan said, though the words left a bitter taste in his mouth.

As he turned, he heard Dorothy Gardner say, "Yes, much like life. Hmm. And your outbursts only drain me of energy. Is that what you want, Ernest?"

"No. I apologize, my dear. I don't know what came over me."

Having had enough creepiness for the day, Dan walked over the cash register, because that's what his dad would have done, and checked on the day's receipts. Carlos stationed himself there.

"I don't know where they come from, Scheff, but this is the first lull we've had. How big is this town?" Carlos asked rhetorically. He and Dan looked out across the diner, wondering what exactly the draw was. "You know what's weird about this place?" Carlos asked.

"You mean how no one comes here alone? They only come in couples," Dan said robotically, unable to peel his eyes away from the Gardners.

"Yeah. What's that about?"

"I wish I knew," Dan said.

He thought back to when he was a kid. Did only couples come in then? He came in with his friends and took them into the kitchen and whipped up a couple of burgers or grilled cheese sandwiches. Sometimes they ate in the kitchen, but most of the time they took the food with them to the beach or park. He really couldn't remember what the diner felt like then, but he doubted it felt like this.

"What are you thinking?" Carlos asked.

"Be honest. Does this place seem strange in anyway? I mean, what vibe are you picking up?"

"Vibe? What's with the 1970s flashback?" Carlos remarked, laughing. "It feels like a diner. It feels warm and friendly."

"You sure?" Dan pressed. "That's it? Nothing else?"

"Old. It feels old. Not that that's a bad thing."

"That's it. It hasn't changed since I was a kid," Dan muttered, as he looked over at Gardner who, for once, wasn't staring back.

"This is a good crew," Carlos said, getting back to business. "Not much to do yet. No issues, except that somehow a picture was knocked off the wall by the door. I found it when I unlocked the front door. Not sure how it happened. You know what's strange though?"

"You mean there's more?" Dan asked, studying the diner walls closer. In many ways, it resembled what Josh had done to his salon, but felt outdated, while the salon felt nostalgic.

"It should be in more pieces. I mean, it fell off the wall. At the very least the glass should be broke. The frame looked like it had been pulled apart rather than broken. There was a newsletter sticking out of it. I think it's a union newsletter from the auto plant. Apparently it was a Chrysler plant before Honda bought it and retooled it. At any rate, it's on your desk. It can be repaired easily enough," Carlos said shrugging his shoulders in surprise.

"I'll look at it later. What did you mean by 'not much to do yet'?" Dan said, as he walked over to pour some coffee in a large tumbler, followed by cream and ice.

"This place can run itself if nothing changes, and I'm not saying anything needs to change. But I know you, the moment anything feels tired or old, you do something about it. We don't go a month at the restaurant without trying something new. It's why people keep coming back, to see what we'll do next."

Dan smiled.

"What?"

"I'm not sure any of these people can handle anything new," Dan replied. "Listen, I'm going to hang out here through dinner, and then I'm going to meet an old friend. Do you mind closing? I'll open in the morning."

"Of course not. No worries." Carlos went back to closing out the register and clearing it for the dinner hour. He was used to tracking receipts for one serving period, dinner. Now he had two more, breakfast and lunch.

Dan wasn't worried about Carlos, but nothing about the diner or the town was making him feel all that comfortable. Before heading into the kitchen, Dan gave Milt another look. He was tempted to walk over and toss everyone else out of the booth and grill Milt for answers. Now he and Frank Schneider were talking, making Milt look more like the Milt he saw outside. Their wives were huddled up close to them, too close for Dan's comfort. The whole scene made Dan uneasy, but he had no idea why.

Christine walked in front of Dan. She was busy checking the coffee creamers and putting those that needed refilling into her bus tray. Dan couldn't get over how much she looked like Angela from behind. If it had been Angela, he would have gone over and patted her on the ass. He always loved her rear end. "It's your best feature," he would tell her. "It takes one to know one," she'd shoot back. Christine turned quickly around and caught Dan in full stare. She smiled back and wiggled her behind. Embarrassed, Dan quickly looked away and turned to refill his iced coffee. Sweat beads began to form on his forehead.

Maybe she really didn't see me staring. She wiggled her butt at me. Idiot. Just like Angela used to do. Of course she saw. At least she didn't slap her ass like Angela did. That would have really freaked me out.

He wanted to turn around and see what she was doing, but couldn't.

Play it cool.

His only refuge was in the kitchen.

"How goes it, Ray? Any issues?" Dan forced out trying his best to sound like business as usual.

"Not a thing. He's got it, Dan," Ray said, of James, his new apprentice. "I'm going to stay a little longer and train James to help with dinner. Sound good? He wants to learn. So…"

"Fine by me. Run it by Carlos."

"I did. He's fine."

"Good. Show him all the tricks," Dan said, his words fading as set the iced coffee down on his dad's desk.

Dan fought back the emotion as he fell into the old oak chair that swiveled and rotated releasing an annoying ear-drum-shattering creak through the kitchen. Despite the smell of grilled meat and French fries in the air, Dan was certain he could smell Old Spice after-shave float up around him as he sank into the seat cushion. He laughed thinking that Buck applied Old Spice to his ass. As he looked around the kitchen, he understood why his dad had the desk in the corner by the supply shelves. From here, he could see everything that was going on in the kitchen, while hearing the murmur of customers in the diner. He imagined his dad sitting and peering at Ray through the shelves of the steaming prep tables. Even now Ray and James were walking up and down from the broiler past the grill to the fry station. Ray was talking, and James listened intently. Dan pictured his dad sitting behind the desk, watching Ray closely as he plated up an order and making sure everything was done as it always had been. Off to the side, Dan could see the soup, salad, and garnish station where the waitresses finished the plates while sharing stories of their lives.

Dan decided to settle in behind the desk. It quickly became clear that Carlos had been here as the paper that had littered the desk earlier was now separated into neat piles of time cards, inventory sheets, orders, etc. In the center of the desk was a check book with the payee, the amount, and date filled out. All that was required was Dan's signature.

I'm going to have to give Carlos a raise.

The broken picture was on the corner of the desk. He'd get to that in a moment. First he wanted to explore the desk drawers. He knew each one would harbor a boatload of memories, so he thought he'd go through them one at a time, maybe even one a day. In the top left drawer was a baseball signed by Ernie Banks, Ron Santo, and Billy Williams, his dad's favorite Chicago Cubs. It's why Dan became a Cubs fan, because of his dad. Dan studied it like it was an ancient artifact. There were also a few Cubs game ticket stubs, pens, paperclips, and a bunch of outdated office supplies.

"Hungry, Mr. Scheffelin? I mean Dan," James said from behind the counter. "How about a serving of our famous macaroni and cheese?"

"He doesn't eat that," said Christine coming through the kitchen door. "Never liked it, even as a kid."

Christine walked over to the sink with a bus tray of dirty dishes and empty creamers. Dan traced her every step with his mouth open in shock.

"What kid doesn't like mac and cheese? This stuff is amazing. Ray showed me how you do it. I could live on it. Of course then I'd be two hundred pounds. Scheff, what do you say?"

"He's good, James. He'll make what he wants. Let's get ready for dinner. It's Monday, so it's Salisbury steak night. First we need…" Ray took him over to the refrigerator and went through the recipe step by step.

"My mom makes Salisbury steak. It's great," James said.

"I'm sure she does. Did you like the mac and cheese?"

"Yes."

"Then wait till you taste this."

"How the hell did you know I hate mac and cheese?" Dan asked, leaping off the chair and making his way over to Christine.

"Really, how do you know I don't like mac and cheese?" he asked again, getting as close as he could without touching her.

"Because…," she replied calmly, reaching across

The Diner

his body to retrieve a towel to dry the creamers. Her arm brushed across his. "That's what you always told me."

Dan's arm tingled.

Christine gathered up the clean creamers and walked over to the dairy refrigerator to fill them. Stunned, Dan paused for a few seconds then followed close behind as Christine nonchalantly went about her chores.

"What? When?" he asked, reaching for the cream to help, rubbing his arm.

Both of their hands held the cream, neither releasing it. Dan's hand overlapped hers. Christine blinked once and stared at him. After a long pause, she opened her eyes, and Dan was trapped. He knew those eyes. He had been lost in them so many times before. They were beautiful.

Angela's eyes.

"You mentioned it when we were at the Brookfield Zoo. Remember when we were both so hungry, and they had nothing but gross fast food to eat. The macaroni and cheese looked best. You remember," she insisted. "It was months before we opened in Chicago."

Dan nearly fell to the floor. He looked around to see if anyone else had heard what she said. They were all busy. He was on his own. Lost for words, he looked back at Christine who never took her eyes off him. It was in her eyes. That's where the words came from, from the eyes he missed so much.

Angela's eyes.

Dan released her hand as he fell against the table alongside the refrigerator. Christine smiled and went back to filling the creamers as if nothing happened.

Like she was performing surgery, she never diverted from the task at hand. Stunned, Dan gasped for air, because there wasn't any left in his lungs. Speechless.

Finished, Christine replaced the cream in the refrigerator and picked up the bus tray, ready to go back to the diner to set them on the tables.

"Are you feeling all right?" she asked. "You look pale."

"Brookfield Zoo? How would you know that?"

"Know what? What are you talking about? It sounds like you're the one that doesn't remember. And besides, you're the one that doesn't like macaroni and cheese. Everyone loves it. Quit being so silly, Daniel."

He stood there, frightened and confused. All he could do was watch her walk toward the kitchen door. He quickly looked around the kitchen. Someone had to have heard the exchange between them. Still no witnesses.

"Christine, hang on a minute."

"I'll be back in a sec. Besides, this gives you another chance to check out my ass," she said and then spanked her ass and walked out the door.

As quick as she exited, Carlos came walking in.

"Scheff, I'm sure you saw those checks on your desk. How about you sign them, and I'll get them out? Geez, you look like crap."

"Huh? Yeah, yeah. Just going through my dad's stuff in the desk. Memories, you know?" Dan said, trying to catch his breath.

"I'm sorry. I forgot. I didn't throw anything away. I only organized things a little. Sit down, and I'll bring you a fresh coffee. Looks like you could use it. Iced or regular?"

The Diner

"Huh? Regular. Thanks."

Dan stood still and watched Carlos leave the kitchen. He took a slow, deliberate look around the kitchen. It was busy with people and activity; still he felt lost and alone. Shaken, he was ready to burst through the kitchen doors and confront Christine. It was impossible for her to know those things. Only he and Angela knew about how they spent their day at Brookfield Zoo, and though the details were vague to him, he knew they were true. Christine recalled it like it happened yesterday.

"Play it cool."

Dan wasn't sure how much longer he could contain the anxious energy building inside, but he knew he had to. From Milt to Christine to Gardner, he felt like they were closing in on him, trapping him in a corner. But why? There were no answers, only questions. But one thing was certain; there was time to figure it all out. For as long as he owned and operated his own business, slow and deliberate was always his strategy. "If you cook fast, all you get is fast food," he'd tell his staff. Even though he wasn't cooking, it was going to take time to figure out was going on with the people of the town and his diner.

"Here you go," Carlos said, setting the coffee down on the desk. "By the way, Mr. Gardner said he'll wait. What the hell is he talking about?"

"I wish I knew. Wait for what?"

"I thought you might know."

Just as he was beginning to calm down, the mention of Gardner, like Pavlov's dog, had his nervous energy boiling over. Refusing to react, Dan relegated himself to the desk to sign checks. With the last of the checks signed and the register closed, all Dan could do was think and he did, about everything.

Sitting back, he savored the cup of coffee. The first sip brought back memories of his parents.

I guess if you make coffee this good and serve good food to a perpetually packed diner, why would you change anything?

"Because you need to keep it fresh and not boring."

"What's that, Scheff?" Carlos asked.

"Nothing, just mumbling to myself.

"What do you want to do about that?"

Dan reached for the picture frame. Behind the glass was a collection of newspaper articles on the closing of the Chrysler plant and the eventual transition over to Honda. It was a huge event. Without Honda, there was no telling what would have become of Circle Lake, Wander Lake, and the surrounding communities. Dan pulled out the cardboard backing that everything was pasted too. It seemed easy enough to fix. A blue, four-page newsletter put out by the local United Auto Workers Union stuck out from the rest. The glue was now too dry to keep it affixed.

The front page touted the efforts of the union to work out a deal with Honda. Their angle was, if it hadn't been for them, the plant would have closed. Uninterested in what happened because, after all, the plant was there and thriving, he opened the newsletter. There were a few small articles on safety, membership efforts, a calendar of events, and a small section entitled "In Memoriam."

"Son of a bitch!"

"Something wrong, Dan?" James asked as he mixed ground beef with spices under the watchful eye of Ray.

"Don't mix it too much," Ray instructed, never looking up at Dan.

"All good. Listen to Ray," Dan said mechanically as he sprung up from the chair and blasted his way through the kitchen doors with the UAW newsletter in his hand.

"Dammit!"

Chapter 13

Dan stopped cold in the middle of the diner. There were three couples all sitting at separate tables. Two of the couples were unfamiliar. The other was the Gardners watching Dan's every move. Rosie, Molly, and Christine were getting ready for the dinner rush, which was still hours away.

Carlos threw a nod at Dan to signal the Gardners hadn't left yet.

"Screw them. When did the Waldens leave?"

"Sorry, not sure who they are."

"They were a four-top, the middle, by the window," Dan said pointing.

"Three or four minutes ago."

Dan flew out the front door.

"Milt! Milt!" Dan shouted as he looked up and down Lake Street. Not seeing the Waldens, he ran around the corner to the back of the restaurant and shouted out again.

"Son of a bitch!"

Dan stood at the back corner of the restaurant, under the shade of an oak tree whose roots had the sidewalk heaving in all directions. Breathing heavily, he looked down at the newsletter again hoping he misread it. He hadn't.

Four sentences in the Union newsletter was all Milt got for his twenty of years of service. "In Memoriam.

We are saddened by the passing of Milt Walden, foreman, first shift, transmission line. Mr. Walden died of complications from pneumonia. He is survived by his wife Mae and two children William and Audrey. Funeral services tbd."

"Yep, I'm dead. It's accurate."

"What the hell? You can't be." Dan reached out to grab Milt's hand but glided right through it. Dan's hand was freezing cold and tingling as if he had been electrocuted. Dan started to stagger, feeling light-headed.

"Don't pass out on me, kid. You need to stop all this."

"Stop what? Jesus Christ…Jesus Christ. What's happening to my arm?"

Dan held his hand out wanting to reach out again, but the energy vibrating off Milt was too intimidating.

"Something you won't understand. At least for now. Just know it's building. Listen, I can't stay here. I need to go."

"What's building? If you're dead…then my parents, Milt. What about my parents?"

"They're not here, kid. They're at rest, where I want to be. We need your help. Gardner will be out any second. Play it cool. Don't say anything. I'll find you."

"How? When? And what do you mean, 'We need your help'?"

"I'm not alone. They're coming. See ya, kid."

Dan looked over Milt's shoulder toward the front corner of the restaurant. No one was coming yet. He had more questions for Milt, but as soon as he looked back, he was gone. Dan reached out to where Milt was standing. The air was frigid but warming. His legs felt like they weighed a hundred pounds each. He nearly tripped over the cracked sidewalk as he lumbered back to the diner. Looking up, he could see the Gardners coming toward him. Eying the kitchen entrance at the back of the diner, he took two steps in that direction but stopped. Just because he wasn't fond of them, he had no intention of avoiding them.

They know something.

Straightening his back, Dan met them head on.

"What do you have there, son?" Mr. Gardner asked, pointing at the newsletter with one hand while he held his wife's in the other.

"I'm not your son." *You asshole. What business is it of yours?* "This fell out of the picture. It's an old UAW newsletter."

"Find anything interesting in it?"

"Yes, I did."

"And that would be?" Gardner asked.

Dan assumed that everyone in town jumped when Gardner spoke and immediately became subservient. He had no intention of following that model. He wondered if Mrs. Gardner behaved that way. She stood with a firm, straight back but with her eyes closed as if she was praying.

"It's really nothing, certainly nothing that involves you. Thanks for coming. Good day." Dan stepped aside to the let couple pass.

"You can't always believe everything you read, son."

"Once again, I'm not your son. Got it? Please come again," Dan said, rolling his eyes when he saw that Dorothy's eyes were still closed.

"Look, you need to understand this place creates

lasting memories. You won't take away the lives and loves of so many."

"It's a goddamn diner, serving food from yesteryear for crying out loud. It's my business, and I'll do whatever I damn well please. Now if you'll excuse me."

"I'm sorry. I can't let you do whatever you please. If your father were here, he'd tell you. But alas, he decided…" Gardner started to say as he blocked Dan's path. "No matter. You're here now, and as such I must see to it that you leave the diner untouched. You see the lives you affect, include your own. We'll talk more soon. You'll see it my way."

"What did my father decide? Tell me."

"In due time you will learn all you need to know," Gardner said, as his voice rose in anger. "You will leave the diner as is!"

"I don't think so. You can open your eyes now, Mrs. Gardner, I'm leaving." Dan bumped Gardner out of the way and headed to the front of the diner. He considered pressing Gardner for more information, but why. As long as Gardner was doing the chasing, Dan felt that he held the upper hand.

****

"It seems Daniel will need more convincing," Mrs. Gardner said, opening her eyes.

"Indeed. Let's hope your project is beginning to take root, otherwise, drastic measures will be necessary."

"Death is only a last resort. Do I make myself clear?"

Gardner nodded.

"Ernest. Do I make myself clear? You have drained

me of too much energy as it is putting our current clients at risk."

"Yes, my dear," Gardner replied as his mind raced.

"I must rest. Take us home," Dorothy said and walked ahead of Gardner.

Gardner turned to look at the diner.

"Well, Daniel, I see you will take more convincing. My boy, you have no idea what you've started."

Chapter 14

"Gees, Dan, you look like you've seen a ghost. What's up?" asked Carlos as he wiped down the diner counter.

"You wouldn't believe it. But hey, it's all good," Dan replied, deciding to keep what little he knew to himself. "And it's nothing I can't handle."

Dan walked over to the counter and picked up the receipts that Carlos had already reconciled.

"Something you need?" Carlos asked as Dan sorted through the paperwork.

"I never finished my coffee. Do you mind? I'm going back into the kitchen. I want to go through these and see what people are ordering."

"Coming up. There is one trend. See if you can spot it," Carlos said.

The kitchen was quiet. Everyone was busy cleaning or taking a break. Dan was relieved that no one said anything to him. He wanted to be alone and distract his mind with a simple task. However, he couldn't help noticing Christine, sitting on a stool, making herself a spinach salad. He recalled how when he made a spinach salad, Angela would always pick off the bacon. She hated spinach, saying it made her teeth feel dirty.

Dan smiled yet still felt unsatisfied that he never got answers to how Christine knew about his dislike for mac and cheese. Like every mystery so far, it would have to wait to be sorted out.

Christine smiled back.

Dan laid the receipts out on the desk, took a deep breath, and began reviewing them one by one. With more than a third of completed in a heap off to his left, Carlos walked in with his iced coffee.

"Spot it yet?"

"Not through them all, but if I had to guess, they all had coffee. Right? Did anyone not order coffee?"

"Nope. Every single customer. I've never seen that before. Damn good coffee, I guess. I haven't tried it," Carlos said and returned to the dining room.

"Told ya," Christine said. "There's something about this coffee. They love it."

"'Cause you made it, right?"

"Actually, I don't remember. I'm sure I made a pot or two."

"Whatever keeps them coming back," Dan said. "That's different for this place," he said referring to the spinach salad, almost saying "different for you."

"It is, isn't it? I mean we have spinach here, but we only use it for a spinach omelet, not a salad. It doesn't make sense. I suggested it to your dad, but he was like…I'm sorry."

"I know. He said something like, 'There's plenty on the menu to choose from.' "

"I think that's exactly what he said," Christine replied as she crumbled bacon on top of her salad.

Dan wanted to ask her about the macaroni and cheese incident at Brookfield Zoo, but as he looked at her, there was something different about her. She looked like Christine, not Angela.

110

"This salad needs something."

"It needs some chopped hardboiled egg, perhaps some pecans, and a quality balsamic vinegar dressing," Dan replied walking over to the refrigerator. "I'm afraid all we have in this kitchen is the egg and almond slivers, which will be okay. I don't think a bottle of balsamic vinegar has ever been within twenty miles of this diner. Here let me help."

Dan sprinkled the almonds on the salad and then chopped up the egg wielding the knife so quickly and effortlessly.

"Look at you go," Christine said smiling.

Dan enjoyed showing off his knife skills. As he slid the knife under the pile of chopped egg and moved it over the salad, their arms touched. Electricity shot through him. It reminded him of first time he held a girl's hand and the adrenaline rush of a first kiss. They stood frozen in place for what felt like minutes.

"Wow!" Dan was the first to speak, not realizing he said it aloud.

Christine came to life and lifted herself onto the stainless steel counter and started picking at the bacon on the salad. Dan was looking straight into the eyes of Angela.

"No matter what you make, you always do it with…"

"Flair," Dan finished her sentence.

He knew it was coming. How and why she said it, he had no clue.

"This is good bacon. You should get this for Scheff's, Daniel," she said, winking as she continued to pick the salad clean.

"We need to talk," he said as his hand touched

hers.

"We don't have to talk. There are other things we can do."

"Doesn't she have lovely hands," he recalled Mrs. Gardner saying. And Christine did. His hand didn't move. It felt warm and wonderful. It was a touch that he missed so much. He simply didn't have the strength to move.

Carlos walked back into the kitchen startling Dan.

"Gees, Scheff, these people eat an early dinner in this town. It feels like we're in a retirement community. Christine, we need you out here," Carlos added and then walked back out to the dining room, but not before taking another look at Dan and Christine. He shook his head and smiled.

"Later, Daniel."

Dan stared at her in amazement.

"I'll put your salad in the refrigerator. You can eat it later."

"Don't be silly. You know I don't like spinach. It makes my teeth feel…"

"Dirty…I know."

Dan stood shocked for a few seconds and then finally made his way over to the desk. He reached for the cup of coffee but didn't drink it. He stared at it.

"What the hell is going on around here?"

Chapter 15

Gardner pushed his horse hard all the way to the lake. Coach was more than up to the challenge. Gardner wished all his employees followed orders like Coach. A ride along the shoreline was what he needed to clear his head. It was his favorite part of his acreage, or as he called it, his kingdom. There was always a breeze off the lake, and the sound of the waves lapping the shore calmed even the most anxious of thoughts. Dan Scheffelin was proving to be an inspired challenge.

"No matter. Plenty of people have tried standing up to me and my enterprise for what I believe to be for the betterment of our town. The kid's got more backbone than the old man. I'll give him that. He may not be so easy to manage," Gardner said to Coach.

Gardner was certain his father would be proud of what he had created. His dad, Andrew Gardner, and grandfather, Horace Gardner, dedicated their services to the folks of Circle Lake. And that was only if a client came to them. No one was forced to participate. It was a free service. Ernest Gardner saw so much more. He saw it as an enterprise, a multi-million dollar enterprise. "Who wouldn't pay to be with the one they love for the rest of their life?" He decided to change the business model.

For years the Scheffelin family supported the elder Gardner's service to the town. No one was ever hurt in the process. When Ernest took over the business, the service stayed the same, but he expanded his market beyond the Circle Lake city limits. Furthermore, rather than doing something for the people of the town, he was doing something to them. He began dictating how life after death will be conducted. His service was now required for anyone living in town. As a result, the trust and friendship between the families deteriorated. Buck tried numerous times to remind Ernest of his father and grandfather's purpose for bringing the service, as they called it, to the town. "Narrow minded and short sighted," Ernest replied. "Why do for only a few when so many more can benefit?"

Buck didn't have the know-how or the strength to fight Ernest. The threat of Diavolo, the devil of Circle Lake, was all too real. The whole town knew how one of their neighbors, Jim Clancy, had suffered at the devil's hands. He was found in his garden with a pitchfork through his throat. On Clancy's chest was the word "Diavolo" written in his own blood. Though, Gardner didn't like taking the life, the message had to be sent. To live and die in Circle Lake took obedience and suicide. They were the only two options. Buck couldn't win against Gardner. All he ever wanted to do was own and operate the diner. It was all he knew.

Ernest was running a business, a business clients paid dearly to become a customer of. Of course, there was a reduced rate for the citizens of Circle Lake. That was a promise he made to his father before he died. One thing the business couldn't accommodate was a vessel for his father's soul to occupy. The same was true for his grandfather. The Gardner family was one of kind. Their search proved that there wasn't a vessel anywhere

The Diner

on earth. Therefore, the same fate awaited Gardner, but that was many years away. However, Gardner liked the idea that the town believed he wouldn't die. It made him seem invincible. Should his own energy source be removed, his life would end. And when that time came, the business would be handed down to his son, David, who was away, learning and perfecting his craft.

Staring across the lake toward the Scheffelin property brought some clarity.

"He needs to know that I am in control of this town and ultimately in charge of the diner. Yes, a message must be sent. And then our diner and town can get back to normal."

Gardner gave a single sharp pull on the leather reins and guided Coach back to the compound. Thundering hooves pounded the dry ground stirring up a trail of dust as Coach glided like a missile through the tall, bronze grass.

Gardner saw a couple farmhands loading a pickup truck with fence mending supplies. Their heads turned when they heard Coach in the distance. The six man crew stood motionless as Gardner slowed Coach to an easy trot. He liked surveying his employees from the saddle as he entered the compound. It made him feel like a sixteenth century warlord on his trusted steed. He turned his head left and right, looking each crew member in the eye, staring them down until their chins hit their chests. Near the maintenance barn he saw Emil Matchak. Emil, the foreman and Gardner's most trusted employee, was staring down one of the new employees who seemed to be busy talking rather than doing what he was assigned to do. Everyone knew the guy as Mills.

Gardner stopped Coach. It was clear Emil was

115

about to remind Mills exactly who was in charge. At six foot four with a shaved head, muscles that bulged even when he was scratching an itch, a nose that had been busted more once, and a scar over one eye, Emil was an intimidating figure.

"You know, Mills, it seems you'd get a lot more work done if you kept your mouth shut," Emil said.

"I'm the one doing most of the work already. And if you don't like my talking, don't listen," Mills replied as he returned to loading the bed of the truck with more supplies.

Gardner watched Emil standing like a statue. Emil eyed Mills as he walked to the truck. Mills would cross his path again when he walked back into the barn.

"This should be interesting, Coach," Gardner said, patting the horse's neck.

Mills walked passed Emil, staring him down the whole way. Emil's head never moved. He looked straight ahead at the truck.

"Hey, Mills," Emil said.

Mills stopped and turned. The power and force of Emil's punch sent Mills staggering and slowly crumbling to the ground. Shaking his head, he pulled one knee up, took a deep breath, and got himself back on two feet.

"I've got work to do," Mills said smiling, as he brushed the dirt and dust off his pants and turned to head back into the barn.

Gardner nodded at Emil. Emil lowered his arms and unclenched his fists. He then pointed at one of his men to walk over to take the horse, but Gardner shook him off.

"Emil, I have an assignment for you. It takes

The Diner

priority. We're going to need to send a message, much like the one you just delivered, to Mr. Scheffelin. His cooperation must be encouraged. Let's not make it too severe though. Keep it meaningful. And take care of it at the diner. I want him to know that there is no place in this town that I can't reach."

"Yes, sir. I'll handle it myself," Emil replied.

Gardner always insisted on a verbal response. No head nod or shake. "Yes, sir" was the most preferred.

"I'd rather you didn't. Take that kid, Bostwick, and Mills. Mills is big enough and should now follow orders without question. Should something go wrong, they can easily be replaced."

"Yes, sir."

"Head over to the diner as soon as you can. Mrs. Gardner and I will be there shortly for dinner. Understood?"

"Yes, sir." Emil released the reins.

Chapter 16

The aroma of Salisbury steak triggered another round of childhood diner memories for Dan. The smell always made him hungry, and today was no different. While still in culinary school, he'd occasionally help out his dad in the kitchen. Anxious to apply what he learned, he'd try to modify the recipe. His dad always stepped in and grabbed his hand before he could shake a different spice into the ground beef.

"When you get your own restaurant, you can make everything the way you want."

"And I will," Dan replied defiantly.

"Good. Never settle. But don't be surprised if not everyone loves it though."

"What do you mean?"

"It may be how you want it, but is it what your customers want? This Salisbury steak is just how my customers want it. Like everything else on the menu."

Pulling his eyes away from the grill and ovens, he rubbed his eyes trying to stem the tide of tears. Dan started sifting through the other drawers in the desk. He found old receipts, coasters, pens that no longer worked, and a few photos. Other than a few odds and ends, there was nothing in the desk of value. As he closed the middle top drawer, just under the desktop he heard the sound of paper flapping and getting caught on an edge. Opening and closing the drawer repeated the

The Diner

sound, but there were no loose papers that he could find. He took the drawer out and placed it on top of the desk just as Ray walked over with plate of Salisbury steak and set it down.

"Still as good as ever, Scheff. I'll get you a fork."

"Thanks, Ray. It does smell good. Nicely done, James."

"Thanks, but maybe you should try it first," James replied.

"Ray, remember that discussion you, Buck, and I had?" Dan said. One thing that irritated Buck and Dan was when someone plated up something that they felt less than confident about. Ray made that mistake once. Dan handled most of the conversation with Ray, surprised that his dad didn't interrupt. Afterwards, his dad pulled Dan aside and said, "Nicely done. Teach, not preach, right? Give them something to think about. A few clues make the lesson sink in deeper."

I miss you, Dad.

"James. Walk with me for a minute," Ray said across the kitchen. "Let's get Scheff a fork."

With a puzzled look on his face, James followed Ray out to the waitress station.

Dan reached under the desktop and felt an envelope secured to the underside of the desk top with tape. Dan pulled it free. There was no name on it, but it was dated two weeks prior to his parents' death. Dan looked around the kitchen. No one was paying attention to him. He tore into it quickly before Ray and James returned.

A handwritten note on a single page of lined paper was inside. He recognized his dad's handwriting immediately.

Daniel,

I'm sorry we left you alone with so much to figure out and so many souls to take care of. Your mother is sick and I need to be with her…only her. I can't begin to explain why or what the diner is and has always been. And knowing you, you've already begun searching. I hope I've taught you to never settle. You can't, especially now. You'll soon learn everything about us, the town, and why our diner is so important.

Our diner is a good place, Daniel. So many people in our town, your town, need it just as it is. Remember, change for the sake of change isn't always a good thing. Still there are good family friends out there that need your help. Your mother and I couldn't do it. It's up to you, son. We know you have the strength to find a way. Know that we'll be at rest and have found our way to the other side. We love you very much. Tell Milt and the others we'll see them soon.

If this letter remains hidden may God find a home for the many souls that wander.

We love you,
Mom and Dad.

Dan read the letter three times. He could hear Ray and James approaching. Wiping his eyes dry, he folded up the letter and put it in his pocket. With the drawer replaced, he began tearing up the envelope.

"What are you up to, Scheff?" Ray asked.

"Tearing up the payroll. You guys don't want to get paid, do you?"

"Heck, no. We should be paying you," he said handing Dan a place setting.

"We good, Ray?" Dan asked as he stabbed at the Salisbury steak.

The Diner

"Yep. Everyone gets it."

"Perfect. And James, I'm talking about the special. Nicely done."

"Thank you. I knew it would be," he said, smiling.

"Ray, I'm going to do a few more things and then head out."

Ray nodded and went back behind the counter to show James a few more diner tricks, which brought a smile to Dan's face because it confirmed what his dad had written. "The diner is a special place."

No one else has a clue that something is going on around here. But there are clues, right Buck?

"Either they were too naïve or simply accepted it as that's how things work at Scheff's Diner in Circle Lake," he muttered.

Dan patted his pocket to make sure the letter was still there. He planned on reading it at least another dozen times, thinking there had to be a clue in it that he was missing. The list of questions continued to grow, but he knew getting the answers wouldn't be easy.

He hoped Josh had some answers. He had intimated as much. Dan put his plate in the bus tray and went to check on Carlos before leaving. The diner was at half capacity. He couldn't believe it. It should be empty. Though as he thought about it, it was the same when he was a kid.

Some things don't change.

"Carlos, I'm heading out. Looks like everything is in good shape here."

Out of the corner of his eye, Dan saw Christine looking his way. He tried not to look at her but couldn't help himself. She smiled. He smiled back. He wanted to walk over and talk to her but couldn't think of what to

121

say. All he had were questions, and something told him that she didn't have any answers. He patted the letter in his pocket again.

"All good, Scheff. Look at the street. More cars are pulling up," Carlos replied.

Dan gazed through the diner windows and was amazed at how a small town's main street could fill up so fast. Once again, he felt like he was seventeen as it all looked like it did years ago. He even saw an old Ford F150 drive by, the kind Mike Miller used to drive.

Crazy.

"Should be a good night. See you tomorrow. Call me if you need anything," Dan said as he walked back into the kitchen. It was something he always said. Not once did Carlos ever call.

"Ray, James, see you both tomorrow."

"G'night, Scheff," they said in unison.

Dan didn't look up until he heard the kitchen door close behind him. When he did, he saw three huge men leaning up against his car. He could see the faces of two of them. One had a broken nose; the other looked like a stupid kid, like the ones he used to meet out at the Dairyland. He couldn't make out the third. He had a beard and a weathered Cubs hat pulled down over his face.

Emil was the first to approach Dan. It was the Dairyland all over again. Dan could feel it.

"It seems you're making plans to change things around here," Emil said. "This town and this diner get along just fine as is. Why don't you just leave well enough alone?"

"Maybe I will, but probably won't. That's not how I do things. Now if you'll excuse me."

The Diner

"Bostwick, reinforce my point will you?"

This was a first for Dan. Usually people talk before acting. Not Bostwick. The punch landed square in Dan's stomach, knocking all the air from his lungs. Dan bounced off the diner dumpster and then off the kitchen door. He hoped someone had heard the commotion. He also wished he was in better shape. There was no way he could fight all three, and there was nowhere to run.

"Hang on. Let's talk a minute." Dan relied on what he knew. The guy in the Cubs hat shook his head. Dan was certain he heard him laughing too, but he was too busy catching his breath.

"Mills, why don't you show this clown how we talk things through," Emil instructed. "Then maybe he'll understand how things operate around here."

Mills stepped between Emil and Bostwick. He kept them only a foot behind him.

"You haven't changed a bit, have you, Scheffy? You can't talk your way out of this. Let me see if I can help you this time…"

Mills left elbow flew up and caught Emil in the throat followed closely by a hammering foot to the groin. Bostwick stood stunned. With a quick right hand, Mills hit him squarely on the nose, sending blood and cartilage flying. Emil began to straighten up, when Mills landed another left to the jaw.

"How's it feel, asshole? No one fucks with my friends. And it's Miller. Mike Miller, dickhead."

Emil hit the ground, writhing.

Bostwick's head swiveled around. He was lost and by the shocked look on his face, he clearly didn't expect events to go this way. Mike grabbed him by the shirt and lifted the young man's 240 pound frame off

123

the ground and threw him against the diner brick wall. Bostwick slid down the wall like cold maple syrup on a stack of pancakes. Mike picked him up again.

"This is your chance, you fat fuck. Get out of town and never come back. Get a job at the plant. Do something with your life. If I see you again, I won't be this cordial," Mike said as his knee came up and flushed any remaining air out of the kid's lungs. "If you want to join the rest of the ghosts walking around this town, then go ahead and stick around."

Mike set the kid on his feet and shot him a cold, hard stare. "Now git!!"

Dan stood there stunned.

So Mike Miller turned out to be one hell of a badass.

Bostwick stumbled all the way to his car. They could hear Emil beginning to come around.

"Where the hell have you been?" Dan finally found the energy to speak.

"Hang on, Scheff. This piece of shit needs to have his nose fixed." Mike bent over Emil and picked him up. "You know what, Evil? Your nose bothers me. You fucking asshole."

With his hands on Emil's shirt sleeves, Mike head butted Emil and threw him against the trash cans.

"He's nothing but a piece of fucking garbage," Mike said walking over to Emil again hoping he'd get up. Nothing. Emil was out cold.

"Scheff, give me your keys," Mike said as he opened the BMW's driver's side door. "Move that big fat ass of yours and get in."

Hitting the edge of town, Dan finally broke the silence.

The Diner

"What the hell was that all about? I knew this town was stuck somewhere between 1950 and 1970, but geezus, that was like the Wild West back there."

"I'm sure that's not the last we'll hear from Gardner," Mike said, pushing the bill of his hat higher on his head, revealing the creased forehead and eyes that Dan remembered.

"Gardner? What were you doing with them?"

"I work for him, at least I did. Guess I'll have to find another job," Mike added, flashing a wry smile.

"Don't worry about that. I can take care of that…"

"Same ol' Scheffy, always trying to fix things."

"What?"

"Never mind. I was trying to find out how Gardner could have such a grip on this town."

"Fuck him. I'm gonna kill that son of a bitch," Dan said, pounding the side door with his fist.

"I'm not sure you can kill him."

"What?"

"How do you kill something that has no soul?"

Chapter 17

"What the hell happened?" Josh asked. "I don't know why, but I expected to see you guys a little more cut and battered." He quickly ushered them inside. As soon as he got to the bar, he poured them each a Scotch on the rocks. "Mike called me and said Gardner was going to teach you a lesson. I offered to help, but he just laughed. Asshole. So tell me, what happened?"

Dan looked over at Mike who motioned with his hand as if to say, "The floor is all yours." However, Dan was still a bit in shock and struggled to put two words together let alone describe what had happened at the back of the diner.

"Somebody better say something," Josh demanded.

"You tell him. I'm still trying to figure where the hell you came from. And apparently you guys know something I don't. You never told me you and Mike connected," Dan said to Josh and then went about walking around his house like he was in a museum.

"You never asked. Just take a minute and relax and acclimate. It takes longer than you think," Josh replied.

As much as Dan wanted answers, he couldn't process anything now still reeling from the attack. Wandering around Josh's house helped even though it felt like he had entered a time warp.

How many more memories are there?

Most everything in Josh's house looked the same

as it did when they were kids. He figured Joshua only redecorated what he felt comfortable doing. That's what he would do. Dan knew it wouldn't be easy replacing his parent's memories.

He walked over to the sliding screen door that led from the family room to the deck. Josh's house sat directly west from Gardner's farm. It was a beautiful view looking through a runway of a finely manicured lawn cut through large white pines and then out across the lake. From the deck directly off the family room, Josh had a perfect view of the sunrise. Dan wondered if Josh ever got up early enough to see it. He promised himself that he would start enjoying sunrises very soon. And at sunset, as the lake mirrored the colors of the sky, the view was even more perfect. It was all so tranquil and best of all, it was the farthest point on the lake from Gardner's property. Dan liked the distance, though he knew it still wasn't out of Gardner's reach.

Dan sipped at his scotch and stared through the screen at Gardner's shoreline. His disdain was palpable. Turning around he caught the end of Mike's version of what went down behind the diner. He was surprised that Mike stuck to the facts, not one ounce of exaggeration. Joshua looked over at Dan.

"No, that's about it," Dan added. "Hey, how the hell did you end up with Gardner's bunch anyway?"

"I'll give you the short version. Josh, I'm sorry Joshua, knows all this already," Mike said to which Joshua reacted by flipping him off. "I showed up and got a job. How else do you think I got a job?"

"Would you knock it off and give Scheff a little more history," Josh interrupted.

"Just messing with ya," Mike replied flashing a big

smile. "Yeah, I worked at the plant for a while, and then went into their engineer training program. I did quite well. I actually have a couple of patents. I'm not as fucking stupid as you guys thought I was."

"Plus, now you're stinking rich," Josh added.

Dan shook his head feeling a little embarrassed and now understood the Mike's sarcastic tone when he said, "Same ol' Scheffy. Always trying to fix things."

"I have a few bucks," Mike joked. "Even after two ex-wives, I still can say that," he continued with a nonchalant shrug of his shoulders and a smile. He finished his scotch after a final, long gulp and then continued. "Then I got involved with these guys and their crossfit, kick boxing idea."

"He owns KickFits," Joshua interrupted again. "What, about 300 of them nationwide and growing? Plus a piece of my salon. I could have never opened it without…"

"That's enough out of you, Jingle Bells. Yeah, you might say, I'm not only a client of KickFits, but the owner." With that he flexed his muscles. "That's where I learned all my sweet moves," he said smugly, while rubbing his forehead. "That head butt thing though, I hope that's the last one of those I need to use."

Dan got up and paced as nervous energy was getting the best of him. He wanted Mike to get to the part with Gardner. Mike sat down.

"Then about a year and a half ago, my dad got sick. It was early in the summer. They hid it from me. Lung cancer." His eyes glazed over as he looked at no one. "I've always come home on that Friday before Labor Day. This time I was later than usual. I had a new store opening. That was back in the day, when I made each opening. Can't keep that schedule up anymore. Anyway, I found them both. In bed. Dead. Sleeping pills. I don't know what possessed me, but I hid the pills and then called the cops. I never thought about an inquest or autopsy."

He stopped talking. Dan walked over and sat down next to him on the couch. Joshua sat across from them.

Silence.

"The coroner said that his dad died from the cancer and his mom from natural causes. Can you believe it?" Joshua said.

"They went on to say that it wasn't uncommon for people who have been married so long to die right after the other. When one heart stops, they both stop. It's fucking bullshit," Mike added, jumping to his feet and walking over to the sliding screen door. "That bastard."

"Are you sure it was the pills?" Dan asked.

"Yeah, I'm sure. Trust me. They committed suicide, and I have no idea why."

"Mine too," Joshua added, shuddering his shoulders. "They drove straight into a truck, an eighteen wheeler. Died on impact. Barely a scratch on the semi. I don't know if either of them was sick. They wouldn't have told me anyway."

Dan pulled the note from his pocket and read it again. It was right there in the first line. *First, I'm sorry we left you alone with so much to figure out and so many to take care of.*

"Son of a bitch."

Dan swallowed hard on the last of his scotch.

Chapter 18

"Sorry, Scheffy. But I'd say your parents took their own way out too," Joshua said refilling everyone's glass.

"Sorry, Danny," Mike added. "Somehow that bastard across the lake is responsible."

"I don't know. How can you make someone commit suicide? Our parents died in a car accident. I mean…I don't know," Dan replied.

Dan looked at the letter again. *Your mother is sick, and I need to be with her…only her.*

"I know, it doesn't make any sense. At least they left you that. Can I see it?" Mike asked. "There's no question in my mind that your dad is telling you that there is something going on around here and it has to do with his…your diner."

"But what? What does the diner have to do with it? And why does Gardner care so much that it stays the same? It's insane," Dan said.

"I don't know. That's why I went to work for him, thinking I could find how and why he wields so much power in this town."

"Wait. What?" Dan asked. "I realize Gardner must be involved, but how?"

"It doesn't take a genius to figure out who's running this town. Everybody bends over backwards when Gardner's around."

The Diner

"That doesn't explain why you went to work for them?" Dan asked.

"I asked him the same thing. He told me not to worry about it," Josh added.

"Because you have a business to run. You worry about that," Mike added, while walking closer to Dan.

"Why didn't you tell me that you and Mike got together?" Dan asked Josh.

"I don't know. I figured you'd do what you always do and start peppering me with questions. Let's face it, Scheffy, you love to question things. I knew you and Mike would connect eventually, so here we are. Let it go. That's not what matters now."

"You're right. No worries. Sorry. So what did you find at Gardner's?" Dan asked.

"Let me ask you guys something first. Have you noticed that there's not a single home property up for sale in Circle Lake?"

"Now that you mention it…" Joshua added.

"It's because Gardner buys them all, often at above market price. And get this. He sells them, almost as quickly as he buys them. I think the longest he's held onto a property is about sixty days. And even more crazy is that he often sells them for less than he paid. He works it all through some Chicago real estate attorney. I suspect you'll be hearing from the guy soon, Scheffy."

"Well, I'm not selling. You guys didn't. Good for you."

"I almost did. I needed the money for the salon, but Mikey here…well, you know."

"That's enough out of you. You'll pay me back. But not only that, most of the farmland around here is

131

owned by him. Any new housing development that goes up, he finances. The population of Circle Lake keeps growing, but the infrastructure doesn't change. The town is dying."

"That still doesn't explain his connection to the diner. At my parent's memorial, John McQueen said, 'Don't sell the place to Gardner,' so the people around here must know what he's up to."

"Probably. I don't know for sure," Mike said, pacing as he spoke. "I do know that he did business with your dad. Or should I say they had some kind of arrangement. I guess he still does, with the diner anyway. And I bet you didn't know that his father had the same arrangement with your grandfather. He was the one that opened the diner, right? By the way, do you know how he and your grandmother died?"

"My parents never told me," Dan replied. "I never thought about it. But now I am. Maybe they were trying to protect me from something. But from what?"

"What do you mean?" Mike asked.

"I don't know. My father takes the time to write this letter, but does so in code. Why not just tell me what hell is going on? Then he leaves me to figure it out on my own."

"You're not on your own. We're all in this," Mike responded. "And maybe he couldn't find the words to explain it. Had someone handed you this letter immediately after you found out your parents died, would you have believed any of it? Probably not. What's more you'd think your dad was making up some outrageous story and yanking your chain. Regardless, you'd let it go. Buck knew what he was doing. Now more than ever, you're not going to let this

The Diner

rest until you get answers. It's just that none of us know what we're looking for. But you're right. Why the hell couldn't he have told us?" Mike added after a long pause.

"'Cause it wouldn't have brought our parents back," Joshua said after remaining conspicuously quiet. "If we had the answers, we might stop searching and then it, whatever 'it' is, would happen to someone else. Mike's right, your dad definitely knew what he was doing."

Without realizing it, all three guys were now standing shoulder to shoulder in Joshua's family room looking through the double sliding door across the lake toward Gardner's farm. Dan felt safer standing on the inside of the screened door. He wondered if the others did too.

"I just love this high school boyfriend sandwich I have going on here," Joshua said standing between the others and extending his arms out and embracing them.

Mike peeled away quickly toward the kitchen.

Dan stood by Joshua and said, "Geezus, you're a sick puppy."

"Funny too," Joshua replied.

"Yeah, you are. We needed that."

Joshua walked away and sat at the granite bar that divided the kitchen from the family room. Dan watched Josh shake his head as he watched Mike wander through his kitchen. It was more amusing than staring out at Gardner's property which only instigated more questions. He was growing tired of the list of what he didn't know getting longer. He walked over to join his buddies. It felt good to be around them again.

"Hey, at your place you said we'd talk later. What

133

exactly did you want to tell me?" Dan asked Josh.

Mike walked over after grabbing a beer from the fridge and bag of potato chips from the pantry.

"Help yourself," Joshua said sarcastically.

"Thanks. I will. Now tell us what you know."

Chapter 19

Ernest Gardner entered the diner with Dorothy on his arm and Emil Matchak walking close behind. Gardner looked directly at Carlos, who was busy staring at the light fixture above the entrance, which brought a smile to Gardner's face.

"Not here. Wait outside and we'll talk there," Gardner said to a battered and groggy Emil. "I must talk to my wife first."

Emil walked out, with his shoulders slumped.

"Dorothy, it's clear that keeping Dan in line is going to be far more difficult than his father. Please conserve your energy should a more direct lesson be administered later."

"Ernest, we'll have none of that. Do you really believe that course of action will help me with my work? Now go deal with Emil, and I'll order our dinner."

"Very well," Gardner said, feeling less than satisfied. "I'll be back momentarily."

"So Emil, tell me, exactly how did you fail?" Gardner demanded, in a quiet yet forceful tone.

"It was Mills. Mike Miller. He's obviously a friend of Scheffelin. I heard him say…"

"Say no more. That's what you get for hiring off the street. I assume you've learned a valuable lesson."

"Yes, sir. And I will have my revenge."

"You will have no such thing. Is that clear?"

Emil remained silent.

"Do I make myself clear?"

"Yes, sir," Emil replied quietly.

"Regardless of the outcome, a message has been sent. Daniel and his friend will be expecting you to pay them another visit. Let them spend their time and energy preparing for another confrontation. Instead, I'll increase the pressure on what really matters."

"What is that?"

"Matters you can never begin to understand. These are matters of the heart. Where the heart goes, the head must follow," Gardner waxed philosophically. Looking at Emil, he could tell his words had been wasted on him.

"Yes. Well. Head back to the compound, and make sure the accommodations are ready for our guests. They'll be arriving in a few days. There are many preparations that, as always, I personally will be attending to."

"Yes, sir," Emil replied, again barely above a whisper.

"And Emil, my orders will be followed. No harm must come to Daniel Scheffelin."

"Of that you can be certain," Emil replied, turned and walked away.

Gardner watched Emil until he was out of sight. He had lived too long, compounding years of experience, to trust anyone.

"The seed of revenge, once planted, needs to be nourished," Gardner said to no one.

As Emil disappeared over the horizon, Gardner made a phone call.

"I believe Emil is going to be a problem. Is Ansel ready? Good. Have him deal with this threat. Are we clear? Good."

Gardner put the phone back in his pocket and looked around the town like a proud father looks at his children.

"Well, young Mr. Scheffelin," Gardner said to no one before he went back inside the diner, "you will learn what is best for you and my town."

He shot an insincere smile at Carlos as he walked in. Carlos smiled back and looked up at the ceiling. No flash. Carlos shook his head and went back to work.

Gardner sat across from his wife and took her hand in his. He was certain that without her, his life would be meaningless.

Dorothy was the love of Ernest's grandfather, Horace, and then of his father, Andrew, and now she was his. She wasn't the mother of Andrew or Ernest. Ernest never knew his birth mother, just as David would never know his. Dorothy was the love of these men and a servant to them. She was also a Spirit shape shifter. She could make herself look physically different while altering her age, twenty-one or eighty-three, it didn't matter. How she looked was entirely up to the men she served. She genuinely loved these men having fallen in love with Horace while he was in Jamaica looking for coffee to sell in the States.

Dorothy's family owned a struggling coffee plantation. Her father saw Horace as a means to improve his business by exporting his special coffee blend to the United States. After weeks of dating, her father sat Horace down and told him of the power his daughter and his coffee had. "Imagine harnessing immortality. My daughter possesses the power to help souls cross over to new vessels. And my coffee delivers the energy from this earth. My Dorothy will open the portal for you, the vortex of energy that will keep spirits alive, while my coffee feeds the required energy to sustain the vessel."

Even though he was intrigued by the idea, Horace remained reluctant; however, a visit from Diavolo convinced him otherwise. And having Dorothy by his side made compliance even easier. Once back in the States, Horace sought out Dan's grandfather, Tom Scheffelin. The portal to the vortex had to be located in a public place where everyone would gather regularly. The diner made sense. The elder Scheffelin loved the idea of serving a great cup of coffee. He felt it would help grow and support the diner. As far as what Horace had in mind for the dead, Tom was fascinated with the idea of immortality. "I don't believe it, but if you can do it, I see no harm." That was what Horace needed to hear. He took care of the rest. It worked beautifully; everyone benefitted.

After a few years, Horace's son Andrew was born. When he turned eighteen, he was sent to study in Jamaica where he not only learned how to continue the business but also how to conjure up the power of Diavolo, should it ever be needed. It wasn't. Ernest Gardner mastered it, because he did need it.

"Fine. Is everything in order?" Dorothy asked.

"Of course. However, I need you to make more time with our young lady friend. It's time that we advanced young Christine's transition and provide Mr. Scheffelin with a clear picture of what's possible."

Chapter 20

"I'm not sure what I know. I can only tell you what I've heard," Joshua said, reaching in the refrigerator for two beers and handing one to Dan. Dan didn't reach for it at first. Something caught his attention out on the deck.

"Dan, here you go," Joshua said. "Stay with us, ol' boy. What are you looking at?"

"Nothing. I'm sorry."

Truth was he thought he saw Milt standing next to someone. They were both peering in through the sliding glass door panel. It was only for a second, and then they disappeared. He wanted to mention it to the guys but wasn't comfortable sharing that bit of news just yet.

He looked at Mike who gave him a reassuring smile and wink.

"My parents had been gone less than a month when I was at the salon. It was still under construction. We were opening in two weeks, that is, if everything was completed in time. The place still needed to be painted and for some reason, I was running into problems finding a painter. Finally, I spoke with one of the other store owners who recommended this guy. Maybe you guys know him. Max Karel. He lives in Circle Lake. Moved here, I don't know, maybe two or three years ago. Moved from the Czech Republic. God knows why he came here. Ever heard of him?"

Dan and Mike both shook their head.

"Dan, it wouldn't surprise me if you do run into him."

"Why?"

"I'm getting to that point. I decided that since he lives in our home town that I should give him a call. He picks up right away, which is always a good sign. Not only that, he says he'll be by my store in the morning."

"Get on with it," Mike said impatiently and looking toward the screen door and shaking his head.

"What? Did you see something?" Dan asked quietly, hopeful.

"Huh? Nothing," he whispered back. "Get on with it, Joshalina."

"Oh, that's mature. You're such an ass. At any rate, the guy shows up at 8:30 a.m., wearing white overalls, though you'd never know it with all the paint dotting them. I mean these things were covered in paint of every color, like he had been in front of a paint ball firing squad. At least I can see that he's a real painter. Though, I don't know how good he is," Joshua digressed. "At any rate, he's wearing overalls. Do you understand what I'm saying? When was the last time you saw anyone other than a farmer wear overalls."

"There's nothing strange about a guy wearing overalls, especially a painter," Dan interjected, getting a little edgy, wishing Joshua would get to the point.

"I guess, but very old school, if you ask me. And this guy is carrying a lunch box and a thermos of coffee. I mean he stepped right out of 1970 or something. I even mentioned it."

"Mentioned what?" Dan asked.

" 'So, you got yourself a thermos. I haven't seen

one of those in years,' I said to him."

" 'It was my father's," he says in broken English. 'Still keep coffee hot. I like coffee hot.' "

" 'I get my coffee at Stan's doughnut shop up the street. You should try it,' I say. 'It's very good. So are the doughnuts.' "

" 'Oh no,' he says, visibly upset, shaking his finger at me."

Mike and Dan lean in closer as if they were kids sitting around a campfire and Joshua was telling them a ghost story.

" 'No worries. I'm sure your wife makes a fine pot of coffee,' I say, not really knowing what to say."

" 'Oh no, my Martha. She no make coffee. Maybe someday. She new. Just started. I get coffee at diner in town. Best coffee,' he says, slapping the thermos like he's holding some kind of precious elixir."

"What the hell did he mean by 'She's new'?" Mike asked.

"Well I asked him, 'Oh, so how long have you been married?' I'm thinking maybe it's his second wife. I don't know. Just making conversation, figuring the more I get to know him the better the price he'll quote me. He says, 'We've been married thirty-eight years come this June. Yes. God bless diner. It keep my family together.' "

"Now I don't know what to say. I mean, they've been married thirty-eight years and he's saying 'She's new. Just started.' None of that makes any sense."

"So what did you say?" Dan asks.

"I didn't know what to say to be honest. I asked him, 'How does the diner keep your family together?' He hesitates for a minute, like he's afraid to say something or doesn't know how to explain it.

"He says, 'It's the place where the dying go to live again. Yes. Yes, bless the diner. So what color do you want? Let me take a look at your place. Not so much work…'

"I didn't have the heart to press him anymore. Frankly, I thought the old guy was a little nuts. Though as it turns out, he's one hell of a painter and fairly priced."

"There has to be more to the story," Dan asked.

Mike nodded.

"Not with him, but I did ask a few more people about the diner. I mean, after he blessed it. We grew up in it, and I doubt any of us would bless it. No offense, Dan. Most people I asked would say, "Great food and great coffee" or not say anything at all. It was like they were afraid to speak. I don't know. But something's going on there. 'Where the dying go to live again.' What does that mean?"

Dan looked to see his friends staring at him.

"I don't have a clue," he said, though he couldn't help thinking about Angela and Christine. He didn't dare share any of those thoughts. Not yet anyway. He hadn't wrapped his head around that experience yet. "I can tell you this, that everyone that came in today, ordered coffee. Sure it's good coffee, but…"

"Even the kids?"

"You know, I haven't even seen a kid in the place," Dan said after a long pause. "I mean I've only been there for a couple of shifts. The more I think about it, I haven't seen a child anywhere since I've been back. Frankly, I can't remember the last time I saw one. Can either of you?"

Mike and Joshua both straightened up and looked at each other.

"Damn it. What the hell is going on around here?" asked Mike.

"I wish I knew. But I'm going to find out," Dan said, walking back over to the screen door.

The sun had nearly set. Lights of the homes that dotted the shoreline rode on the waves and cast an eerie shimmering glow off the surface of the lake.

"Why won't you guys just tell us what to do?" Dan said to two shadowy figures hovering a few inches above the deck. They nodded and vaporized into the air. He knew they'd be back.

"Yeah, they don't talk much, do they?" Mike whispered just behind Dan.

"What are you guys talking about?" Joshua asked.

"Nothing. So does anyone have an idea what we do next? We know Gardner's not going to take too kindly to Mike beating the crap out of his men. So we need to be ready for what they may throw at us."

"He's not coming after you. I'm not saying he's done with you. Quite the opposite. He needs you. He needs you to keep the diner running the way it has for years. So, he'll come at you from another direction. Me? Yeah, I pissed Emil off, so he may make another run. Gardner will distance himself from that and stay squeaky clean. I'll take care of it," Mike said confidently.

"So what do we do?" Joshua asked.

"You don't do anything," Dan replied.

"That's right. We'll take care of Gardner. I don't mean this as it might sound, but we don't need you for anything right now. You've got a new business to take care of. Right Scheffy?"

Dan looked at his two old friends. "Yeah. Listen, Josh. This involves my parents and the diner. How? We have no idea, but we'll find out. Mike got himself involved by…well by kicking some ass. The way Gardner's been acting around me, it's clear he's not going to stop until he gets his own way. Trust me, if we need you, we'll call you. Make sense?"

"What? Just like that, I'm out?" Josh replied.

"Josh, c'mon. This is gonna get even more crazy. You don't do crazy, but I do. Just get us a couple more beers while Scheffy whips up something for us to eat."

"I get it," Josh said. "But I'm not happy about it."

"I wonder how many am I cooking for?" Dan said, not thinking anyone heard him as he looked out through the sliding door to see people appearing and disappearing like they were Christmas lights blinking on and off.

"I know. It is crazy, isn't it? Since you've been back, they're really coming out. Don't say anything to him," Mike said, seeing Josh reaching into the refrigerator for the beers. "I know for sure Josh doesn't see them. No reason to freak him out. And they're why I got involved with Gardner. I didn't see them then, but I heard them. They told me that Gardner needed to be stopped."

"What?"

"Not now. Don't worry, Scheffy. We got this. Try to relax."

Dan nodded and walked off into the kitchen and whipped some grilled cheese sandwiches.

"To Buck," Dan said, raising a grilled cheese sandwich in the air as a toast.

Chapter 21

"Was everything to your liking, Mr. Gardner?" Carlos asked, never looking up from behind the cash register as he organized the daily receipts.

"As good as always," Gardner said, pulling two twenty dollar bills from his gold, diamond-studded money clip. "I trust you will do what you can to keep it that way."

Gardner held the bills by his side wanting Carlos to reach for them.

They should all come to me. I will never go to them.

"That's up to Dan. He'll do what it takes to make this the best diner around. Are you ready to pay your bill or is it change you're looking for?" Carlos asked, continuing to shuffle through receipts.

"It will always be the only diner around. Do you understand? And, as you can see from the constant stream of satisfied customers, nothing should be changed," Gardner said sternly, reluctantly extending his hand with the bills.

"Again, that's all up to Mr. Scheffelin. I'll make sure he's aware of your comments though," Carlos said as he looked over Gardner's shoulder.

Gardner turned to see an elderly couple walking in.

"I'll take care of your bill in a moment, Mr. Gardner, after I seat these guests. Please excuse me."

"What? Yes, yes. Of course," Gardner replied, visibly irritated. Perturbed at being treated like any other guest, he decided to check on Dorothy's progress with Christine.

Dorothy had Christine locked in a hypnotic stare. Even if she could divert her eyes, Gardner was confident that she wouldn't break free from Dorothy's grip. At first Christine's shoulders were raised in resistance, and her forehead furrowed. Gardner suspected that she may have grown annoyed at spending so much time with Mrs. Gardner over the past few days. Now smiling and shoulders relaxed, Christine listened intently. At this point in the process, Gardner was confident that every one of Dorothy's instructions would become etched in Christine's mind. As Dorothy explained it, it was more than the simple power of suggestion or a type of hypnotism; it was her touch that made her words come alive. Gardner hoped Christine, like others before her, would experience the pleasant outcome if she followed Dorothy's instructions precisely.

Mr. Scheffelin should be happy with our choice of vessel as well.

Gardner smiled confidently. After meeting the vessel, clients were nearly always pleased with the results. Gardner and his network of "Doppelganger Operatives," or DO's as he called them, had an uncanny ability of finding someone who looked amazingly like the departed. Back at his compound, two barracks housed a sophisticated network of computers with access to countless databases from each state's driver license database to all of the social networking sites. Gardner boasted that he had a picture of everyone in the world over the age of sixteen. Once the vessel was secured, Dorothy handled the spirit transfer process.

When a client was brave enough to express their dissatisfaction, Gardner reassured them that the likeness would change as long as they nurtured the soul of their loved one. "It's up to you to rekindle the loving memories needed to allow the spirit to change the appearance of the vessel." To date he claimed a 100% customer satisfaction rate, not that anyone had the courage to complain. A visit from Diavolo was always enough to encourage satisfaction and was more than enough incentive to follow the maintenance instructions.

Caring for the vessel and spirit were simple. First, treat them as you would your spouse; after all their spirit was in the vessel. Touch was incredibly important particularly for transferring memories and fueling the spirit, "so rarely leave your vessel alone." In addition, a minimum of one meal per day must be consumed at the diner. It wasn't so much what they ate or that they ate, but they needed be in the diner for a minimum of forty-five minutes. That's how long it took for the energy from the vortex in the diner to be absorbed. "So why not enjoy a nice meal," Gardner added. "Earthly nourishment such as food and water fuels the vessel. And the energy from the vortex fuels the spirit." To make sure the energy was totally absorbed, a minimum of two cups of coffee had to be consumed. Gardner called it the "Spirit Energy IV." The coffee sped up the vessel's metabolism which helped the absorption of energy received from the vortex.

Should a day be missed, it was imperative that the vessel be brought to the diner for a minimum of two meals the next day and consume at least four cups of coffee. Replenishing the spirit's energy was critical. Spirits were free to wander; after all they were spirits. To call them back to the vessel, simply touch them. "Why wouldn't you want to embrace the one you love anyway?" Gardner stressed.

If more than two days at the diner were missed, Gardner might be able to help, but that would require corralling a spirit that was probably off wandering, and could ultimately wander the earthly plane forever lost. "Lost souls eventually find a portal to cross over. We've closed the ones we know of. There aren't any others in town to pose a threat. Still they are out there, so my instructions must be followed," Gardner would explain.

"You see, we know that the spirit doesn't cross over immediately. How many times have we heard stories of our loved ones being visited by the departed?" Gardner would say to the surviving spouse. "In their way, the spirits are saying goodbye. We harness them before they enter the white light. My Dorothy speaks to them and keeps them from crossing over. It is up to you to keep them here. Should they cross over, they can never be retrieved. The vessel then would be left to perish. Without a soul, nothing lives. Let's not have that happen. Are we clear?"

Yes, Daniel should be very pleased.

Holding Christine's hand, with her eyes closed, Dorothy hummed and swayed. The transfer of energy that emptied the mind and opened the recipient's soul continued to amaze Gardner. With the warm, tender touch of the palm of Dorothy's hand on Christine's cheek, Christine nodded and smiled. Dorothy's work

The Diner

was done. Gardner smiled.

"Yes, I'm sure nothing will change now," he said to Carlos who returned to his post behind the cash register. "No need to worry about Christine," Gardner continued, seeing Carlos staring at her and looking like he was about to break them up. "It's perfectly acceptable to let my wife take a special interest in those that work here. Christine, certainly anyone in this diner, should be honored."

"The employees here must spend equal time with all those that frequent this diner. We can't have favorites."

"Oh, but you will. Certainly, Daniel will."

"Mr. Gardner, please understand…"

"I'm not interested," he said throwing up a hand to halt Carlos. "You will see to it that the waitress gets the change," he continued, throwing the two twenty dollar bills on the counter. "Come along, Dorothy."

The Gardners walked toward the door hand in hand, proud of their accomplishment. A brilliant flash of light sparked above them. Gardner turned toward Carlos, who was staring at the ceiling.

"No need to concern yourself with that. The diner shall remain as it is," Gardner said and walked out.

Chapter 22

"Do you feel that?" Dan asked Mike feeling the goose bumps on his arms multiply.

"Feel what?"

"It feels like the temperature dropped twenty degrees as soon as we got close to the car. It's freezing. How can that be?"

"I have no idea. And I'm not feeling it…yet," Mike replied. "I have to tell you though; it feels better knowing that I'm not the only one seeing them. I thought I was going crazy. What I want to know is where do they go when they disappear. I mean, is there a real afterlife? What actually happens when we die? Is it a better place than what we have here? Imagine, exploring the afterlife. If only I could ride along with them."

"You are crazy. I want to know why they're here. Why can't they just move on like our parents did?"

"I think they're here for you."

"Who are they?"

"I don't know. None of them look familiar to me."

"So you can see them now?"

"I did before, but none at this moment. I can feel them though," Mike replied, rubbing the chill from his arms. "That's what happened when they told me to stop Gardner. I was in my parents' house only a few days, and I kept hearing noises and voices, but I could never make out what they were saying. It happened at the strangest times, mostly before the sun came up or late at night. You know, times when no one is usually up and around. When I wasn't hearing things, I was seeing things. Chairs pushed over, stuff on my kitchen counter pushed all the way into the corner and stacked. Lights would turn off and on. It was crazy. Then I saw them. It freaked me out at first. They always seemed to appear when I was going through my parents' things. Then I relaxed. I don't know why, but I did. Then I heard them say, 'Stop Gardner. Gardner is why.' But now that you're here, they're not talking to me and I rarely see them."

"I still want to know who they are," Dan asked as his anxiety level began to rise.

"I was hoping you would know. All I know is that when they appear, electricity fills the air and it gets cold," Mike said as he walked around to the passenger side of the car and tossed the car keys to Dan.

"So they are ghosts. Right?" Dan asked.

"I don't know. I mean, ghosts imply that they're haunting someone. I don't think they're haunting anyone. They seem more like lost souls or spirits. That's what I was saying earlier. I think our parents found a way to cross over on their own. These souls haven't."

"Or can't," Dan added. "Something or someone is keeping them here."

Dan and Mike stood on opposite sides of the car, each with his hand on the door handle. Their heads swiveled around thinking they saw movement. The moonlight was playing all kinds of games casting shadows through the white pines dotting Joshua's yard, making distinguishing between a simple shadow and a spirit impossible. The wind howling through the pine needles did little to calm their nerves. Conspicuously missing were the sounds of animals, birds, and squirrels rustling through the trees or raccoons and deer foraging in the forest. Nothing.

"Let's get out of here," Dan said as the chill began to leave the air. "If they were going to show themselves, they would have by now."

"Just go to your house. I'll walk home from there," Mike said.

"It's not that much further. I'll drive you home."

"Afraid to be alone?" Mike kidded.

Dan looked around the property one more time before pulling out. The stillness was palpable. He didn't know exactly what to do next but knew he had to do something. This was when he'd typically turn to Angela. They'd open an expensive bottle of wine either at the restaurant or at home and talk it through. The solution always seemed to magically appear and neither one of them realized who discovered it. At least that's what they used to do. Months before her death, Angela had become more independent and was always too busy to talk, constantly meeting with someone that "was critical to the restaurant's continued success. You'll see." Then there was work. The restaurants were beginning to consume him. He and Angela were always heading out in separate directions. That translated into an increase in the number of nights they slept alone.

Was she sleeping alone too?

The only people he saw regularly were his employees and his customers. He had lost touch with his old friends. It took death to bring them back together. It took death for him to realize he had lost his wife before she died.

"Scheffy. You in there? Let's go," Mike said. "I thought for a minute there that a spirit had possessed you.

Dan shook his head, dropped the car in drive, and hit the gas. The headlights of the BMW pierced the darkness. Nothing was darker than the night around Circle Lake.

"Geezus..." Dan exclaimed as he checked the rearview mirror. "That's Milt."

Mike turned around and saw a group of people fading fast as the red tail lights got further away.

"Do we go back?" Dan looked right at Mike.

"Scheffy! Stop!" Mike yelled.

Dan hit the brakes. The BMW drove straight into a crowd. Dan winced expecting to hear bodies bouncing off the hood and windshield. The only sound he could hear was the wind whistling through the pines.

They were surrounded. The air grew colder, so cold in fact that Dan could see his breath.

"Friends of yours?" Mike asked rhetorically.

"Possibly. Some of them do look familiar. I don't see Milt, though," Dan replied looking around his car.

Dan and Mike sat in the car surrounded. All the spirits were elderly. Some wore dated clothing, others wore relatively modern clothes. Some of the spirits seemed to glow. Some faded and disappeared only to be replaced by someone else standing there in vivid detail. Their arms hung down by their sides. Their skin changed from pale to bright and lively to back to pale. They didn't smile, they didn't blink. They weren't breathing. Dan was drawn in by their eyes. While every other part of their body was expressionless, their eyes looked alive. Some looked surprised. Some looked sad. But mostly they all looked lost, and they were all looking at Dan. So was Mike.

"What do they want?" Dan asked.

"How the hell should I know? Ask them."

"Hello," Dan said as his voice stammered and shook. "What can we do for you?" Dan asked with both hands on the wheel, like he was talking into a speaker at drive-through restaurant. He needed answers. It was the only thing that kept him from hitting the gas

Silence. Though a few of them pointed at him.

"Not we, Scheffy. It what's you can do for them."

"What? What do you want from me? Mrs. O'Neill, is that you?" Dan asked seeing an elderly woman breaking through the crowd. She didn't walk, she floated to the front.

"Home."

Mrs. O'Neill's lips never moved. Dan heard it in his head. "What about home? My home? Your home?

"What home? Who are you talking to?" Mike asked impatiently.

"Hang on," Dan replied.

"It not us," she said.

"Who's not us? What do you mean? I don't understand."

"Scheffy. They're beginning to disappear. Hurry up. Get an answer." Mike's head bobbed and weaved all around the car. The spirits were rapidly disappearing.

"Home."

Dan heard it again, and then she was gone. The night grew darker, and the summer warmth returned.

"Fuck me. That was some weird shit. That's the most I've ever seen. What did they say?"

"I think that lady was Mrs. O'Neill. Remember her? She used to come to our school and teach music. I can't be sure, but I swear she was at my parents' memorial. I never spoke to her. She was there with her husband. I don't recall his name only that he was doing most of the talking."

"Who cares? What did she say?"

"Home. She said 'home.' And then she said, 'It's not us.' What the hell does that mean?"

"I don't know. But something tells me you better find out, or there's going to be more of them visiting you."

"I need to speak with Milt. There's something he's not telling me," Dan said as hit the gas. "What the hell are they all doing here?"

Chapter 23

"If only there was a way to summon them," Dan said nearing Mike's house. "Then we'd be able to ask them what was going on. What we do know is that there's a connection between Gardner, the diner, and our parents. But what is it? You certainly can't go back to work for him. Emil wouldn't let you get through the front gate."

"Ha, I guess not," Mike replied, laughing. "I've been waiting to nail that asshole for weeks."

"Well, you did. It's not over. You know that, right?" Dan advised, scouting the area as the shadows from the trees continued to play games with his eyes. "There has to be more answers at the diner. Buck hid the letter; maybe there are other clues hidden there. Why don't you come help me look? I'll pick you up around 10:00 a.m."

"Might as well. I don't have a better idea," Mike replied, leaning forward in his seat and peering through the windshield. "Hey, pull over and turn off the lights."

"Why? I can take you right to your door."

"Scheffy, just do it. Do you have your golf clubs in the trunk?"

"Huh? Yeah, but…" Dan said pulling over.

"Good. Let's get a little night golf in."

With a puzzled look on his face, Dan reluctantly popped the trunk and got out.

The Diner

"Since you hit the three iron better than I do, you take it. I'll take the four iron," Mike said, laughing to himself as he started walking down the driveway. They were less than a hundred yards from his house.

"What's up, and why do we have these?" Dan asked, shaking the golf club in the air.

"Always gotta be talking, don't ya, Scheffy. Look. See it? There," Mike said pointing to a pickup truck parked in a clearing just off the driveway. "I saw the taillight reflection when we came around the turn; it's Emil's. The asshole doesn't know when to give up."

Dan stayed a step behind Mike as his heart felt like it was beating through his chest. He gripped the club tightly and walked on the tips of his toes trying to minimize the sound of the gravel crunching under their footsteps. They stopped and crouched down. Dan held the club in the air, ready to strike anything that came near him. Mike wormed his way to the back of the truck. Slowly, he stood up and peered over the tailgate.

"There's no one in it. They have to be up at the house," Mike said. "Let's go."

As they walked, the moonlight cast dancing shadows on the ground as it did at Joshua's house. Dan could have easily let his imagination run wild as the squirrels and deer foraging in the forest sounded like footsteps, while the owl's screech might be confused with the scream of a murder victim. Seeing Mike march ahead gave Dan the reassurance to ignore it all. What was real, however, was the movement outside Mike's house. Dan could only make out two people. Mike saw them too and again dropped low to the ground. Waving Dan closer, he guided them through the forest and stopped at the edge before popping out on the back lawn.

"Geezus," Mike whispered. "I can see his shaved head all the way from here. I wonder which inept sidekick he brought with him this time. Let me handle this, Scheffy. You just stand by in case I get in trouble. By the way, I'm not getting in any trouble. So just hang back. Ready?"

"Hi, boys. You up for a round of night golf?" Mike said as he approached the two men patrolling the back of his house.

Dan moved out from behind Mike to get a better look at the guys. It was clear they had surprised Emil and his friend. Dan kept a firm grip on the golf club hoping he wouldn't have to use it.

"It's about time you showed up," Emil said, pulling a twelve-inch hunting knife from the scabbard on his belt. "Looks like you brought some help for yourself. Won't matter. I believe you know Smitty. He's never liked you either."

"Don't care. Listen, I'd invite you both in for a beer, but I'm a little tired, so maybe some other time."

Seeing the knife sucked the air from Dan's lungs. He preferred trying to talk to them, but knew Mike wasn't going to have any of that, so he did his best to appear calm. Dan watched Mike as he stood his ground, clearly letting Emil make the first move.

"Tell me, Emil, exactly what is your plan?" Mike asked, turning toward Dan. "Feel that, Scheffy?"

Dan nodded. A cool breeze sent a chill down Dan's spine. He wanted to look around but didn't dare take his eyes off Emil and Smitty. Then he saw movement behind Emil and Smitty as the night air grew colder.

"Its payback time, Mills. See, I owe you."

"Do you?" Mike replied.

"I figure I owe you one ass whooping," Emil replied, quickly turning around as if something or someone caught his attention.

Dan knew what it was and smiled as the temperature continued to drop. Across the yard, spirits were materializing in random points and converging toward Emil and Smitty. They were so vivid in appearance, yet they didn't throw any shadows on the ground. Their faces weren't quite expressionless. In fact they looked pissed, like they hadn't slept in days. Whoever they were, Dan hoped they were on his side.

"You mean you didn't get enough earlier today? If this is what you want, bring it, because I'm tired and would like to go inside and relax," Mike said, twirling the golf club from hand to hand like a baton.

Emil whispered something to Smitty. Smitty, a short round man with a crazed look in his eyes, wielded a tire iron, smacking it into the palm of his free hand. He laughed at Mike's remarks. It was a laugh that turned into a sinister sneer. Dan looked over at Mike, hoping he was ready. Instead, Smitty charged Dan. Before Dan could take another breath, Smitty was nearly on him holding the tire iron high in the air. Without thinking and out of sheer fear, Dan swung the three iron wildly. One swing was all it took. It caught Smitty square in the gut. As Smitty doubled over, the tire iron flew out of his hand and rocketed into the air. Dan took a step to the side to set up for another swing just before the tire iron came crashing down on his head. Now in full panic mode, he started swinging the club wildly and caught Smitty in the jaw, sending him crashing to the ground.

159

Dan's whole body shook. He'd never hit anyone before, let alone knocked them out.

"Way to go, Scheffy. Look at you. But you can't have all the fun." Mike turned toward Emil. "C'mon, numbnuts, let's end this."

"You son of a bitch," Emil screamed.

Nearly hyperventilating, Dan could see his breath freeze in the air as the spirits drew closer. Emil raised the knife and charged after Mike. Dan raised his club ready to swing. Mike never moved. He was standing in the middle of a crowd of spirits. They weren't coming and going, they were multiplying. And they were solid, not translucent, standing shoulder to shoulder. He reached out to touch the back of a spirit. As his hand went inside an elderly woman, he immediately pulled it back out as if he had been electrocuted. The woman never turned around.

Wham!

Emil screamed having crashed into something he never saw. The spirit wall created a force field of energy that he hit hard and sent him collapsing to the ground. He lay there writhing in agony as if he had tangled with an electric fence.

The crowd of spirits began moving and floating away from Mike. Many of them began to dissipate and vanish. Their work was done. Emil and Smitty were moaning and squirming on the ground as the spirits, three men and a woman, converged on them. The only spirit Dan could recognize was Bob Radke, the town barber.

"We'll be taking these two back with us," Bob said.

"To where?" Mike asked.

"Wait. What's going on? What are we supposed to do?" Dan yelled.

"We're getting stronger. You don't want that," Bob replied as he raised both his hands and pointed at Dan and Mike. The golf clubs jumped from the guy's hands and flew across the lawn like spears and pierced Mike's house with a thud.

"Let us rest or no one will," Bob said. Then he and his friends formed a spirit barrier around Emil and Smitty that glowed. They bent over the two men and closed in, slowly compressing into a sphere. The orb wobbled on the ground, like it was chewing on the bodies. Then it grew smaller and began to hover in the air. The orb began to move, almost dance, and then darted away, disappearing into the forest.

Chapter 24

"That was insane. Where the hell did they go?" Mike asked. "And if they can do that, why don't they do it to their own spouses?"

"Probably because Emil and Smitty didn't know what hit them. They had no recourse. I'm sure their spouses have some kind of power over them. They must. One thing is for sure, we won't be seeing Emil or Smitty again. Should we check out the rest of your place?"

"Go home, Scheffy. It's over for tonight. Pick me up in the morning. I'm gonna grab a beer and turn in. See ya tomorrow."

Mike walked toward the house, looked up at the two golf clubs in the house, and then went inside. Dan stood in the backyard looking around. He wasn't satisfied. There were too many questions unanswered. As the temperature and sounds of the night air turned back to normal, he walked back to his car and drove home.

Parking outside the garage, Dan looked up at his house and noticed a few lights on. He couldn't recall if he had left them on or if Buck had them on a timer.

"Maybe the spirits are throwing me a party?" he said, humoring himself.

As he approached the door, he heard jazz music playing inside the house.

The Diner

Angela always loved jazz.

Even though he thought it was strange to hear music, he had experienced so much "strange" for the night, he thought nothing of it. Besides, he was too tired to be afraid so he walked straight in.

"I wondered when you'd be home. I opened the wine. Would you please pour it?"

Dan took a few steps inside and then stopped cold. She had her back to him standing at the kitchen counter slicing cheese into little squares so they fit neatly on the crackers. Her hair, the way she swayed to the music, her shapely legs leading down to her cute bare feet, one foot flat on the floor and the other resting on its crinkled toes, it was all Angela until she turned around holding a tray of fruit and cheese. It was Christine looking innocent and lovely as ever in one of Angela's beach cover-ups.

"What are you doing here and where did you get that?" he asked pointing to the cover-up.

"So many questions when there are so many other things we can talk about. First, I've made us a little snack. As for this cover-up, you've never complained when I wore it before. As I recall, it never stayed on very long anyway," she said with a smile followed by slow, deliberate blinks.

"Something wrong?"

"No, just something in my eye. I bet I left this here the last time we visited your parents. Anyway, I thought that after the long day, we could unwind with a nice bottle of wine. Remember that bottle we had when we were searching for a location to open in Miami? Actually, I should say bottles, though I don't think we finished the third. I don't think we do that enough anymore," she said pausing slightly.

It wasn't only the hesitation in her voice but the wavering smile that caused the creases in his forehead to deepen. He wanted to react, but couldn't get past how much Christine looked and sounded like Angela. It was uncanny. He couldn't tell if it was because she was wearing Angela's clothes, the look in her eyes, the mood she set, or the way she conjured up so many specific memories.

We never did finish the third bottle.

"Why don't you bring the wine and glasses, and we'll sit in the family room. C'mon," she requested in a delicate voice that was impossible to ignore.

Dan wanted to scream, "What the hell are you doing?" but the curiosity of what she would say or do next had the better of him, so he followed behind her with the wine in one hand and the glasses in the other.

A warm orange glow filled the room from a half dozen lit candles.

Angela always preferred candlelight.

Sitting on the couch, she patted the cushion for him to join her. She nibbled on a piece of cheese while drawing Dan in with her eyes. Angela's eyes. Staring at her like she was the last woman on earth, he sat beside her and handed her a glass of wine. Nervous energy raged in his stomach.

"Christine, what are you doing here?" he asked, after composing himself and looking around the family room which looked perfectly ordinary. Ordinary was something he welcomed.

"She's gone now," she replied, as her eyes closed and chin dropped to her chest. When her head sprang up, Angela's eyes emerged.

The Diner

"Relax. Try the cheese. I think you'll like how well it pairs with the wine. Hand me a slice of apple, will you please?" she said, sliding her body over into the corner of the couch and laying her legs across Dan's lap.

While the knot in his stomach was tightening, somehow every other muscle in his body relaxed. Dan melted into the cushion of the couch as he passed the tray of apples and cheese to Christine.

"That's better, don't you think?" Angela said.

Dan sighed. The warmth of her legs began to seep through his pants and send waves of sensual energy coursing through his body.

"Try the wine. You'll feel better."

Nearly hypnotized, Dan reached for his glass, his arm brushed across her leg. A soft, electric charge shot through his entire body. Mustering what strength he had, he took a sip of wine as his head fell back against the couch. His eyes closed slowly. He felt free. He hadn't felt that liberated since a year or more before Angela's death. A cool breeze blowing in off the lake brought him around. He opened his eyes and watched her nibbling on a wedge of apple, devouring it in small bites like a rabbit. Without realizing it, his free hand was running up and down her legs. They felt so warm, smooth, and inviting. Her toes wiggled the closer he got to her feet. It was Angela's way of telling him that her feet were tired and required special attention.

Her tongue teased the tip of the apple. It was Angela's subtle signal to Dan that she had plans for his body. He traced her with his eyes. The cover-up, the only layer of clothing she had on, hugged her body beautifully. Every curve of her body accepted the light

165

fabric like a magnet to steel. His hand slid down her leg from her knees to her bubble-gum-pink painted toes. As he rubbed her feet, he remembered how Angela loved to have them tickled. With the tip of his index finger he ran it slowly from her heel to the tip of her middle toe. She sighed.

"This is nice," Dan said, closing his eyes and laying his head back.

"I hate apples" is what Dan thought he heard, causing his head to snap back and his eyes to fly open.

"So juicy and sweet," she said.

Another breeze blew in from through the windows, this time much cooler than before. A shroud of frigid air blanketed them both. They shivered. Closing his eyes again and taking a deep breath, Dan considered putting an end to the seduction but couldn't muster the willpower to stop. There were simply too many feelings urging him on. He could feel Angela with every touch, in her breath, and hear her sighs. Opening his eyes all he could see was Christine. His hand pulled away from her feet. Her eyes widened.

"Danny, I'm getting chilled."

She pulled her feet off his lap, and Dan figured she was going to close the windows. Instead, she stood in front of him, straddling his legs and smiling. Another cool blast of air rushed through the windows knocking her off balance. Dan put his arms around her waist to steady her. Out of the corner of his eye, he saw rows of spirits huddling around the window. Some were beginning to appear in the room.

Christine's placing her hand on his face distracted him from the spirits. Their eyes locked, and all he saw was Angela. With her free hand she untied the belt on her cover up. Her skin was milky smooth, inviting to be touched. With her hand still on Dan's cheek, she pulled his head between her breasts. The warmth of her stomach was a wonderful contrast to the cold air consuming the family room. Dan pulled his head back to look her in the eyes when he saw Angela turn slowly toward the window. She smiled to the spirits and dismissed them with a shake of her head. They didn't leave. Instead they increased in numbers.

"He's not yours tonight," she said.

At that moment, Dan was confused. His mind told him to stop, but his heart and memory urged him to continue. He felt consumed by her touch. It felt so familiar and awakened so many feelings he long abandoned. His arms came up around her waist and pulled her closer.

Before he knew it, Dan was standing and being led into the bedroom. Her warm hand held his firmly. He could have broken free had he wanted to. He didn't want to. A single candle on the nightstand lit their way. As soon as they crossed the bedroom's threshold, the frigid air followed them in. Angela released a deep sigh. Dan could see her breath hanging in the air, which served as a reminder that this was not a typical evening. Before he could react, he was pulled into the bed and buried under a layer of blankets. The chill didn't stand a chance against seal of the comforter and the heat from their bodies.

They each knew their way around the other's body. They rolled across the entire bed, never releasing the other. They kissed. They touched. As was Angela's way, she wrapped one leg around Dan's leg and put one hand on his back and pulled him closer but not inside her. He loved being teased that way. The anticipation of what she would do next along with the heat of her body drove him insane. They had a routine. When the moment was right, she would wrap her other leg around his, squeeze his ass with both hands, and guide him in.

Dan winced as the nails of her right hand dug into his lower back. It took all his strength to wait and not ravish her body. He wanted so badly to reconnect with Angela in a way he hadn't in months. Her left hand stroked the back of his head. He moaned with pleasure. Her fingers danced around his shoulders and neck and then down his spine ever so delicately.

The blankets fell off them. The contrast of her heated touch to the freezing air raised the level of intensity to something he had never experienced before. He wanted to open his eyes but simply didn't have the courage. He knew the spirits were gathering in numbers and closing in.

"He's mine," Dan heard Angela whisper, followed by, "No."

The spirits closed ranks. They were shoulder to shoulder, blending into one mass. The energy from them could have powered a small city. Dan had hoped they would have given up by now and left them alone. The spirit energy had dropped the temperature in the room to near freezing temperatures. He'd never felt a room so cold.

Angela cupped her hands around Dan's face, ran her fingers through his hair, and then pulled herself up and kissed his ear. Her hot tongue licked the edge of his ear and then nibbled on his ear lobe. Her every touch drove him wild. Lightly kissing his face, she locked on his lower lip and bit softly. A sexual energy he never

The Diner

knew before coursed through his entire body. He wasn't expecting it. Angela never did that before. Dan's chest heaved anticipating what would happen next. His body began to vibrate uncontrollably.

With her right hand wandering down his spine, Angela spanked him hard and pulled him in closer. Pleasantly stunned and with the heat rising from her body, Dan melted into her skin. As he was about to enter, he could no longer keep silent.

"Angela, I missed you. I love you."

"Oh Ryan…I love you too."

Chapter 25

The wind whipped into the family room causing the blinds to rattle and flap wildly, sounding like a drum roll on a kid's toy drum. A summer storm was in the making. Dan did his best to stay asleep, but the noise and lumpy couch cushions weren't making it easy. Reluctantly, he pried his eyelids open after what he figured was three, maybe four hours of sleep and got off the couch. The door to the bedroom, his parents' bedroom, was still partially closed just as he had left it.

He felt compelled to check on Christine, but since she was still sleeping, he decided it best to leave her be. He walked out onto the porch that overlooked the lake and stared at the waves. They were churning up all kinds of madness, no crazier than last night however. When Angela said Ryan's name, every ounce of energy, pain, and passion drained from him. He died inside.

Dan had hopped out of the bed to be joined by the spirits in the room. He shivered in the cold, night air. Christine was lying on the bed, but it was Angela's voice pleading for him to come back to her. She started apologizing, rationalizing and excusing. Mostly didn't stop talking. That's what struck him most, all she had to say were words. Not once did he hear any emotions. Maybe it was the shock or maybe it was the insanity playing out in front of him, but Dan stood at the foot of the bed, motionless. A voice in his head, perhaps that of a spirit, told him not to say a word.

Angela's spirit began to rise while Christine's body thrashed about. Names and places, apologies and memories flew from Angela's broken soul while spit flew from Christine's mouth.

"Daniel, you know I love you. Ryan means nothing. It was a mistake."

Dan said nothing which only infuriated Angela more. Listening to lies that were in support of a love that had deteriorated long ago tore him up inside. The last year with Angela had become crystal clear. It was no longer Angela and Dan. It was Angela and whoever she wanted to be with. And most recently it was with Ryan Billings. There were no words that would alleviate that pain. Now seeing Christine suffer because he couldn't manage his life with Angela tore him up inside. Tears ran down his face.

As Dan watched Christine battle Angela's spirit, it was clear Christine wasn't trying to escape, she was fighting. She could have jumped off the bed and run, but she didn't. Angela tried to get up and grab Dan, but Christine managed to wrestle her back. Where she was getting the energy from, he had no idea. The spirits moved in closer staring straight at a vibrating Christine. A low hum filled the room.

"It will end shortly."

Dan heard the words from behind him. He didn't need to turn around to know it was Milt.

"We'll take Angela out of here, but we won't be able to hold her for long. End this, kid."

"Daniel, I'm sorry. Ryan meant nothing to me," Angela screamed, as the spirits converged around her.

171

There was no escape. In an instant they formed a tight ball of light, floated, and then disappeared.

"You bitch." Christine sprang up and screamed and then fell back on the bed.

She passed out. At first her breathing was rapid, but then slowly it returned to normal. Dan covered her with the blankets and then sat on the edge of the bed for an hour, just watching her. It was only then that he realized that the bedroom had been redecorated with new blankets and furniture. Unlike the rest of the house, the room looked remodeled and resembled the master suite in his condo.

Looking back at Christine, he knew she didn't deserve any of this. Someone had forced this on her, played her like a pawn, all for the benefit of enticing Dan into a relationship with her.

"Gardner. That asshole is going to pay."

Only after he was certain Christine was resting quietly did he leave her alone to sleep. He almost touched her hand but remembered that was how all this started. Rather than going upstairs to his room, he went to the couch in case she woke or Angela returned.

****

The wind continued to whip up, and white caps bounced on the surface of the lake. Before the sky opened up, he went to pull the boat back up on shore and stow the outboard engine in the garage.

Approaching the garage, he felt what was now becoming a familiar event. The air became colder the closer he got.

"Oh, c'mon, guys. Now what?" Dan muttered.

He heard rustling in the garage and sound of tools hitting metal.

The Diner

"You guys better not be messing with my car," he stated as he walked through the side door.

There were eight spirits milling about. However, getting an accurate count was tough, because as soon as one appeared two or three would disappear and vice versa.

"Hi, kid," Milt said peeking out from under the hood of the Mustang. "How's Christine? You shouldn't leave her alone for too long. She's going to have a ton of questions."

"And what am I supposed to tell her? What the hell are they all doing here? And where do they keep going?"

"They're interested. And as you have probably figured out by now, they're often summoned back to their vessel. Something's happening, kid. I used to need their energy to speak, but not any longer. We're all getting stronger. You heard Bob Radke last night, 'you don't want us getting stronger,'" Milt said with a menacing look.

Dan thought that he had seen Milt's eyes glow orange for a minute.

"What do you mean by vessel? And why don't I want you to get stronger?"

"C'mon, kid. Open your eyes. You're smarter than that. The body that's the vessel…their spirit, my spirit, resides in the new body. My body had a heart attack. Not sure how they found that guy. Why do you think you sometimes see three people, when there should only be two?"

"So is every spirit here? I mean do they all wander away?"

"They all can, but not all do. Some are happy in the

173

vessel. Not us and as I said, we're getting stronger. We're going to rest one way or the other. If need be, we'll take anyone we want back with us. By the way, you should try her now, she'll run great."

Dan looked puzzled.

"The car, kid. The car."

Milt came around the car, walking not floating.

"Take them back where?"

"To where there is nothing. A void. A place that is neither Heaven and is far worse than Hell. It's where we took Emil and Smitty. You won't see them again."

"What about Angela?"

"We can't hold another spirit forever. We don't possess that kind of energy."

"Who can?"

"The one that's keeping us here."

Dan took a couple of deep breaths. He looked at the faces of the other spirits. Some looked straight at him with the eyes of someone in desperate need, while others looked at him with eyes that could kill.

"Who?"

"You already know the answer."

Dan nodded.

"Listen, kid, you can't take Angela back. As long as you reject her, Christine will be safe. That doesn't mean she won't try, but you need to reject Angela, not Christine. Got it? To be safe, don't touch her."

"Yeah. But why and how is all this happening?"

"Breakfast must be starting," Milt said as the spirits around him began to fade. "The diner, kid."

"What about the diner? And how?"

"You already know. Trust your…"

Milt vanished.

The Diner

"Trust my what? Dammit!"

"Danny!" a voice called out.

Dan dropped the motor and ran to the house. Christine was standing in the doorway trembling. She was wearing one his mother's robes she had found in the closet.

"It's all right. I'm here. I'm here."

She held out her arms. He almost did the same, but recalled what Milt had said.

"No, I can't. We can't."

The look of disappointment on her face was obvious.

"What's going on? How did I get here? What happened last night? Did we? Charlie?"

"I'm sure he's fine. As a matter of fact, my guess is that you probably called him last night. Why don't you try him now? And I'll make us some coffee."

Thinking about what he was going to tell Christine, Dan poured water in the coffee pot and then went to the pantry for the coffee. A can of Maxwell House drip grind was right in front of him.

"Son of a bitch!"

Chapter 26

Gardner strolled up and down the shoreline never taking his eyes off of the Scheffelin property. Even though wind kicked up strong enough to knock most men back, Garner never wavered. Coach ignored the wind and the shoreline and grazed. Each time Gardner turned to retrace his steps, he looked down at his watch. Ansel would be arriving at 8:00 a.m., and like every appointment, Gardner would keep him waiting. It wouldn't do for him to wait for anyone, so he never did.

Gardner replayed last night's plan in his head and couldn't come up with anything he'd do differently. Still he couldn't decide if no visible activity at the Scheffelin property was a good sign or not. Growing impatient he retrieved the binoculars from the saddle bags and spied the Miller property. Mike was busy removing the golf clubs from his house.

"Well, Coach, it seems that the report is correct. Mr. Miller may have dispatched two of our employees," Gardner said, referring to Emil and Smitty, since neither had shown up for work and neither had a history of being late. "I guess that saves Ansel the trouble. Though we must keep an eye on Mr. Miller to make sure he no longer creates any issues."

After Gardner surveyed the lake, he checked his watch again.

"Twenty minutes past the hour, Coach. Let's go

greet Ansel." With a light tug of the reins, Coach darted off.

As Gardner entered the compound, he could see three large men milling about. The crew looked to be moving in slow motion as they regarded the men while maintaining a safe distance from them. They slowed even further when Gardner appeared.

The three appeared to be in their early thirties. All stood taller than six feet and could have easily been mistaken for professional wrestlers. Each of them showcased well defined muscles that stretched their T-shirts to their limit. Ansel was dressed in all camouflage, while the other two wore basic black. Ansel had chiseled features made even more angular by his razor sharp crew cut. His face was clean shaven but covered with scars. Muscles popped from his arms that were visibly absent of any tattoos. Meanwhile the other two were heavily tatted up, with shoulder-length hair, one blond and the other with black hair. Both had a perpetual five o'clock shadow. Blondy's hands were scratched and scabby, the scars of a recent fight that most likely didn't end well for his opponent. Blackie looked to be the calmer of the two. Whatever Blondy couldn't finish, Blackie surely would end.

Gardner studied them and looked deep into their eyes. They gave nothing away. Gardner appreciated that. To his way of thinking, it meant that any secrets they had would be taken to the grave.

Gardner looked at the crew who shifted their gazes from him to Ansel's gang. He knew that in short order, they would quickly realize that they all had fallen to the fourth rung on the corporate ladder. Ansel walked up with Blackie to greet Gardner. Blackie joined Ansel only to handle the horse. As Gardner dismounted, the deep dark soulless eyes of Ansel not only excited him but gave him the chills.

"Let's walk, shall we," Gardner said, already walking once he got off the horse. He waited for no one.

Ansel caught up quickly. He held his hands behind his back which made his triceps ripple. Gardner didn't question the level of punishment that Ansel might inflict. He doubted that Mr. Miller would be out cleaning up around his house had Ansel handled this from the beginning.

"I assume you have read the full brief," Gardner started. "Still there is much for you to understand. You see, Ansel, your main mission is to protect the infrastructure of Circle Lake. My little town provides its citizens a place where love and life never ends. Furthermore, as an added incentive, I see to it that my fellow townspeople pay next to nothing in taxes, which helps many of the area's retired couples. Meanwhile the businesses in town provide all the services anyone would ever need and all at a fair price. However, my business, like any business, needs a list of satisfied clients. Therefore, those that make their home here are required to use my services for their loved ones that pass on. Leaving is an option, but not a financially wise one. I see to it that homes will not sell at a price that makes a move possible. And as an incentive to move here, I make sure affordable new homes are available— one of my many enterprises. Unfortunately, some folks are reluctant to use my services as the end nears and decide to take their own lives. Death is their choice, even if it is a poor one. You see, living forever with our loved one is what matters most. My business model is simple. Our service is available for a nominal fee to those that live here. However, since we only take a few outside clients per year, they are required to pay a far more lucrative fee. What we do takes energy, my Dorothy's energy, so she cannot be stretched beyond eight to ten clients per year. Since we don't advertise, word of mouth is how we grow. One more time, you are here to see that our infrastructure is maintained.

"To make sure that we're clear, we have four guests arriving in two days. Our latest addition has been challenging. Christine, the vessel, and Angela, the spirit, have an independent streak that has been difficult to control. We'll need to monitor this transition closely. We're in the process of bringing Daniel Scheffelin in line. Any further action against him will be my decision and mine alone. Mr. Miller, Daniel's friend, could prove to be problematic, but I don't want any action taken unless you clear it through me. You see, I insist on keeping bloodshed and death to a minimum in my town.

"In addition to Christine, two of the three vessels are new residents of Circle Lake today, while the third is a longtime citizen of our fine town. Mr. Lloyd Harper lost Helen, his wife of thirty years only a few days ago. He's been difficult to deal with. However after a visit from Diavolo, I'm sure Mr. Harper will come around. Diavolo is very effective at encouraging cooperation. He's never subtle; therefore the message rarely needs to be sent twice. You see Mr. Ansel, some may prefer that I simply call him the devil, but Diavolo isn't some religious entity designed to provide a contrast to their God, thereby making him seem more attractive and pure. In each one of us, there is that ugly and horrific spirit that is intent on inflicting pain and destruction. Some of us are simply better at managing it than others. Historical figures from Genghis Kahn to Hitler to mass murderers such as Jeffery Dahmer have been manipulated and controlled by the spirit of Diavolo. Fortunately, none of my clients' loved ones possess the level of evil of these men. Still in their souls we can find evil. This is why these renegade spirits cannot defeat me. Their energy fuels me. And only I can call upon and command Diavolo to make sure that our tradition of living endlessly with our loved ones continues." Gardner's eyes went hollow black, lifeless.

Ansel shuffled his feet and cleared his throat. Visibly nervous, he began to lag behind Gardner.

"Come along, Ansel. Now back to our guests. Mrs. Harper's body and the others arrived earlier in the week with their souls intact. They are in Barracks Two, which is strictly off limits to you and your men. Are we clear?"

"Yes, sir."

"Good. You see, without the knowledge of the soul's location, our job becomes much tougher, but not impossible. Finding Mr. Scheffelin's Angela was relatively easy. She was all too willing to participate, but as I mentioned earlier, containing her has been trying. Nonetheless, she should be harnessing her vessel as we speak. One more point, we can't hold on to the souls forever, so time is of critical importance. My two assistants take care of all the details. For our purposes, you may refer to them as the nursing team."

"What happens if the souls are lost?"

Gardner stopped and turned toward Ansel.

180

The Diner

"Then the soul is lost. But Mr. Ansel, losing souls is not my business. Are we clear?"

"Yes, sir."

"The transfer," Gardner said, with raised eyebrows expecting Ansel to know that he was referring to the soul inhabiting the new body, "happens as soon as our guest arrives."

"And to maintain that transfer, the diner does the rest," Ansel added.

"That is correct. We can only start the process. We couldn't simply keep the couple here at my compound. No, they need to be returned to an everyday way of life. The diner keeps the process alive. It provides not only the ongoing life blood, but the energy to sustain the spirits in their vessels. How it all works is not for you to question. We are custodians of the process. And remember, the life blood, as it were, is also part of my business. There are those who deal in addictive narcotics such as cocaine and heroin. Mine is a special blend of coffee, Mr. Ansel. It keeps the vessel and soul together. They desire it. They must have it. Make sure the inventory is maintained. We cannot run the risk of it running low."

Ansel nodded.

"Excuse me," Gardener said firmly.

"Yes, sir," Ansel replied.

"Good. Let us go and introduce you to your new crew."

Chapter 27

"What is it?" Christine asked, making her way to the kitchen table.

"The coffee. Look," Dan replied holding the can of Maxwell House.

"That's not what we use at the diner."

"I know. I know. I'm sorry, how are you doing?" Dan asked, doing his best to settle his voice down. He knew the last thing Christine needed was a hysterical discussion about coffee.

"Honestly, I don't know. You were right, though. I did call Charlie last night. He's fine. He's having fun with his grandpa," Christine said, falling hard into a kitchen chair. "What happened last night?"

Dan set a cup of coffee in front of her and then sat down. He didn't know where to begin as he watched Christine stir a half teaspoon of sugar into the coffee. All Dan could do at the moment was look at her, more specifically, study her. She was all Christine, and she was beautiful. As he continued to regard her, he looked around expecting Angela's spirit to pounce. Everything in the house was calm and quiet, while outside the wind howled furiously.

"Smells good," Christine said, taking a sip. "Not the same as the diner though. That's odd. I'd expect your parents would be using the same coffee as in the diner. Oh, I'm sorry."

The Diner

"No worries," Dan replied. "That's what I expected too. So you don't remember any of last night? Think hard. First, how did you get here?"

Christine closed her eyes.

"The Gardners brought me here. But there were other people too. I remember a truck or something. I really can't be certain."

"Makes sense. It's how they redecorated the bedroom. It appears they'll stop at nothing. Go on."

"I was in bed. Naked. You were standing at the foot of the bed. Naked. Did we?"

"No," Dan said, blinking slowly and sighing heavily. "What else do you remember?"

"You were in pain," Christine replied, speaking slowly and looking off into space. "I could feel it. And then I was…but that couldn't be. It must have been a dream. Actually, more like a nightmare."

"What?"

"I was fighting with your wife. She was hurting you. Actually, I could feel that she was torturing you. It all seemed unfair, like you had no choice but to take it. That had to be a nightmare, right? I mean she's dead. And if we didn't make love, how come we were both naked?" Christine asked growing more agitated.

"This is going to sound crazy, so before you react, promise me you'll listen to it all. Will you?"

Christine nodded.

"Somehow my wife's soul, Angela's soul, is still with us. I mean, she's not here now, but she's around and she's trying to take over your body." Dan paused to let the statement sink in.

Christine fell back in the chair.

"Take over my body?" she exclaimed.

183

Dan watched her closely. He didn't know her well enough to know if she was about to explode or just break down and cry.

"Yes."

"That bitch….that bitch. She was cheating on you, wasn't she? I remember now. That bitch."

"That doesn't quite cover it for me," Dan replied as the anger and bile rose in his throat. "I'm just beginning to process it all."

"So how did all this happen?"

"I'm not sure how any of it happens or when it happens. I just know that when we touch, it initiates some connection. Either you're tapping into my memories, or it gives her soul a pathway from me into you. I mean, up until last night, I was hanging onto every memory of Angela. I wasn't letting her go. Maybe she was using me to get to you. I don't know. All I know is that it's happening. It's happening all over town."

"Damn! What do you mean it's happening all over town?"

"Haven't you noticed that no one ever comes in the diner alone? They're all couples. And I think that one person from that couple is not the original. I know…I know, that doesn't sound right," Dan said, seeing the puzzled look on Christine's face. "What I mean is…well, take the Waldens, Milt and Mae. That's not the original Milt."

"How do you know that?"

"'Cause I know Milt." Dan wasn't sure if Christine was ready for more, but if they were going to get through this, she needed to hear everything. "I've been talking to his spirit."

The Diner

"His spirit? Do you mean ghost?"

"I guess I do. But they're not the 'boo' kind of ghosts."

"What do you mean, they're not? How many are there?"

"I don't know. But their souls aren't at rest because they're trapped in another body. A body that begins to look like the person of the soul."

"This is nuts. I gotta move," Christine said walking over to the kitchen.

"Tell me about it. Even as I try to explain it, I'm trying to believe it. Still, my parents killed themselves, just like Mike and Joshua's parents did. They're high school buddies of mine. What we don't know is why they killed themselves."

Christine turned. The simple beauty that was all her returned to her face. A feeling came over him. He felt it in his gut. He was more than just a little attracted to her and had no idea what to do about it.

"Maybe they had no choice. I mean, what if everyone around here can't die…I don't know."

"That has to be it. They had no choice. Still…to take their own lives. How did they conclude that that was the only way?"

Christine looked at Dan. The look in her eyes was one of pure sympathy and tenderness.

"Because rather than living with the soul of their loved one in the body of a stranger, they decided to travel together to their final resting place. They figured death was their best option to be together forever," Christine said.

Dan sat stunned. He believed Christine was right. His mother was dying, and she and Buck didn't know any other way out. He wished they had come to him. He would have figured something out. Instead, they crashed into a tree.

"Sonofa…"

Dan's face fell into his hands as tears filled them. He could feel Christine moving closer. As much as he wanted to feel her touch, he couldn't risk it.

"I could have helped them."

"How?"

"They could have come and lived with me. Or I'd have bought them a place somewhere close by. If my mom was going to die, why did my dad have to go too?"

"Because he loved her. I understand that. And I think you do too."

"But I could have gotten them out of here."

"And then what would have happened to the diner?"

"Who the hell cares?" Dan snapped back.

"The town does and so did Buck, otherwise he wouldn't have left all this for you to fix. He must have sensed that things were worsening."

You don't want us growing stronger.

"And as far as the diner goes, they knew you'd do the right thing."

"And what the hell is the right thing?"

"I don't know. But you need to do something. What do we know? Only couples come to the diner. Everyone orders coffee so that has something to do with it. And the more I think about, where are the kids in this town?"

"I know. It's crazy. But why me?"

"Your dad believed you can make everything right

The Diner

with this town. Milt apparently believes you can too."

They stared at each other for what felt like an eternity.

"Can I ask you something? Why didn't you just jump out of bed and run? Why did you keep fighting with Angela?"

Christine turned away and stared into nothing. After a few seconds, she turned slowly toward Dan. "I could feel the pain she was causing you. It was a piercing pain, right in the heart. I know it all too well. Why would I let that happen to somebody else? Besides, I knew I could take her."

Christine smiled.

Dan smiled back her. "Thank you. So you kicked her ass, but if you want to quit, I understand. Charlie needs you, and you don't need any of this."

"I'm going to take a shower, and then we're going to the diner," Christine said.

"What?"

"What makes you think they're going to leave me alone? And, of all the things that Charlie needs, topping that list is a mother who doesn't quit."

Chapter 28

Dan introduced Christine to Mike as he climbed into the back seat.

"You know who you look like?" Mike said.

Dan and Christine looked at each other and shook their heads followed by Christine's exaggerated eye roll.

"What?" Mike asked.

Dan filled him on his conversation with Milt and what he and Christine had been through but so as not to embarrass her, he left out the intimate details. Next he mentioned the coffee.

"How can it be the coffee? That's nuts," Mike asked.

"That's what you react to? The coffee? Not anything else I said?"

"Listen, I knew Gardner was into some crazy shit. I just couldn't figure it out. Now we're finally getting close, Sheffy."

"We're almost to the diner. What are we going to do?" Christine asked.

"I'm not sure," Dan replied, gazing at both sides of Main Street. "Though, I'll tell ya, I think that the reason this town is always so quiet is because it holds so many secrets."

They all nodded.

"Here's what I think we need to do. First, Dan you

The Diner

do whatever it is you do in a restaurant. I guess you call it work," Mike said smiling. "Christine, act like nothing is wrong. Just take care of your tables and make the customers comfortable. I'll look around. We'll find something. The answer has to be there."

Christine looked at Dan. He gave her a reassuring nod and pulled into his parking space at the back of the diner.

"Sorry we're late, Ray," Dan said as he walked in. "Everyone, this is my good friend Mike. He's going to be looking around the place. You know, to see what improvements we can make."

"Problem, ladies?" Dan asked, seeing Rosie and Molly shuddering and acting nervous as if they had been told the diner was closing tomorrow.

They shook their heads and took their plates out to their guests, but Dan could see the look of fear on their face.

"Trust me, anything we do will be for the better. I promise," he said.

"What's that, Scheff?" Carlos asked as he walked in.

"Nothing. How are we doing? All good?"

"On automatic pilot really. Christine, you're needed out there," Carlos said, nodding toward the dining room.

Dan introduced Carlos and Mike.

"He's going to be looking around. We need to get a better handle on what makes this place tick, you know?"

Carlos nodded.

"I can tell you that the trend continues," Carlos said. "Everyone's ordering coffee. I've never seen anything like it. I almost poured a cup myself, but I don't drink the stuff. And Dan, look at the file in front of you."

Sitting at the desk, Dan opened the file. He leafed through a couple of more papers and then handed the stack to Mike.

"We're not paying for it," Dan said.

"Nope. Your dad must have had some great relationship with the supplier," Carlos said as headed back out.

Dan and Mike looked at each other. Mike raised his finger indicating to wait until Carlos left.

"Oh Mike, you wouldn't happen to be an electrician or know anything about lighting would you?"

"Why?" Dan asked.

"The light above the entrance flashes from time to time. It's incredibly bright. What's strange, though, is it doesn't happen every time."

"I'll take a look at it," Mike said, shrugging his shoulders at Dan.

"Thanks," Carlos said returning to the dining room.

"This is Gardner's company," Mike said. "About every two months there's a delivery. I've seen them. Each time the writing on the truck is different, but the packages are usually the same. I've never seen the contents of the boxes and pallets, but the scent of coffee is unmistakable. As best as I can tell, it comes from Jamaica. But with all the routing it's difficult to know."

"Voodoo," Dan said not sure if he believed it or not. "Maybe they cast some kind of weird mojo on the coffee."

"Or it's laced with something," Mike added. "I

don't know."

"Check out the rest of the inventory; maybe there's something else from Gardner's. I'm going out there to see what's going on out in the dining room."

"Good idea."

Carlos was right; nothing in the dining room looked any different. In a way it comforted Dan because it reminded him of his folks. There were only a few familiar faces enjoying a late breakfast, but the only couple he could recall by name was Rob and Barbara Sanders. They nodded and smiled. Some of the other couples ignored him, seemingly immersed in their morning meal routine. Once they ate their last piece of toast and took a last sip of coffee, and it was always a last sip of coffee, they'd leave, looking fully energized and ready to get on with their day. Dan felt like an intruder in his own diner. When someone did look his way, their gaze cut right through him while their spouses looked into space or down at their food.

Still he felt like his feet were shackled and his hands were handcuffed. And the person holding his arms behind his back was sitting at his usual table, with his wife Dorothy, who once again had her claws wrapped around both of Christine's hands.

How did Christine get caught so quickly?

Dan was ready to run, even dive over there and break them up, but seeing Gardner stopped him. Gardner's stare was different from all of the others. His had purpose. It was chilling. It was exhausting. Most of all, it was challenging. Dan walked over to him intent on making sure he never had to see or feel it again.

"Hello, Dan, I trust you had a wonderful evening," Gardner said. "I only wish we could have done more for you to make it special. Consider the redecoration a gift and my commitment to your happiness."

It took all his strength not to react or comment. The last thing he wanted to do was say something that would imply Gardner had control. That wasn't going to happen. Furthermore, he had no intention of returning Gardner's gaze. Sitting across from Gardner was Dorothy speaking softly to Christine while she held her hand.

How did she take control of Christine so quickly?

Dan couldn't make out anything Dorothy was saying. Upon seeing Christine's eyes it was clear that she wasn't listening as much as she was processing every word. She was in a trance. He concluded that Dorothy was somehow the catalyst for the transfer of Angela's spirit. The air around him grew colder while the flame of anger burned inside him furiously. This scene had played out too many times and needed to end.

"Christine! Christine, it's time you waited on the rest of your tables," Dan said sternly, trying to keep his voice from rising above the rest of the diner conversation. He looked around at all the tables as the air continued to swirl around him and grow colder. He didn't see any spirits and then looked back at Dorothy.

Christine didn't move. Dorothy didn't respond. She behaved as if she was safe in her own world as she continued to whisper and chant.

"It's no use, my boy. This is for the best. You'll see that in time. You and Angela should be and will be reunited. Isn't it beautiful when we can be with our one true love forever?"

Prying his eyes away from Christine, Dan leaned

across the table. Now only a foot from Gardner's face, he said "Fuck you, old man. Whatever game you're playing, it's over."

"Christine!" Dan shouted, surprisingly only attracting the interest of a few customers.

With his heart pounding in his chest and his head feeling like it was going to explode, Dan ran out words. He reached for Dorothy and Christine's hands and pulled them apart. Dorothy fell back into the booth and shook her head.

"My dear boy. Do you really think that's all it takes? The transfer that I complete cannot be stopped or undone. Many young souls have tried and failed. Still. You seem different. There's an energy…no matter." Dorothy paused, looking Dan over. "Embrace her, won't you?"

"Hi, Daniel. Tonight will be different. You'll see."

It was Angela. Dan could see her in Christine's eyes, in her face, her posture. It was all Angela. He released her hand.

"This ends now," Dan said, turning toward Gardner.

Gardner smiled confidently.

It took all his strength not to grab Christine by shoulders and shake her until Angela spilled out and landed helplessly on the floor.

"Angela, you're not wanted. Leave Christine alone."

"This bitch isn't going to have you," Angela said. "You're mine, and we are going to take back the life we had."

With his face flush with anger, Dan turned back toward Gardner.

"Let it go, my son. You have this one chance to be with your wife. Second chances don't come around very often. Now do the right thing," Gardner said, matter-of-factly.

Dan took a deep breath.

"Angela, I don't want you here. You can go to hell, and while you're at it, take these two back with you," he said in a voice that got barely above a whisper. He punctuated it with a searing look that blanketed Gardner. Gardner's once confident smile quickly faded.

"Carlos, can you please help Christine with her checks?" Dan asked, thinking it was the most plausible excuse to extricate Christine from Dorothy's control that didn't draw the rest of the diner's attention. "See if it matches what you have at the register."

As Christine and Carlos walked past the entrance and over to the cash register, flashes of light sparked wildly. Dan ignored it. He was more interested in the three burly men that had walked in moments earlier. They were huddled around the Gardner's table. It was obvious that they were here for him, and not waiting on a table of their own. Dan stared them down as he walked to the middle of the diner.

"Steady, son. I've been very patient with you. You don't know what type of energy you're dealing with. It can turn darker than you ever imagined. Accept Angela and accept your responsibility to this diner and to this town," Gardner said sternly.

"Can I have everyone's attention?" Dan announced to the diner. He knew he was beginning to get to Gardner. Confronting him in front of the diner guests would only infuriate him more.

Not everyone looked at him. Seeing those that

The Diner

continued to stare off unconsciously into the distance only reinforced what he had to do. Out of the corner of his eye, he saw Mike meandering his way into the dining room. Mike regarded the three men walking in. They were fanning out in the diner. Mike nodded at Dan as if to say, "I got them. You go ahead."

"Many of you have been concerned about the fate of our diner. The reason my family has been doing this so long is because of you. So, thank you. As you all know, the restaurant business is in my blood. One thing I've never done is settled." Dan looked over at Gardner and Dorothy, who watched closely. "It's imperative that my restaurants never become stagnant, so we'll be making changes to your diner. New furniture…"

Gardner sat up straight.

"A new menu."

Gasps and groans filled the diner.

"We'll paint the walls. We'll upgrade the kitchen equipment. And how about some iced coffee or even flavored coffee? You'll love it."

"Scheff," Mike interrupted and nodded toward the window. Spirits were lining up beyond the glass as the sky outside grew darker. Lightning flashed outside and inside the diner.

"My boy. I'm warning you. It wouldn't be wise for you to press me any further. The force I can bring down on you is far worse than anything you can ever imagine," Gardner said as bent over and spoke to Dorothy. Dan didn't hear a word. Dorothy stared at Gardner for a few seconds, then nodded slowly. Gardner straightened up and shook his head in the direction at Ansel and his men.

Despite the spirits lining up three deep outside, the

menacing and darkening conditions in and outside the diner, and with his heart nearly beating through his chest and fists clenched, Dan pressed on. "I trust you will find these changes only make the diner a better place for you and your families."

Rob and Barbara Sanders were already standing up. Rob fumbled in his wallet for a twenty dollar bill to cover a twelve dollar tab.

"Hurry, Rob," Barbara pleaded.

He threw the money down, grabbed her arm, and headed for the entrance. Dan stepped in front of them.

"Thanks for coming. See you soon," he said.

"Your dad was right, you wouldn't back down," Rob said, pushing Barbara ahead of him and toward the door. "Buck tried, but never had the strength to see it through…probably because your mom was so sick. I'm sorry, Dan. Do what you can. Please save this town. We can't move."

Dad tried? Gardner must have bullied him down.

The anger building inside him was at a boiling point. A huge rush of cold air swirled around Dan and prevented him from walking over and tearing Gardner apart.

Dan watched as Rob and Barbara pushed their way through the crowd and out of the diner. He looked up at the entrance as the Sanderses walked out expecting to see another bright flash. Nothing. Gardner and Dorothy rose from the booth and walked toward him. There was strength in the old couple that Dan hadn't noticed before. It shook him. Seeing the Gardners converging, the other diners followed suit. Dan felt the diner close in on him. Lightning flashes in and outside the diner persisted. The sky opened up with a torrential, angry

The Diner

downpour. Darkness deeper than any midnight encased the town and approached the diner like a dust storm in the desert.

"Sorry, kid," Milt said from behind Dan. "We can't help you in here."

"Then why come here?" Dan said as the dining room grew colder and crowded with spirits.

"You know why. We had to make sure you didn't back down. If you had, I'm not sure what would have happened. Look at them. They're restless. Their energy is building," Milt said of the wandering gazes of those spirits that had been trapped in vessels that never had a choice and who had lost their own souls.

Dan felt the pain in each of the vessels and the wandering souls. And there were so many souls, but the pain of those that were discarded to make room for another was what he felt most. It was the sting of being in trapped in a relationship that was loveless. Having recently experienced that same hurt, he would never wish it on anyone else.

Dan saw Gardner look over at Ansel. Blondy started to move as did Mike. Blondy headed straight for Christine who was now engaged in her own war with Angela. Carlos tried to grab her and calm her down, but she tossed him aside like a rag doll. It was clear, the combination of Christine's strength and Angela's power was more than he could handle. Dan tried to run over but was slowed by the converging customers.

It was getting difficult to see as the diner grew darker. Dan could barely make out Blondy as Blondy reached for Christine's arm. He almost had it in his grip when Mike dropped him with a hard right cross. Christine bent over and gasped. When she stood up, she

197

looked like Christine again. She started to wobble and certainly would have collapsed on the floor had Mike not caught her. He sat her down slowly on the floor as something caught his attention. Dan saw it too, but didn't move. A pair of perfectly manicured women's feet in peek toed high heels floated toward him. Her legs were tanned and shapely. Dan knew those legs. They were the legs of a woman who rarely walked over to a man. Dan now knew they were the legs of a woman who walked all over a man.

"Daniel, isn't it time we put an end to all this?" Angela said, now hovering in front of Dan.

She raised a hand to caress his face, but Dan pulled away. Despite what he now knew about her, he couldn't help but be captivated her. Running her hands up and down her slender body, she looked like a runway model wearing the latest designer fashions. There was no question that her short black dress, hugging every curve of her body, would drive any man insane with desire. Despite the dimming lights of the room, her hair caught what light was left and bounced it back. Her eyes sparkled. Her lips were a fiery ruby red, matching her stunning fingernails. Angela glowed. Dan saw the beautiful woman he married. He also saw a woman in a black dress. The same dress she wore when the paparazzi lit up the New York skyline by taking thousand of pictures of her and Ryan Billings leaving the restaurant. Then he saw Christine sitting on the floor, exhausted. Her eyes pierced through the sea of spirits and met his. In her stare he felt her kindness and compassion, and maybe even love, a love he never knew. Still there was still sadness and emptiness in her eyes he could actually feel. Regardless, he knew

The Diner

Christine was real, far more real than Angela ever was when she was alive.

"I thought I told you to go to hell," Dan said to Angela as he started walking toward Christine.

"You can't win this," Angela screamed, her body rising and settling back to the floor. "You never win. I was the one that made everything happen for us. And I will again. Without me all you'd have would be this lousy diner."

"This diner has more to offer than any restaurant I've ever opened. It's serves memories." It came out so naturally. For the first time Dan felt like he was not only fighting for what his parents had created, but he was fighting to preserve their memories. And his. He never felt more resolve.

"And Angela, hell shouldn't be hard for you to find. You put me through it enough," Dan replied with twice the venom of a diamondback rattlesnake.

Christine and Dan started walking toward each other, when she was intercepted by Blackie. Mike lunged at him and grasped nothing. Dan couldn't take another step. He was trapped in the middle of the deep, dark gray madness of the diner as the guests and spirits all surrounded him. He swung his arms through frigid air and into bodies sending them crashing into the diner chairs and tables. A fractured energy of good and evil hovered in the air fueling every living and dead thing while the diner hummed like old stereo speakers. Despite his efforts, he couldn't break free to get to Christine.

A white hot lightning flash rocked the diner.

Christine screaming his name was the last word Dan heard before the diner and town went pitch black.

Chapter 29

With the diner under a cloak of frozen darkness, Dan couldn't see his hands in front of his face. Breaking the silence was the random sound of someone stumbling into a table or chair. Seconds dragged until the front door clanged open. The diner lit up as if it was under a dozen strobe lights. Dan, Mike, and Carlos watched in amazement as everyone seemingly disappeared through the front door. The three of them tried to move, but an enormous weight of energy kept them cemented in place. Slowly the lightning flashes ceased. The temperature returned to normal, and the diner and town began to lighten. It was still overcast and rainy, but beams of sunlight were beginning to break through. It now looked like noon rather than midnight.

"Where's Christine?" Dan yelled out. His head shifted about in every direction never once focusing on the disarray the diner was now in.

Finally able to move, Dan, Mike, and Carlos scrambled searching in and outside the diner, while the rest of the diner staff went about straightening up the diner, seemingly uninterested in why the place was a mess. Dan wanted to understand how they could react that way, but figured they had probably become used to seeing crazy come to life in their town, especially the diner.

The Diner

There was no sign of Christine, Gardner, or his men. No more than five minutes had passed when Dan rushed in from the kitchen and was amazed to see guests walking in and looking forward to their lunch as if it were just another day.

"Scheff, what the hell is going on around here?" Carlos asked, as he picked up a couple of chairs and set them around a table. "Gardner has Christine, doesn't he? Why?"

"Yeah, he's got her, and we need to go get her," Dan replied. The panic in his voice was obvious to everyone.

"Steady," Mike replied. "We will, but we just can't go out there and storm his compound. Gardner knows we'll be coming, so let's not make it easy for him."

"I'm not going to sit here while he has Christine," Dan replied, starting to pace the entire length of the diner, constantly looking out through the windows, amazed that the town could so quickly return to normal.

"We're not going to just sit here. Think about it. He's not going to harm her—quite the opposite. He's the one behind Angela taking over her body. So Christine's not in danger, plus they need you there, right? So we're going, but not without a plan."

Dan looked at Mike for a couple of seconds and then finally nodded.

"Good. We need to know what we're dealing with. Carlos, what did you see?"

"First, I saw the Sanderses get up to leave. You know it's weird; the entrance light never flashed when they left. Odd. Then I saw you deck the guy trying to grab Christine. Then Gardner got up and everyone did the same and started to walk toward Dan. Next, the place went nuts, freezing air, lightning flashes, pitch darkness, it was freaky."

"So you never saw the spirits," Mike stated, shaking his head as he dodged the waitresses as they put fresh condiments and place settings on the tables.

"What spirits? Do you mean ghosts? I knew this place was haunted. I mean, there is some strange shit going on around here. And look, it's only been a few minutes since the storm, lights and pitch-black darkness and now look outside, people are getting out of their cars and heading straight over here like nothing ever happened. I don't get it. This diner and the whole town seem to be wired for insanity," Carlos said as opened the front door to let the guests in.

"It is nuts," Mike said, waving at Dan to join him behind the counter. "Those lights have been bugging me too. Both Rob and Barbara appear normal, right? You know, neither one of them has a spirit in them. Here's what I'm thinking. Anyone walking through that door that doesn't have a spirit inhabiting their body goes in and out without event. When a spirit is along for the ride, the light flashes. It must have something to do with their energy. Who knows? At least we know who or what is coming into the place."

"But what about the flash when Gardner walked out? Are you saying he has a spirit in him or Dorothy?" Dan asked watching in disbelief as Rosie was taking a guest's order.

"Who the hell knows? They both may be spirits. Doesn't matter really, but my guess is we'll find out."

Carlos joined the guys behind the counter after picking a few napkins off the floor.

"So let me get this straight. We have ghosts

wandering around the place. Not only that, we have spirits inhabiting people's body. What? Like the body snatchers?" Carlos asked.

"Not quite," Dan said hesitantly.

"Maybe it is," Mike interrupted, seeing Dan struggling. "Angela's spirit is trying to inhabit Christine's body to the point of turning Christine into Angela. Christine's body becomes the home for Angela's spirit and soul. Maybe half the people of this town are walking around with someone else's spirit controlling their body. Who knows how many really? And as best as I can tell, the spirit is that of their dead husband or wife. What I don't get is what happens if one of them dies? I mean, suppose the body with the spirit has a heart attack or what if the living spouse dies? Where does the spirit go then?"

"Does it matter?" Dan asked rhetorically. "I'm sure Gardner has an answer. Whatever it is, I'm sure it's not good."

"That's messed up. But why are they coming to this place?" Carlos asked.

Silence.

"The coffee," Dan and Mike answered simultaneously.

They both turned around to face the coffee urns. Carlos walked over and poured a cup and stared at it.

"The coffee? That's insane! What's so special about it?" Carlos asked.

"Somehow it's like their spirit blood. How the hell should we know?" Dan snapped.

"Then why not just drink it at home?" Carlos asked innocently and then walked over to the sink to dump it out. He watched it go down the drain as if he was expecting something to rise up from the from the bottom of the sink.

Dan and Mike looked at each other with blank stares.

"Damn. He's right," Mike said. "What else is it about this place?"

They all turned and surveyed the diner. Some of the tables still needed to be cleaned while a few napkins, forks, and knives littered the floor. Truth was the diner looked like it did after a breakfast, lunch, or dinner rush.

"It's probably provides some type of energy source that without it, the coffee would be useless," Carlos said without really thinking. "Then again, maybe I watch too much cable TV."

Again Dan and Mike looked each other unable to come up with a better explanation.

"What do you mean?" asked Dan.

"Did you ever see any of those ghost hunting shows on TV? There is always some energy source like water, limestone, or electricity that fuels the spirits. And sometimes the vortex can be altered when someone renovates a house or hotel. Heck, knock out a wall, and you can open or close a portal to the spirit world too. I really don't understand any of it. I actually didn't believe it until this all happened."

"That's why no one wants me to change anything. If I do, the energy could shift."

"How could putting an iced coffee on the menu change the energy?" Mike asked.

"It probably can't. It isn't one change that they're afraid of. It's the ripple effect of many changes, particularly if I start renovating the place."

The Diner

"Screw 'em. Change the whole fucking place," Mike said. "Whatever is going on around here, your parents, mine, and Josh's killed themselves because of it. Who knows, I bet there were others too."

"What?" Carlos asked, now holding a bus tray and a damp cloth about to go clean the tables.

Dan took a deep breath. "Mike and Josh, another friend of mine, each had a parent who was terminally ill and rather than having their soul trapped and living in another body, they chose to…let's just say, move on to the afterlife together."

"You mean they had no choice. Who made that rule? And how the hell is it enforced? And where did their souls go?" Carlos asked, setting the bus tray on the counter.

"We don't know for sure, but we think that death was the only way for their souls to be at rest together. Gardner's behind all of this, and my guess is our friend over there will know what happens if someone doesn't follow Gardner's rules," Mike said pointing to a spirit standing outside the diner.

"What or who are you pointing at?" Carlos asked, straining his neck to look around Mike.

"Nothing you need worry about. Just keep the place running. We'll be back soon. You got this, right?" Dan asked.

"Whatever you need, Scheff," Carlos said, picking up the bus tray and making his way over to clean the tables while Dan and Mike walked outside. Mike looked back at the ceiling as they exited. No lights flashed.

"Hey, kid. You're heading out to Gardner's, aren't ya?" Milt said walking around the corner of the restaurant.

"He has Christine, so you bet your ass we are," Dan replied. "But first you need to tell me, what is it about this diner? Why doesn't anyone want me to change anything? Because right now I'm thinking I'm going to turn this place inside out."

"Screw that," Mike interrupted. "What does Gardner have over these people? How's he getting them to do everything he says? Our parents killed themselves. Josh's parents too….son of a bitch. What is it?"

"It's about time you boys got pissed," Milt said, motioning the guys to follow him around the corner to the side of the diner.

"What does that mean? C'mon, Milt. What the hell is going on?" Dan asked, looking up at the clearing sky, amazed how the weather had returned to normal.

"I don't have much time," Milt said looking down at his feet as they disappeared and then reappeared. "You're going to have trust me that what I'm about to tell you is the truth. The diner holds a vortex of energy that powers the spirits. More than that, it's home to a portal for us to move on to the other side. The vortex can't exist without the portal, but the portal is closed. We need it opened, otherwise we can't cross over and be at rest. Gardner wouldn't let your dad open it up."

"That doesn't make sense. People are dying all over the planet, and I doubt they're coming to my diner to move on," Dan said, looking around to see if anyone was watching them. There were people on the street, presumably heading into the diner, but they never looked Dan's way.

"That's true; there are portals all over world.

The Diner

Spirits know how to find them. However, Gardner and his wife teach the surviving spouse how to anchor the spirits here to this time…to this town…to this diner. Do you think I'd be here if I could break away? Mae won't let go. Somehow she and the others use the energy from the vortex, their mind, and their touch to keep us here. If they don't let go, and they never do for long, we can't move on. Plus that damn coffee does something to the vessel that keeps us here. But know this, we also can use the energy from the vortex to break free, but with the portal closed, it's useless."

"But you said that you and the spirits were becoming more powerful. Why can't you use that energy to break free?"

"It's not the same power. What we tap into is the destructive power that is fueled by all the negative energy of your world, not the spirit world. At Mike's with Emil and that kid, you've seen what we're capable of. More and more spirits are joining the fight and have the power to destroy everyone and everything in this town. We will be at rest, one way or another."

"Then why don't you all use that energy to fight Gardner? Why drag me into this?" Dan asked.

"Again, if we could, don't you think we would? He's too strong for us. He has a way of neutralizing our power. We're hoping you can weaken him, then maybe…"

"How?" Mike asked, shifting from side to side. Clearly not getting any answers was beginning to get to him too.

"Listen, guys, I don't know. All I know is that you have to do it, and you have to open the portal."

Dan stood still, shaking his head and trying to

make sense of what Milt was saying. He thought of what his Dad had written to him. *"It's up to you son. We know you have the strength to find a way."* Milt and his father were counting on him to save the town. "Yeah, and they're both dead," Dan muttered.

"What's that, Dan?" Mike asked.

"Nothing. So Milt, where is the portal and how I do I open it?"

"I don't know." Milt was beginning to fade. "Find it though. Before you do, get out to see Lloyd Harper. You need to know what you're up against."

Milt disappeared.

"Lloyd Harper?" Mike asked, pacing with his fists clenched in anger and needing to hit something. "What does he have to do with this?"

"I don't know. I haven't seen him in years. Is his wife Helen still around?" Dan asked.

"Oh shit. You don't think that…" Mike started to ask.

"Yeah. Call Josh and have him meet us there!"

Chapter 30

Dan brought the car to a creeping halt in the driveway leading up to Lloyd Harper's garage. Mike was about to jump out when Dan grabbed his arm.

"Hang on a minute. Something doesn't feel right."

"I'm not feeling anything," Mike replied.

"It's here."

"What is?"

"I can't really describe it. It's an energy and not a good one."

Through the windshield, they could see Lloyd Harper sitting alone in his garage fully consumed in the task of cleaning a shotgun. Like a pilot going through his preflight checklist, Lloyd inspected every centimeter of the gun. He pulled the gun up to his eye and aimed it off in the distance. He pulled the trigger. No burst from the barrel. No sound. However, Dan detected the briefest of smile appearing and then fading on Lloyd's face. Lloyd then returned to wiping down the gun barrel.

"I'm going to go talk to him," Dan said. "You stay here."

"Well, that's not happening. Are you crazy?"

"I'm telling you, there's a negative energy building, and let's face it, it has nothing to do with you. It's much like what I felt at the diner. My guess is it's about to converge on Lloyd's garage. If something happens to me, I need you to go get Christine."

"After that, should I go and save the town while I'm at it?" Mike replied facetiously, as he scanned the sky and began to rub his arms. "Ok. I'll give you this one. Go talk to Lloyd, and then let's get out of here."

As Dan walked over, the sky continued to grow darker. In just twenty short paces, lightning and thunder crashed and echoed around him. As if on cue, the sky opened up and the rain fell hard. Dan bolted inside the garage as the lightning flashes came in rapid fire and lit up the sky. The breeze transformed into a howling wind that was no longer refreshing but frigid.

"Lloyd. It's me. Dan Scheffelin. How are you doing?" Dan asked as Lloyd held the rifle across his lap. He never turned toward Dan. Instead, he stared off into space with a glazed look in his eyes.

Three quick burst of light caused Lloyd to jump off his stool and cower under the workbench. Dan ducked too, expecting a rhapsody of thunder any second, but no sound followed. He looked around as the air grew heavier and even more ominous.

"Lloyd. Lloyd," Dan shouted. Lloyd didn't respond. He stood up staring at the entrance of the garage as if someone was walking in.

Dan followed his stare but couldn't see anybody or anything unusual. Icy air rushed in and filled the garage. Outside, the rain fell sideways. The wind whipped up and pelted the garage along with heavy rain drops, nickel size hail, and broken tree branches. Paint cans, rags, and tools flew off the workbench and crashed to the floor and against the walls. A loud, murmuring hum caused the rafters of the garage to shake and creak. A mixture of dirt, dried leaves, and month-old newspapers rode the cyclone of air that started along the inner perimeter of the garage and then transformed into a swirling three-hundred-sixty-degree wall of racing debris in the corner of the garage. Dan could see the panic-stricken look on Lloyd's face. Dan wasn't feeling all that safe himself. He thought about running back to the car, but he couldn't bring himself to leave Lloyd. Dan moved closer to Lloyd, squinting as dirt and sand pelted his face. Over the jet engine noise of the wind, he shouted at Lloyd again. Either Lloyd couldn't hear him, or he was just too frightened to reply.

Dan's blood began to race seeing Lloyd reach for a couple of shells, load the rifle, and bringing it up to fire. But at what? There was nothing but a cloudy wall of trash to shoot at. Lloyd struggled to hold the gun barrel level as the end of it seemed to be pulled down. His entire body began to shake. His breath hung in the air like a patch of fog and then was swept away in the swirling dirty gray dust trail. The shotgun fell from his hands and slid a few feet away and then rose into the air, pointing straight at his chest. The cyclone grew tighter in front of Lloyd and formed into a crooked, floor-to-ceiling pillar of dark, empty energy.

The two of them stared straight into an endless tunnel of midnight blackness that seemed to stretch on to infinity. As best as Dan could sense, it was every type of negative energy imaginable. Despair, helpless, sadness, loneliness…Dan couldn't label it. The conical black hole began suck in every loose object in the garage. Then heavier objects such as power tools, logs, and bricks began to shake and vibrate. One by one, they sprang into the air and began orbiting in a tightening spiral and then flew into the dark mass. Lloyd's body began to wave like a flag as it was being drawn into the cyclone.

"So glad to see that you've joined us, Mr. Scheffelin. Now you will witness the extent of terror I can unleash," said a gravelly, disembodied voice. "You would be wise to not have me repeat this exhibit."

With that, a plume of gray, grime-filled air shot out from the cyclone like a punch from a heavyweight boxer and sent Dan flying across the floor and crashing into the far wall.

"Now, Mr. Harper, is this really what you want? I warned you. I can bring about a death more painful, cold, and empty than anything you can imagine."

Barely able to lift his head, Dan strained to look at Lloyd as his eyes grew bigger and his back began to bend. His stomach protruded toward the dark emptiness. Lloyd struggled to keep his feet planted on the hard concrete floor of the garage.

"Who…who are you?" Lloyd spat out.

"You know exactly who I am. The devil of Circle Lake. But you will refer to me as Diavolo."

Unable to right himself as his head pounded and body ached, Dan strained to look at the top of the spinning cylinder certain that he saw the face of Ernest Gardner forming in the shadowy gray mass. But it was a deformed a face, a sunken face, one that you might find on a corpse.

The shotgun cocked.

"Or perhaps, we should scatter your brains all over your garage and see that Helen's spirit finds someone new," Diavolo said in a voice that pierced Dan's eardrums like a screechy air horn.

"No. No. Please, what do you want?"

"Accept the soul of Helen in another," Diavolo replied as the empty mass pulled Lloyd closer with the shotgun now only inches from his chest.

"Yes, yes, of course."

"I don't believe you," Diavolo shouted in guttural voice that reverberated throughout the garage.

With Lloyd shaking, Gardner's face protruded from the black hole. His eyes were a fiery crimson, with black hollow pupils against an ashen, withdrawn shallow face.

"On your knees and pray for the soul of your wife to be free in the vessel of another."

Lloyd crumpled to the ground. Tears ran down his face. The butt of the shotgun flew across his face sending him crashing to the ground. Before he could throw his arms up to fend off another blow, the shotgun got sucked into the black hole and disappeared.

"I said kneel."

The garage shook.

Lloyd got to his knees but not before pissing himself.

"Accept her soul."

"I do…I do," Lloyd said as he trembled.

"Hell is waiting for you should you betray me and her soul," Diavolo said as Lloyd's body was lifted off the ground. He had nothing to hold onto.

As Lloyd's body hung in the air like a rag doll, his arms and legs flailed about aimlessly. Dan got himself up on one knee.

"Noooo!" Lloyd cried out as he floated into the hollow emptiness.

Dan jumped up and wrapped his arms around

Lloyd. Using every ounce of strength he could muster, Dan tried to pull Lloyd back but couldn't drag him back an inch. Now they were both floundering inside a deep, dark emptiness. As Lloyd cried uncontrollably, Dan punched his hands all about in the vacuum. He felt like he was swinging at emotions. Lifeless. Loneliness. Eternal sorrow. Then tears ran down his face thinking of the love he lost with Angela and the love he may have found with Christine. With his eyes closed, he felt like he was floating. His feet were unable to find purchase with the ground. There was nothing for his hands to hold onto.

"Helen, my love. I'm sorry," Lloyd muttered with his face buried in his hand. "I tried to convince the devil…Diavolo. I just can't…Why didn't he give me a chance? Oh, Helen."

Dan opened his eyes and saw Lloyd lying at his feet. Dan now felt his feet firmly planted on the floor of the garage. Dan reached down and wrapped his arms around Lloyd and lifted him to his chest.

"Lloyd. This isn't the end. I promise."

Still surrounded in darkness. Dan shook his head trying to clear it. He had felt enough fear and fear was getting him absolutely no where.

"Lloyd, we need to stand up," Dan said as the deep black darkness faded into gray. The ground began to warm as did the air. He heard the sounds of birds and the wind through the trees. Lloyd slowly removed his hands from his face. They were now standing in the middle of the garage with the floor and shelves littered with trash. The rain continued outside, but the storm was over. Dan looked around. Everything was there, not in its original place, but it was there. Everything except for the shotgun.

"You can't kill something that's already dead," he muttered to himself.

Chapter 31

"Ansel, I suspect Dan and his friends will be here shortly. Let's make sure Christine and our other guests are safe. Dorothy is working with Christine and Angela...Mrs. Scheffelin now," Gardner said, walking toward Barracks One with Ansel following obediently behind. "I shouldn't have to, but given what occurred at the diner, I feel compelled to remind you that we simply send messages. It is only in extreme cases that someone has to die for our mission. Are we clear?"

"Yes, sir. I'll remind my team." Ansel threw a nod in the direction of Blondy, who stood rubbing his fists.

"Good. Are the barracks prepared?"

"Yes, sir."

Even though they referred to the facility as barracks, it bore no resemblance to army barracks. Rather, it looked like a typical machinery storage barn that one would find on any farm in the Midwest. The exterior was weathered and covered in peeling barn red paint. The windows were trimmed in white with the bottom of the sill at least ten feet off the ground. At that height there was no way to peer inside without being hoisted up or standing on a ladder. The landscaping was simply dirt, scrub bushes, and rusted farm implements, everything you'd expect to see around a barn. Meanwhile, walking inside the building was like entering the lobby of a Ritz Carlton hotel except that

The Diner

there wasn't a front desk clerk or concierge willing to attend to a guest's every need. There was no service help around. The lobby was nothing more than a waiting room for the living to wait for the dead to return to them in the body of another.

"The place looks exceptional. Your crew did a nice job preparing the accommodations. I assume that the clients' rooms are prepared," Gardner said to Ansel. "We'll need Mr. Scheffelin in here soon to help with Angela's vessel. Pull the team in. I'm sure you and your men can handle anyone accompanying him."

"Yes, of course," Ansel replied confidently.

"See to it. I'm going to check on the progress of our guests. Also alert me immediately when Mr. Harper arrives. He's running a little late, but that's to be expected. I understand he had a rough time today," Ernest said with a satisfied smile.

With Ansel leaving to check on his team, Gardner found Dorothy with Christine, who was resting comfortably and nearly asleep. The temperature in the room was near freezing, which meant Angela had been there and now was recharging herself in the spirit realm. Dorothy greeted Ernest with a smile and a nod. She released Christine's hand and walked over to Ernest and took his hand. Her hand was wonderfully soft and incredibly hot. Gardner was amazed how she could generate that much energy and heat when the spirits froze the air around them. He knew that Dorothy was stronger than they were. She commanded them, not the other way around. She led Ernest out of the room.

"She'll be fine for now. But Christine is strong. She fought hard. She's also exhausted. But it won't last; we need Mr. Scheffelin here as soon as possible.

Without his connection, Angela can't take over the vessel."

"He'll be here soon," Ernest said, noticing the concerned look on Dorothy's face. "I've instructed Ansel that Dan is to arrive safely."

"Thank you. Now who would you like me attend to next?"

"Helen Harper, please. Lloyd had quite the experience this morning."

Dorothy shot him a disapproving look.

"It was necessary, my dear. You know I despise having to do it; however, we cannot tolerate disobedience."

Dorothy acknowledged him with a slight smile. "Remember it only makes it harder for me to do my work. Should Mrs. Harper learn of what happened, it will be most difficult to keep her here. And then what of her vessel? We can't let anything happen to it."

"I understand, my love. Now please see to it that Mrs. Harper is ready for Mr. Harper."

Chapter 32

As Mike was about to run up and join Dan and Lloyd, Josh pulled up.

"What's going on out here?" Josh asked looking around the property. "It looks like a hurricane hit this place."

"That's what I'm about to find out," Mike replied. "I thought the world was coming to an end before. It was effin' crazy out here. Torrential rain, lightning...I couldn't even see the garage from the car and now look. The weather is perfect."

"Damn. Geezus, this place looks trashed," Joshua asked as he walked into the garage stepping over paint cans and garden tools.

"Shit. Are you guys all right?" Mike added, seeing the garage looking like it had been turned upside down.

"Yeah. That was nuts. Let's get Lloyd in the house," Dan replied.

"What are you kids doing here? I can't let you in. I have to go. Helen needs me," Lloyd stammered as he staggered into the house.

They ignored him and followed Lloyd inside. Dan looked around and turned his nose up to the musty odor in the house. Dan wondered if it was death that he smelled. With his arm around Lloyd's shoulder, Dan guided him over to the kitchen table. He knew it was the one place where people were likely to open up and speak their mind.

"Why don't you sit down, Lloyd? We need to talk. I was there with you. I saw it all…"

"What the hell happened out there, Scheff?" Mike interrupted.

"Later," Dan replied. "I saw Gardner too. Why was he here?"

"It wasn't Gardner. It was the devil himself. Diavolo," Lloyd said standing and staring through window toward his garage.

Seeing the puzzled look on his friend's faces, Dan put his hand up to stall any questions. Lloyd turned around and stared down at the kitchen table, whispering his wife's name.

"Lloyd. Please. I'm here to help."

"What do you mean? What can you do? Your father couldn't do anything and look what happened to him. He left us. You'll just do the same thing," Lloyd said becoming more agitated.

"I'm not going anywhere. All three of us lost our parents. And we know Gardner's responsible."

"He didn't kill them, though he could. He has that kind of power. He's Diavolo." Lloyd took a long pause. "They killed themselves. It was their only way out. I know that now. But I can't, I won't do it. I have my children and grandchildren to take care of. I promised Helen."

"Lloyd. Why the shotgun?" Dan asked. "Start from the beginning."

Lloyd took a long look at Dan and then nearly collapsed into a kitchen chair, sighing as if he was holding onto his last breath. With tears in his eyes, he looked up and explained.

The Diner

"Nine months ago, Helen got sick. Cancer. We thought she was going to beat it, but we were only fooling ourselves. The cancer had destroyed her body. There was nothing we could do. We wanted to leave here, to get away from Gardner. But how? We couldn't sell our house; he wouldn't let that happen. Besides, my kids and grandkids are here. They need their grandpa. It would be up to me to keep the memory of their grandma alive. All Helen wanted was to be at rest. We decided I was to stay behind and put an end to all of this for us, for our kids and for everyone in this godforsaken town. I'd get away with it too. No one could blame me."

Lloyd took a deep breath and continued. "That son of a bitch and all his bullshit about a life with Helen's soul in the body of another. If I followed his every word to the letter, soon this person, the vessel he called it, would be Helen. My Helen. That's not what we wanted. It's not what so many of us want. Some of us just want our loved ones to move on…to their final resting place. What of our faith in God, of man's goodwill to one another? Someone had to do something. I may be sixty-seven years old, but I've never backed down from a fight in my life and I'm not about to start now. But…Diavolo…"

"The shotgun," Dan interjected.

"It would have been so easy. Gardner has a routine. It would have been so easy," Lloyd said, getting up and now talking out through the back screen door staring at the garage. "He leaves the diner at 10:30 in the morning and reaches the edge of his property by 10:45. I found the perfect spot behind a willow tree. No one would see me. Just before he'd drive by, I'd step out and…I had

221

plenty of shells, not that I need more than two. But now…"

The room fell silent. Dan looked at Mike and Joshua.

I wish you had ended this.

"Somebody has to end this," Dan muttered, as the kitchen table began to shake and a chill crept into the room.

"What's that, Dan? Damn, what are they doing here?" Mike asked, feeling a cool breeze on his neck.

"Back off!" Dan shouted into the air, as he stretched his arms across the table to steady it. "I'm trying to help! How is this helping?"

The table stopped shaking.

"You tell em, Dan!" Mike said. "They're listening."

"Tell who?" Josh asked.

"Later," Mike replied.

"Don't worry, Lloyd," Dan said, seeing Lloyd's gaze dart about the room. "They're here for me, not you."

Lloyd nodded and shivered from the chill entering the room. His head continued to swivel and cower. "What do they want?"

"To make sure I keep my promise. Now tell us what you know."

"Gardner has Helen. I mean he has her body, doesn't he?" Mike asked, shaking his head as more and more spirits materialized and then faded away.

Lloyd nodded again. "She wants to be at rest. She's tired. She had a long fight. There's nothing more for her to do here."

Dan tried to keep his eyes on Lloyd but was

The Diner

distracted by one of the spirits, more specifically by the eyes of the spirit. They were ablaze and glowing a fiery, angry orange color. It was Bob Radke. A sharp shaft of cold air and energy knocked Dan against the wall. Bob picked up a glass. Dan sensed it and righted himself quickly and caught the glass before it crashed against the wall.

"Bob, enough!" Dan shouted. "This isn't getting you any closer to the other side, is it?"

"Sorry, kid," Milt said appearing as Dan placed the glass on the table. "I tried to warn you. They need to be convinced you're going to help. 'Cause if not…"

"Listen, Milt, and the rest of you, I'm…we're…doing what we can. But you have to give me some time."

"Who the hell are you talking to and what the hell was that?" Josh asked, looking around the room after finally peeling his eyes off the glass that flew across the room.

"Mike, you better tell him," Dan said.

Mike nodded and took Josh into the family room.

"Try relaxing your mind and quit being so afraid, then maybe you'll see them too," Mike suggested as they walked back to join Dan and Lloyd who were standing in a ring of spirits.

"What stopped you from killing Gardner?" Josh asked.

"Diavolo," Lloyd cried.

"Who?" Josh asked.

The spirits all stopped moving; all of them but Milt and Bob Radke disappeared at the mention of the Diavolo.

"Better tell your friends, kid," Milt said, as Bob

223

paced with his eyes continuing to glow, but not looking as menacing as before.

Dan could see the fear on the faces of his friends as he pored over every detail of what he and Lloyd experienced. When he described the image of Gardner appearing from the dark, empty mass, everyone's jaw dropped. Dan's hands were balled up into fists as he continued. He looked out toward the garage, looking lost, wondering if the nightmare had really happened.

Mike paced, getting angrier by the minute. "That bastard. So that's what he's doing. He's scaring the shit out of people and threatening them with eternal hell unless they play by his rules. I wish you had blown him away."

"You can't kill the devil of Circle Lake," Lloyd replied.

"So what are we going to do? I mean, if we head out there, there's a chance he turns into this Diavolo and….shit," Josh said, too scared to finish the sentence.

"What are you going to do, kid?" Milt asked, as Bob Radke's eyes began glowing brighter again as he picked up a kitchen chair and threw it against the wall. Everyone jumped and looked right at him, all except for Josh who was staring at the chair. Bob quickly faded with his stare locking on Dan as he disappeared. "The more time that goes by, the more…." Milt disappeared.

"The more what?" Mike shouted. "Jesus, this is getting crazy. What was he talking about?"

"You don't want to know. Trust me, you don't want to know," Lloyd said as he picked up the chair.

"Actually, we do," Dan said calmly, helping Lloyd with the chair. "We're going to get Christine, and we'd like to know what we're up against and exactly who's

The Diner

on our side."

Dan could feel every eye in the room fall on him.

"I already told you. Gardner…Diavolo. What more do you want to know? You saw what he can do."

"I want to know what Milt was talking about. What are the spirits going to do?"

"I'm not sure. What we…others in town…think is that they'll destroy this town if they're not able to cross over," Lloyd said.

"Where are they getting their strength from?" Josh asked.

"Many of us think they get it from the living. From our fear. From our despicable acts of cruelty on others. You see it every day. There seems to be less and less kindness in this town…in this world. It's not getting any better. Their energy is only going to grow. If you're going to do something, you better do it quickly or everyone and everything in this town will be destroyed," Lloyd replied.

Before Dan could speak, his phone rang.

"Hey, Carlos. What's up?"

"Scheff, I think I know where the portal is."

Chapter 33

"No one else sits there? Are you sure?" Dan asked.

"I noticed it when I started reviewing the guest checks. The Gardners are the only people who sit at table one. It's like they protect the entrance. I asked the staff, and no one can recall anyone else sitting there," Carlos said.

"So you think the portal is in the ceiling? The lights," Dan interrupted.

"It has to be. What do you want me to do, Scheff?" Carlos asked.

"Nothing for now. Business as usual. Got it?"

"Sure. Talk with you soon."

"In the ceiling? That has to be it," Mike said. "I can't believe we missed that."

"I don't know. How can we figure it out in a day when Milt, who's been here longer than a lifetime, says he has no idea where it is? It has to mean my dad really didn't tell him. And I doubt opening it will be as easy as removing a few ceiling tiles. Something doesn't make sense."

"Damn," Mike said.

"So what are we going to do? And whatever that is, we better hurry, because I think Lloyd is leaving without us," Joshua said as Lloyd was walking out the door.

"Lloyd, hold on a minute," Dan said.

The Diner

"Why? Why should I do anything you ask? Diavolo will just reappear and then kill me. Then what? Then what?" Lloyd said as his voice crack and tears welled up.

"Give us a minute. Lloyd, please. We're going to figure this out," Mike said, helping Lloyd back to the kitchen table.

"Got a plan?" Dan asked.

"Well, Gardner knows we're coming, right? And he knows Lloyd is coming. What he doesn't know is when and how."

"What do you mean?" Josh asked.

"Lloyd, why don't you go get yourself cleaned up while we work out a plan," Mike said. Once Lloyd left the room he continued. "I bet Gardner thinks we're going to drive up to the front gate? Do you still have that canoe?" Mike asked of Josh.

"Yeah. So?"

"So we take the stealth approach. Lloyd drives up as planned. That way we know some of Gardner's men will be occupied at the entrance. The others will be patrolling the barracks. Meanwhile, Dan and I will come in through the side door, from the lake."

"Wait. If we manage to get Christine, how are we getting out of there?" Dan asked.

"Dude, all the vehicles on the property have the keys in them. Gardner figures no one has the balls to come on his property, so we'll have our pick of vehicles."

"What about me?" Josh asked.

Mike looked at Dan.

"Can you head back to the diner and look around and see if you can find the portal? Turn the place upside

227

down if you have to. Carlos will help. We'll meet you there as soon as we can."

Lloyd entered the room and walked over toward Dan. He had a renewed look on his face, one of resolve and determination.

"Ready, Lloyd? We got this. Go out to Gardner's. We'll be right behind you. I know it will be tough, but if you really want to help Helen's soul, don't touch the body she's in. If you do, you may not be able to release her. We're not sure how it all works, but be strong. Don't touch her. Got it?"

"Yeah. Don't worry about me. I'm not living with another person. I promised Helen she could rest. You boys better see this through, or I'm getting me another shotgun," Lloyd replied and then walked to his car.

Josh shook his head and left for the diner.

"I have to tell you, storming a psycho's compound by canoe doesn't exactly sound like much of a plan," Dan said as he and Mike drove down the road.

"It won't be just the two of us."

"Who else do you have in mind?"

"The spirits."

Chapter 34

"There aren't a lot of places in the diner the portal can be. I guess we'll know soon enough," Mike said as he brought the canoe to the edge of the water and nodding at a few spirits that began to materialize around them. They kept their distance, seemingly there only to observe. "Do you know any of them?"

"Nope. They look like scouts, don't they? Let's get out of here."

"Not yet. I figure it will take us about twenty minutes to get across, so it's still too early. We need to wait until it gets darker," Mike said looking at his watch. "We'll leave in about thirty minutes. Thankfully, there's barely a ripple on the lake, so it won't be too hard to get across."

"And when we get there, then what?" Dan asked when his phone rang. "Hang on, it's Josh."

"I was doing like you said, looking around the place," Josh began. "And as you know, your dad has all this stuff hanging on the walls, but most of it is meaningless. Sorry, but it is. It's nothing but boring news clippings or old ads for furniture and appliances. Frankly, that in itself is strange. Why would he hang those on the wall? I mean, there's one after another. That got me to thinking about that newspaper photo of you and me high fiving at home plate after the conference championship. Remember, your dad kept it up by the cash register. Hanging there now is some old want ads, but here's the thing. It's from page thirty-five. No big deal, right? But all of the news and magazine articles framed on the walls are from page thirty-five. It makes no sense. There's nothing of interest in any of it."

"What does that mean?" Dan asked pacing along the shoreline, swatting the occasional insect buzzing front of his face as Mike went to check out Josh's garage. "Buck would have never hung any of that stuff up."

"That's what's I thought. Anyway, as I'm looking at this want-ad, the light above the entrance flashed as two people walked out. I decided to go into the kitchen and stick my head up there; you know, remove a ceiling tile and see what I could see as someone left the diner. At first, all I saw was a bunch of wires, conduit, pipes, studs, and more ceiling tiles. Then a burst of white light flashed in front of me, but an even brighter flash occurred behind me. It scared the hell out of me. I turned around to see a white light glow coming up from an electrical junction box that was only few feet away. I ducked my head below the ceiling tile to see that the flash had occurred above the refrigerator. I walked over to the refrigerator and there it was, a taped sign that read: "Keep Temp at 35 degrees." Who adjusts the temperature of a refrigerator? No one. Am I right?"

"Damn. That has to be it. Anyone in the business knows to keep the temp at thirty-five. That's Buck's clue. I can't believe I missed it."

"What do you want me to do?"

"Nothing for now. Wait till we get back there." Dan hung up as Mike approached. He filled him in on the conversation with Josh.

"No doubt about it. The portal has to be there. Good," Mike replied. "How did you not notice it before?"

"I don't know," Dan said shrugging his shoulders. After a couple of deep breaths, Dan asked, "So what are we going to do when we get to Gardner's property?"

"We'll snake our way to the barracks; that's where they'll be holding Christine. Gardner knows we're coming, and there are cameras all over the place. His men will see us, no doubt about it. I just don't want to make it too easy on him. I know where some of the cameras are, but not all of them. It doesn't matter; I'll get you to Christine. Then I'll do my best not to get caught while getting us a vehicle," Mike said brandishing a fishing knife he found while retrieving the canoe paddles.

"What the hell are you going to do with that?"

"Hopefully only scare a few people. I'm not going there to create more spirits," Mike said as Dan continued to pace. "What's bothering you, Scheff?"

"Let's say we get out of there with Christine…"

"We will get out of there," Mike interrupted.

"Fine. Then what? What's going to stop Gardner from coming after her or anybody else for that matter?"

"One thing at a time. Regardless of what we do about Gardner, we need to go get Christine. That alone will send a message that we're not backing down. This isn't like some recipe you're cooking from. We don't know how this is going to turn out. We will get it done though," Mike said, as he looked over his shoulder noticing that the spirits were apparently listening to every word. "Hey, Scheffy, why do you think they're so many of them? I mean, if they were scouts, they'd only need one or two."

"I don't know, maybe they're protecting us. Who knows?"

"I hope you're right, Scheffy. I sure hope you're right," Mike said under his breath.

Dan never heard him; instead he stood staring across the water at Gardner's property while Mike continued to gather whatever supplies that might come in useful, including a rope, baseball bat, and six road flares.

"What are those for?"

"You'll see. We may need a diversion."

Mike joined Dan at the water's edge. Lights began dotting the shoreline around the entire lake as night fell.

"Ready?" Mike asked.

"Yep. Are they coming with us?" Dan asked rhetorically referring to the spirits behind him.

Mike smiled, hopped off the shore and into the canoe, and then steadied it for Dan as he got into the front. In less than a minute on the water, they found their stroke and were working in tandem. Mike looked back toward the shore to see the spirits slowly disappear one by one. "I guess the spirits will meet us there."

"I don't think so," Dan replied pointing to the water, seeing reflections of spirits coming and going. When he turned around, only he and Mike were in the boat.

"Damn, that's a little creepy. You can only see them in the water; they're not hanging in the air. Let's get there, get this over with, and get these spirits back where they belong. Still, I'd like to know where that is.

The Diner

I mean what if it's…"

"That's it!" Dan interrupted and shot around, nearly tipping the canoe. "Remember when Milt and the other spirits took Emil and Smitty back with them…to that place you have so many questions about? Well, I wonder if they'll oblige us again. Angela…if they can…"

"I like it. Let's hope the spirits are willing. But from here on out, let's keep the talking to a minimum. Voices really travel across the water."

After a few more silent minutes on the lake, they made it ashore. They scanned the area for Gardner's men and for the spirits. There was no one around.

"So they're going to let us walk up?" Dan asked rhetorically.

"Why not? They want you with Christine. Here take this," Mike said handing Dan a road flare.

"What am I going to do with this?"

"Improvise," Mike replied. "You can't always talk your way out of every situation."

Mike tucked the other five flares tightly in his back pockets; the knife was clipped to his pants. "Damn, it feels good to swing this," he said swinging the baseball bat. "Let's go."

They ran across the field, plowing a path through the tall, sharp grass. Every hundred yards or so they'd stop, kneel down, and scan the area to see if anyone was about to pounce on them. Still no one was near. They approached the perimeter of the compound cautiously. It was brightly lit, like a Friday night high school football game. They could see about a dozen men walking around, always in pairs. Dan watched the men while Mike looked past them, like a football running back studying the defense.

"What are they doing? They're not even carrying any weapons."

"They never do. Gardner doesn't allow them. I guess since he can turn into the devil, why would anyone need a gun? But you're right; they're just loitering around out there. They're definitely making it easy on us, too easy," Mike said. "Here's the layout. There are two sets of barracks. The one closest to us is where Christine is. The one behind it houses Gardner's network, you know computers, telecom, the surveillance cameras, etc. The barn over there is just that, a barn for the horses and equipment. That building that looks like a plane hangar is where they store the shipments."

"The coffee?"

"Yep, among other supplies, feed for the animals, etc. Gardner's house is a quarter mile or so from here. Are you ready? Damn."

"What is it?"

"They know we're here," Mike replied. "They're all wired and wearing headsets. One of them just pointed in our direction and now they're all looking our way. I must have missed one or two of the cameras."

"They're just standing around. Why aren't they headed this way?"

"Because they know if they do, we're out of here and that would only prolong what they want and that's you with Christine."

"Then it's a trap."

"Kind of. But screw 'em. We're going to make them pay. I'm going to bolt for the service entrance on the side of the barracks to draw some of them with me.

The Diner

I'll bang on the doors, so if there are men inside, maybe I can draw them to me. You quickly run in through the front entrance. Once inside, go straight ahead through the double doors at the end of the lobby. There are only four rooms, so you shouldn't have a problem finding Christine. Get her and then get out. Head back toward the canoe."

"Where are you going to be? And why the canoe?"

"So I can find you. First I'm going to drive these assholes crazy with a few diversions."

"What for?"

"What if you can't get out quickly? What if they swarm the place? What if…"

"What if the devil shows up?"

"Then we're fucked. I don't know. One problem at a time. Let's go."

As they made their way over to the barracks, Gardner's men tapped their ears and began to converge on them. Mike and Dan broke for the service entrance. Once they got a few feet from the door, Dan darted toward the front while Mike ran around to the side of the barracks.

Standing inside, Dan was immediately hit with the contrast of the exquisitely decorated interior of the barracks to the weathered and drab exterior. If he didn't know better, he'd swear he had walked into a four-star hotel. He was shocked to see so many expensive furnishings from the furniture to the wall hangings and artwork, to the brass fixtures and the crystal lighting. There was a large sitting area with leather couches and chairs, a big screen TV, and a wall full of books should a guest prefer to read. Behind that was a small kitchenette, with an open pantry well stocked with food and a fully equipped bar. As his feet sank into the plush carpet, he quickly dismissed his awe and chalked up the surroundings to what a rich, psychotic control freak would do with his money. A little surprised there was no one around, Dan figured they were now watching the entrance to make sure he didn't come out. *Mike was right. They wanted me in here.* He made for the double doors, hesitated for a second, and then burst through them like a wild man. He stopped cold.

"It's good to see you. We've been waiting for some time," Ernest Gardner said standing tall and confident, while Dorothy sat obediently by his side in an elaborately adorned chair fit for a queen. "No matter, you're here now. You'll find what you're looking for in our Promise Room. You see, my son, we don't use room num—"

"What the hell are you talking about? Where's Christine?" Dan shouted.

"As I've already stated," Gardner replied calmly. "Angela is in the Promise Room. There…to your right. We find that room numbers are so impersonal, so each of our rooms has been assigned a name. I felt that the Promise Room was appropriate for you and the love of your life. Go to her now."

"Fuck you," Dan said, reaching for the doorknob.

Feeling a bolt of electricity shoot between his shoulder blades, Dan turned to see Gardner's hollow dark eyes embedded with a fiery red cornea. They were aimed at the center of Dan's chest. Chills ran down his spine. He couldn't shake the desperate and dreadful feeling that washed over him as the memory of Diavolo came rushing back. He quickly opened the door to get away from Gardner as much as to find Christine.

The Diner

With the door closed behind, Dan's senses immediately went into overdrive. He stepped inside of an elegantly decorated room that was more suited to the high-rise Gold Coast shores of Lake Michigan, not a small northern Illinois lake town. It was impeccably clean, with freshly painted walls and luxurious, deep cranberry colored carpeting. The cherrywood furnishings, complete with polished brass hardware, were beautifully finished and reflected every beam of soft white light in the room. The king-size bed was draped in satin sheets and pillows alive with colors that resembled a warm fall morning. Decorated more lavishly than most hotel rooms, it still had the staples of a desk in the corner, a flat screen TV across from the bed, and a full bath. None of it shocked Dan after what he saw in the lobby, until he spotted two six-inch dark glass domes mounted in opposite corners of the room.

"That son of a bitch; he's watching our every move."

"Well, there you are," Angela said from Christine's body as she walked in from the bathroom and sat down on the bed. "You've kept me waiting much too long, Daniel; you know how that annoys me so."

He took a long look at the woman sitting on the corner the bed, dressed playfully in beige shorts, a red tank top, and flip flops. It was Angela, the woman who led a life in pursuit of her own pleasure, and it was Christine, the waitress who had awakened the need for real love that had been dormant for far too long.

"I know what you're thinking, but I'll get this body in shape," Angela said as she got up. "How do you like my eyes? I think they're getting better, don't you?"

"Dammit, Angela," Dan said seeing that

237

Christine's eyes had faded from green to light brown.

"Don't worry, they be all brown soon. What does this woman eat? It must be a strict diet of brownies and ice cream. I don't know how someone can let themselves go like this." As soon as she said it, her body flew back on the bed and flopped around like a fish on dry land.

"Let go of me, you bitch!"

Christine's body writhed in pain as she wrestled with the energy of Angela's spirit. Her arms and legs kicked about wildly, like a child throwing a tantrum. Dan took a few steps toward the bed. The hair on his arms stood up as the electric charge increased the closer he got to Christine. His body began shake from both the cold and pain from the negative energy engulfing Christine's body. He had to back off and felt completely helpless.

Christine's body relaxed. The electricity in the room vanished. Christine's body sat up.

"Christine, c'mon, let's get out of here."

"Don't be silly, Daniel, you're not going anywhere. We're staying here until that waitress of yours is no more. Now come here this instant and hold me. Damn it." Christine's body lurched forward and then back. "She may be out of shape, but this bitch is strong," Angela said.

"Angela. I've already told you. I don't want you here. You can go to hell or to whatever the other side is. I couldn't care less. Now release Christine!" Dan said with one eye on the camera in the corner of the room.

"Daniel, she means nothing to you. No one ever did. Now hold me so we can be together," Angela demanded, and leaped up to wrap her arms around Dan.

Dan sidestepped her at the last minute but not before their shoulders touched. Feeling as if he had been launched into a time warp, the memories of his life with Angela came flooding back. From the day they first met, to their first date, their wedding day to opening their first restaurant. As the timeline of memories rushed through him, an oppressive darkness began casting a shadow over each recollection. Dan knew what it was. He could feel it. It was his anger and resentment of her infidelity. The pain of learning the truth snapped him back to reality.

"Let her go, Angela. You need to move on, and Christine needs to be with her son!" Dan shouted, occasionally seeing Christine's eyes shine through. "Christine, Charlie needs you. Don't give in to the bitch."

Dan watched the battle unfold before his eyes. Clearly, Christine wasn't giving up. He could hear it in Angela's normally controlled voice that was now cracking with emotion. Christine was getting to her. Furthermore, in place of her typically steely-eyed stare were a pair of eyes shifting back and forth never able to find focus. Angela stood and tilted her shoulders back. Dan knew her defiant stance all too well. Angela was about to release an "I'll tell you this, Daniel," diatribe."

"Save it, Angela. Actually, go fuck yourself. Where do you get off thinking I'd want to spend the rest of my life with your spirit? You have no spirit, other than an evil one. Let Christine go so she can get back to her family. There is no us and never will be."

"Why are you making this so difficult?" Angela shouted, as she cocked her head menacingly to the side.

Dan expected her to make another attempt to

embrace him. If she held him, she could potentially flush all the pain he remembered and replace it with their most pleasant memories. The energy, all the loving feelings they once had would be rekindled, and she'd have her life back. That thought made him shudder.

Dan was trapped in the corner between the bed and the wall as Angela came barreling at him. Angela jumped on the bed ready to pounce, when she stopped abruptly and crashed into the TV knocking it to the floor. Christine's body twisted violently on the floor. Dan looked up at the cameras and then dashed into the bathroom, grabbed two washcloths, and quickly soaked them under the faucet. He ran back out and placed a wet cloth over each camera lens. He was about to run over to the door and throw the deadbolt, but there was none. Instead, with Christine still rolling on the ground, he grabbed the desk chair and jammed it under the door handle.

"Christine, fight! Think of Charlie," Dan shouted.

He knew if Christine could break free, he'd have to get her out of the room and then out of the barracks quickly. Other than the door, the only other way out was through the window above the desk.

The energy in the room grew in intensity as a buzzing, static sound filled the air. Lights flashed off and on as did the cracked TV. The temperature in the room continued to drop. Dan's head began to throb feeling the pressure in the room increase as if he were on a jumbo jet.

"Your wife is a fucking bitch!" Christine said, grabbing the corner of the dresser to steady herself.

"Christine! Is Angela still in…I mean where is

she?"

"She's not in me. I'm certain of that. One minute we're in what felt like hand-to-hand combat. Neither of us was winning. I heard you say Charlie and that was all it took. I grabbed her by the throat and squeezed...I don't know." Christine nearly stumbled trying to take a step. "I can't explain it. Then Angela vanished, like she was sucked from my soul."

"Let's get you outta of here," Dan said as they heard a crash outside the room door. "I'm sorry, but you still need to fight through this. We're going through that window. Get up on the desk."

"Where the hell do you think the two of you are going?" Angela said, as Christine and Dan stepped on top of the desk.

"Son of a bitch," Dan said, hearing the voice as he opened the window and punched out the screen. The heat of the evening came pouring in. He was about to turn around when two coffee cups flew through the air, one hitting him the shoulder while the other crashed off the wall, barely missing Christine's head. He turned to see Angela not standing, but floating about a foot off the ground. Dan shook his head. Once again Angela was wearing the same dress as the night she was killed.

"Going to see Ryan?" Dan snapped back at her.

"I will once I get that fucking waitress to behave herself. Of course, I need to get her fat ass in shape first."

Angela's eyes glowed red. Emotionless. Her head moved as if was on a swivel and turned toward the TV. Dan saw it coming. He grabbed Christine and pulled her close nearly falling off the desk as the TV crashed at her feet. The lights in the room flickered faster, like a strobe light. A frigid breeze blew in from the window, catching Dan's attention. He looked out and saw Milt with other spirits lining up alongside him. Dan grabbed Christine's shoulders and brought her face inches from his. "You gotta go now. Hit the ground and run toward the lake. I'll be right behind you."

"You two aren't going anywhere," Angela said as she flew through the air toward them.

"Christine, go!" Dan shouted as he stepped in front of her. Angela crashed into him and disappeared into his body. Dan fell off the desk and hit the edge of the bed and slumped to the floor. Memories of his life with Angela consumed him, but the details were different. They weren't from his perspective; they were from Angela's. Each restaurant opening came flashing by. He was looking at his wife. She looked beautiful, but she was looking at Ryan. He saw their first night in the condo. He also saw a week later when she was in the condo making love to Ryan in their bed. "You fucking bitch. You never loved me."

"I did once, but your life was your food. Goddamn food. What kind of life is that? Serving others? I needed more. And I'll have it too. And you're going help me."

Dan couldn't see Angela, but her words rang loud and clear in his head. He fought to come around. Pulling himself up, he retched and doubled over as Angela shot out from his gut. She hovered above him. Her skin color kept fading in and out from a healthy, bronze glow to a pale, ashen white, while her eyes glowed like a blazing bonfire and then faded looking as lifeless as a rock.

She's losing energy.

Another frigid cool blast flew in through the

window. Dan knew what he had to do.

"You're right. You built my restaurants. You created the blitz. It was all you. So if you're going to do this then go get Christine. But I doubt you can accomplish it, since she rejected and defeated you twice. What do say, Angela? Are you going to fail again?" Dan hoped she wouldn't back down from the challenge.

Another heavy thump on the room door made Dan's head spin. The chair against it wouldn't hold out much longer. Angela drifted within inches of Dan, putting both her hands on his face. His face froze and electricity coursed through his body. He was about to pass out when Angela released him and flew through the window. Dan staggered to his feet and climbed on top of the desk. "C'mon, Milt, don't let me down."

Dan jumped up on the desk to see a burst of white, hot light fill the sky about fifty yards away. Christine stopped running and turned around. Milt, and the other spirits, including Angela were gone.

"Christine, I'll be right there," Dan shouted and then jumped off the desk.

He quickly grabbed the sheets off the bed and balled them up at the base of the door. He grabbed a pillow and tore it open. Clumps of goose down floated in the air and fell to the floor. Retrieving the road flare from his back pocket, he struck in and threw it into the pile of feathers. They burst into flames which quickly spread to the blankets. Leaping to the desk, he shimmied through the window and fell to the ground. He could hear men shouting all around, and he knew they'd be on him and Christine in no time. As soon as he reached Christine, a second explosion beyond the

243

barracks lit up the sky. It brought the men in pursuit of them to a standstill. A few short seconds later, another explosion occurred close to the first one.

"What the hell is happening?" Christine asked.

"Mike's been busy. Come on, we need to keep moving," Dan said as he saw the men behind them peel off to attend to the fires.

"Where are we going to run to?" Christine asked.

As Dan was about to reply, a pickup truck came rushing toward them.

"Get down," he shouted, and they sank into the thick, tall grass.

The driver of the truck skidded to a stop only a few feet away from them.

"Scheffy, you did it. Nice," Mike said referring to the burning barracks. "What do you think of my fireworks?"

"It certainly isn't understated. At least you have them scrambling and off our trail for the moment," Dan replied.

Without thinking much about it, he grabbed Christine's hand and trotted around to the passenger side.

"Sorry, Scheffy. I still have a few things to do. I'm gonna bury this place. Take the canoe back to your place. Gardner doesn't have a boat, so they can't follow you. I'll meet you back at the diner as soon as I can. Yee haw!" Mike shouted and hit the gas and sped out of sight.

"What an asshole," Christine said, pulling Dan closer to her body.

"A crazy asshole," Dan said. "C'mon, I have another idea."

Chapter 35

"Oh my God, they're beautiful, but what are we doing in here?" Christine asked, admiring the perfectly groomed horses.

"They're our way out. We don't have time to paddle across a lake," Dan said as he led Coach out of his stable. "Maybe you should call Charlie?"

Christine hesitated, tilted her head to one side, and blinked. "I'm fairly certain I already did. I told my parents that I'd be working at your restaurant in the city for a few days and staying with another waitress. If I call now, I'd only confuse them, and besides, they'll start asking a bunch of questions that I truthfully can't answer."

"What?" Dan asked seeing Christine now looking at him with a puzzled look on her face.

"Why did you suggest that I call Charlie?"

"I don't know. I guess it seems like something we…I mean you should do. I didn't mean anything by it," Dan replied wondering if Christine believed him, particularly since he wasn't sure himself.

"I know. Thanks," Christine said.

Her smile landed heavy on his heart since he felt responsible for all that had happened.

"Well, pick a horse and let's saddle up. Do you know how to ride?" Dan asked, wanting to change the subject.

"You'll be eating my dust, my darling Scheffy," Christine said, walking over to a tan colored horse with white spots on his chest. "I don't know what your name is, but I'm going to call you Patches."

Dan watched Christine in amazement.

She just fought the spirit of my dead wife, explosions going off all around us, and she's talking to a horse like she's getting ready for a casual Sunday ride.

Even knowing that they had to be on their way, he couldn't find the strength to peel his eyes away from her. The words "my darling Sheffy" echoed in his head as he leaned against his horse and held tightly to the saddle, certain if he hadn't, his weakening knees would sending him collapsing to the ground.

"Get it together and get out of here," he muttered to himself.

Christine had her horse saddled in no time. Dan didn't offer to help after seeing how capable she was. Instead he took Coach by the reins and led him to the rear doors and wrapped the reins around a hook. All of the activity was occurring at the front of the barn, so before they headed out, he needed to make sure Gardner's men were all occupied. Mike's incendiary distractions had made it easy to get to the barn; now he hoped it was as easy to get out. *No telling what he's planning next,* he thought. What he witnessed was chaos. Men were running around trying to put out the fires, while others running from truck to truck apparently unable to get any of them started.

"Are you ready?" he asked Christine, seeing no reason to wait. She hopped on the horse with ease.

"Let's get out of here before Mike blows this place

off the map," Dan said running past Christine to open the rear doors of the barn. With less than a four-foot opening, Patches bolted past him with Christine smiling and winking. With a squeeze of his legs around Coach's belly and a tug on the reins, Dan was upon Christine in seconds. Despite the circumstances, it was the first time since his parents' memorial service that he felt like he was beginning to have fun. Christine gave him another warm smile when he got alongside her. This time her smile shot through him and lingered. He knew at that moment that he had to see that smile again and again. Christine peered over her shoulder, and it reminded Dan that first they had to get off Gardner's land and then to the diner. No one was trailing them. *How could they, unless they ran? Mike probably has all the vehicle keys,* Dan thought.

Three hundred yards from the edge of Gardner's farm two strange rows of lights appeared. They flashed on and off. Dan's back straightened as a chill ran down his spine. They brought their horses to a halt.

Chapter 36

The rage Gardner felt inside the guest barracks paled in comparison to what he felt when he burst through the doors to see his life work nearly destroyed and his compound in chaos. The grounds were bathed in a dusty, orange glow from the flames that shot from the barracks and the gravel that Mike's truck spit out from the tires as he tore through the compound. Some men were chasing him, while others were trying to extinguish the fires. Gardner wrenched a man by the collar as he ran by and threw him to the ground.

"Why is that man still able to drive around and inflict further damage?" Gardner shouted as the man crossed his arms over his face in fear.

"Get up and answer me," Gardner demanded, kicking the man in the side.

"He…he…he must of have taken the keys to our cars…no one can find them. Others have flat tires. We don't have any vehicles," the man said finally getting to his feet and keeping his distance from Gardner.

"Put out these fires. Where's Ansel?"

"I don't know…I'll go find him." The man ran off not waiting for a reply.

"Coward. You're all cowards," Gardner said, looking out across the compound to see spirits appearing and disappearing. They flew and floated about. It had been some time since Gardner had seen that many at once. He figured they were turning out as news spread of the destruction.

"You'll all be back where you belong shortly," he shouted, shaking his fist in the air.

Gardner turned to see Dorothy usher the guests away from the barracks. Lloyd Harper walked behind the group, slowly and with a limp, rubbing the side of his face that was badly bruised by the rifle butt.

"Diavolo's message definitely made an impact with Mr. Harper," Gardner said to no one as a devilish grin appeared on face.

The smile quickly faded as Mike's truck barreled down on Gardner. Seemingly out of nowhere, Ansel rushed at Gardner and pushed him out of the way. They both rolled on the ground. Ansel jumped to his feet and reached down to help Gardner up. Gardner pushed his hand out sending a bolt of energy square into Ansel's chest, sending him flying in the air and landing against the barracks door. He was out cold. A few spirits gathered around him and then flew off.

"He's not worth your time," Gardner said, now scanning the grounds for the truck.

The truck slid to a stop and turned, apparently ready to make another run. Gardner's entire body began to shake. His eyes glowed yellow with a blazing, lava orange center. His arms began waving about madly. Slowly his hands came together as if he was packing a basketball size snowball. Letting out an ear piercing, thunderous roar, Gardner released a fiery ball of red energy. It pierced the night sky and barreled down on the truck. It looked like a comet, but flew no more than eight feet off the ground. With it closing in on the truck, a dozen or so spirits lined up in three rows of four.

They absorbed the burning missile and converged around it like an oyster around a pearl. The truck stopped abruptly, kicking up a cloud of dust. Light beams of white, orange, and red burst out from between the spirits' legs, arms, and necks. They closed in tighter finally sealing the energy ball within them. Then like a group of water ballet dancers they all arched their backs sending a stream of light energy harmlessly into the night sky. As the light dissipated, they disappeared one by one.

The truck sped off as Gardner's men came running toward it only to be showered in flying gravel.

"Ernest!" Dorothy shouted, seeing her husband stagger and nearly stumble after he unleashed the destructive sphere. "No more. That will not do anyone any good, least of all yourself. You need to sustain your energy. There is more work to be done. Let Ansel tend to the grounds and that boy in the truck."

Gardner's body slowly stopped shaking. His eyes cooled to a deep brown and found focus on the barn. "I'm making no promises," he said angrily walking toward the barn. He waved at a few of his men to follow, which they did, but none of them got too close. Dorothy was only a step behind and closing in.

"No, Dorothy. I need you to attend to our guests and see that the spirits stay with their vessels. Please take them to our house. We'll have to complete the transfer there," Gardner instructed.

"Once again, your anger is getting in the way of me doing my work. If need be, I can and will see this transfer to conclusion myself. Then I'll have no choice but to accelerate your son's ascension. Is that what you want?" Dorothy asked, clearly annoyed that she had to remind Ernest of her dominant power.

"Of course not. Don't worry. It won't happen again," Gardner said in a failed attempt at reassurance.

Shaking her head, Dorothy walked toward the guests who huddled together far away from the burning building. Lloyd Harper continued to lag behind.

Gardner wasted no time going into the barn. Seeing that the back door was wide open, Gardner walked quickly over to Coach's stall. Gardner turned around with fists clenched and his eyes glowing red.

"Now! Get them all out of here, at once!" Gardner commanded.

The man scattered, each running to grab the halter of a horse and ushering them outside. It only took a few seconds. Now each of them was standing a safe distance from the barn with a horse by their side and staring back at Gardner.

The doors to the barn closed sharply. Only seconds later, a thundering noise erupted from the barn. The ground of the entire compound shook while the blast could be heard from more than a half mile away. A blinding shaft of orange and red light exploded through the top of the barn like a cork from a shaken bottle of champagne. In seconds, the roof burst into flames. A flickering amber glow shone through the windows and doors. Soon the entire building was a blazing inferno. The dry hay and barn wood were as good as any kindling, burning quickly and hot.

The barn roof collapsed. One by one the walls began to fall inward. The last standing wall was the front entrance. Through a smoke-filled cloud and flames of black and orange fire shooting out in every direction walked Gardner, heading straight for the men and horses. Against a hollow, dark gray face, Gardner's eyes glowed fiendishly yellow. Not one article of clothing was burnt, though smoke continued to rise from his shoulders, arms, and legs. All the horses began to tug and pull on the halters. One jumped up on its hind legs and let out a shrill cry that drowned out the sounds of the night. The men stood frozen in place. It was first time they saw the demon Gardner, though they had heard countless tales of the devil of Circle Lake. The men stood frozen in place with eyes wide open. They looked at each other. Still no one moved or said a word.

"Tell Ansel to get off his ass and get over here," Gardner shouted.

"He went after the guy in the truck," one of the men responded.

"Find him and get me transportation into town," Gardner barked back.

No one moved.

"Now!" he roared.

Chapter 37

"It looks like an airport runway of lights, doesn't it?" Dan asked.

"It does, but what is it really?" Christine asked patting Patches on the neck, sensing the horse was getting nervous.

"I think they're spirits."

"What are they doing out here?"

"I think they're showing us the way to go. I mean I was going to take us back to my house from the road, but going through the forest makes more sense. We won't be seen. Don't be afraid."

"Seriously, Scheffy. I just kicked your wife's spirit's ass. What else do I have to be afraid of?"

There was something about the way she said, "Seriously, Scheffy," that persuaded him to look closer at her. There was nothing about her that looked like Angela now. *Hopefully she never will,* he hoped.

"What?" Christine asked looking back at Dan.

"What, what?"

"You're just looking at me."

"Yeah, I guess I was," Dan said embarrassed. "C'mon, let's get out of here."

Just as they pulled on the reins, the ground trembled and the sky lit up as an explosion nearly knocked them off their horses.

"What the heck is going on? Mike?" Christine

asked, patting Patches on the neck to calm him down.

"It's probably something he's done or he really pissed someone off," Dan said, certain Gardner was causing his own brand of chaos.

"Hey, what happened to our lights?" Christine asked.

Dan turned, still looking toward the explosion as the light in the sky began to fade. Bright lights, much bigger than fire flies, flew about in the sky looking like mini shooting stars.

"I have a feeling they'll be back in a minute," Dan replied tracing the sky back to the edge of the woods.

"You're right."

The row of dotted lights began to appear and illuminate their way. They trotted through the line of spirits like they were in a parade. Each spirit watched them closely with sad and desperate eyes.

"Can you feel that?" Dan asked feeling ticklish pulses of electricity pinch his skin as the air became heavier, like someone one was pushing down on his shoulders.

"Yes. It's their sadness. It hurts…I can feel their pain. Look at their faces. We need to help them. They don't belong here."

"Can you really feel them? I mean, how do you know?"

"They're talking to me. Not with words, but with their feeling and emotions. It's like when I know Charlie is hurting without him telling me. Or when my dad is missing my mom, but won't admit it. I can feel those things. Now you're looking at me again."

"I guess I am. You're something."

"I've been called worse," Christine said with a

smile.

Once they passed the last spirit, they all vanished. Dan didn't need to look back to know they had left. The electricity in the air was gone, and the feeling was lighter. He sat up straighter in the saddle.

"Damn."

"What is it?" Christine asked.

"The fence. I was hoping we could ride the horses a while longer."

"Are we heading down that path?" Christine asked.

"Yeah, but…"

"Then follow me." Christine backed the horse up. "Are you ready, Patches?" With a tug of the reins, Patches took off and cleared the fence easily. Pulling the horse to a gentle stop, she turned back toward Dan. "Can you handle it?"

"Damn, she's something," Dan said to no one. He figured Coach could easily clear the fence. "C'mon, buddy, don't make me look like an idiot." In full gallop, Coach charged ahead. As soon as he hit the air, Dan braced himself for the landing, but it was as smooth as landing on a field of pillows.

"Yes, I can handle it," Dan replied as Coach took the familiar position in front. "Follow me," Dan said, relieved that he wasn't picking himself off the ground. "We need to put more distance between us and Gardner."

In seconds they were deep in the woods. The memories of him and Mike exploring the woods as kids came flooding back.

"Do you know where you are going?" Christine asked.

"Sure do. But we'll probably need to dismount and

lead the horses through this. It's going to get thicker," Dan said as tree branches and bushes closed in around them.

They walked along in a single file and in silence. Occasionally a crack of a twig in the distance or a stray shadow startled them, but not once were they in any danger. Even though he could hear Christine and Patches following close behind, Dan constantly looked over his shoulder to make sure they were still there.

"Can I ask you something?" Christine asked seeing Dan looked back at her again. "Why did you come back for me? I mean if you hadn't, then the connection with Angela could never happen. Problem solved."

Dan stopped and turned toward her. He couldn't find the exact words to say. Instead he was caught off guard by not only the question but by her beauty. A beam of moonlight found a path through the trees and landed softly on her face, highlighting her hair and making her eyes sparkle. They were green again. Christine looked at him with a look he'd never seen before on any woman. She wasn't only beautiful, but alluring with a vulnerable quality. Vulnerability was something new for him; he had never experienced that with Angela, ever. She was always in control. *And tried to stay in control even after she died,* he thought. He studied Christine looking for any hint of Angela, but there was none. His insides rolled as one conflict layered onto another. He wanted to hold her, but he barely knew her. And even though he learned the truth about Angela, there was something about her passing only recently that made pursuing Christine feel inappropriate. *She may not even be interested in me that way,* he thought.

He couldn't hold the gaze any longer without replying. "First, the problem wouldn't have been solved. Not at all. What about all the other spirits? They still hadn't crossed over and are only getting stronger and more violent. And I had to come get you and not because it was the right thing to do or because of some high and mighty reason like I always protect my employees. What I mean is that I don't like Gardner. Look at what he's doing to the people of this town and to the town. My town. The town I grew up in. That son of a bitch needs to be stopped. No one gets away with messing with me, my town, or someone that…," Dan said. He couldn't finish the sentence. He knew what he felt but couldn't find the right words to express it. Now he felt vulnerable.

"Someone that…go on," Christine said, moving slightly and catching more of the moonlight in her eyes.

Dan looked at the ground and then back at Christine. "Someone that matters to me. You mean something to me. And no, I don't know exactly what I mean by that. I guess…the way you talk about Charlie and your family. I don't know. Actually, I do. Family matters so much to you and…and for so long the only thing that mattered to me is my restaurants. I'm realizing that's not enough. I need something else in my life."

"Something or someone? I think you need to figure that out first," Christine said and then smiled.

"I'm beginning to. C'mon." Dan smiled back. "We'll be coming out at my house in a few minutes," he said, still not used to the idea that it was his house and not his parents'.

Back on the horses, they easily navigated through

257

woods on a path that had been there for as long as Dan could remember. He looked back again at Christine who had stopped.

"What is it?"

"I don't know. Yes, I do. As soon as we get to your house, it all begins again. All the bullshit."

"It never went away," Dan said, as Christine rode up alongside him.

"I know, but while we are in these woods, it seems like nothing can touch us. It feels safe, you know?"

"Yeah, I do," Dan replied after looking all around him. "Mike could spend hours in here. Me? Every chance I had, I was on the lake. It's the same feeling for me out there. But….I couldn't stay out there forever, and we can't stay in here. You know what, though? Anyone that can kick Angela's ass like you did has nothing to fear. C'mon."

"You're right," Christine replied sitting a little taller in the saddle. "I'll kick it again if I have to."

Dan nodded, shook the reins, and started off. Approaching the edge of the woods, he could see his garage and stopped. Christine came alongside him.

"Here, take Coach's reins. I'm going to walk ahead to make sure there is no one waiting for us."

"And what if there is?"

"Then we'll backtrack and ride the horses into town."

"Why don't we just do that now?"

"We could. But that will take too long. Besides, we know Gardner is certainly going to go to the diner, and he's going to be pissed. If he does come here and sees Coach, he'll go ape shit. And we already know what he's capable of. No doubt the more pissed he is, the crazier he gets. So it's best you hang back. I'll be back in a couple of minutes."

Dan didn't wait for a reply; he took off for the garage.

He hesitated before springing from the safety of the forest. There were no cars, movements, or lights to draw his attention. Everything looked fairly benign. He ran past the garage and up to the house. Again, nothing. Satisfied and not wanting to keep Christine waiting alone too long, he ran back to her, but never made it back to the woods. Instead he found her tying up the horses to a tree on the side of the garage.

"You really didn't expect me to wait for you, did you?" Christine said.

"I guess not," Dan said laughing. "You are something."

"Something or someone?" Christine replied, smiling. "Don't answer yet. So how are we getting into town?"

Dan shook his head, thankful for not having to answer her first question. Before he opened the garage, a cool breeze engulfed them. Christine rubbed her arms. Dan looked around. He didn't see any spirits but sensed that they were around. With one hand on the garage door, he looked around again.

"What are you looking for?"

"They're here."

"Who?"

"Spirits."

"Where? I don't see any."

"You will," Dan said, lifting the garage door.

"Hi, kid. Nice touch taking the horses. It really sent Gardner over the edge. You should see what he did to the barn," Milt said, wiping a wrench clean. "She's all ready and should run great."

Dan looked at Milt, then at the Mustang, and then at three spirits floating about in the garage.

"Who are they?" Dan asked.

"Some old neighbors."

"What are they doing here?"

"C'mon, kid. They don't trust you like I do. Don't let me down. Hey, nicely done there, young lady. You really put a whooping on Angela."

"Thanks," Christine replied. "Where is she now?"

"You have her, right, Milt?" Dan added.

"Yeah, but we can't hold her where we go off to now. You need to open that portal. Have you found it?"

"We think so. What do you mean you can't hold her forever?"

"She's a spirit. She'll break free. Just open the portal, kid. Go!" Milt said, as the other spirits started to fly about the room. The chill increased, cans began to fall off the shelf, and garden tools fell off their hooks.

"Hey, easy does it, guys. I'm doing the best I can," Dan said. "C'mon, Christine, let's get out of here."

"The keys are in it, kid. See you there," Milt said and then disappeared as did the other spirits, but not before causing a few more items to fall off the garage shelf.

Dan turned the key to the Mustang, and it fired right up. Speeding down to the main road was more freeing than the ride on the horses. A small part of him wanted to fly right through town, out to the expressway, and keep going until he found the right place to land in, a place where no one knew him and where the problems of his past could never find him. Seeing Christine in the

The Diner

passenger seat told him that his thoughts were just that, thoughts, and not grounded in any logic and certainly without substance. The fact is, he had never felt more alive and purposeful before. He smiled at Christine as the wind blew her hair all over. She smiled back.

"Are you ready for what may come next?" he asked.

"Don't know how it could be any worse or more frightening than anything that I've already been through. So let's do this."

"I like your style," Dan replied, and hit the gas as they came to the road into town.

It was well past midnight, when they drove slowly past the diner. Dan was relieved to see the dining room empty and the lights dimmed. He pulled into his parking space and hopped out of the car. Christine took her time getting out of the car and stared up at the night sky.

"What is it?"

"Look at the moon. Look at the stars. I don't remember the last time I noticed either of them. My life seems to have raced by. I wonder what else I've missed. It's a beautiful night."

Dan stood still with one hand on the diner's back door and looked up at the sky and then back at Christine. "Yeah, it is." As he said it, he heard the sound of a car engine and then saw the beam of headlights coming down the side street next to the diner.

"Get inside. Carlos and Josh should still be here. They think they've found the portal."

"Why? I want to stay with you."

"Please, Christine. Just do it. Someone's coming."

261

"I'm not sure how taking refuge in the diner is going to protect me. I mean, did you see what Gardner is capable of? Nothing is going to stop him, least of all the walls of this diner," Christine said. "Don't say anything. I'm going inside. Be careful, Scheffy."

Dan was relieved and stood by the back door with his fists clenched. He had never before felt as much strength and resolve. The headlights turned into the diner parking lot. Dan shuffled his feet as anxious energy was getting the better of him. He couldn't see if there were one or six men in the truck. The driver side door opened. Dan wasn't sure if he should attack or stand his ground. Too afraid to move, he stood still.

"Shouldn't you be in there looking for the portal rather than playing doorman? C'mon, Scheffy, we're running out of time. I don't know how long I've stalled them. Come help me with Lloyd," Mike said.

Dan found it impossible to move. The first thing he needed to do was unclench his fists, though he would have loved taking a swing at Mike for scaring the crap out of him.

"How are you holding up, Lloyd? How did you get away from Gardner?"

"While the others were being moved to Gardner's house, I lagged behind. When the barn exploded, I took a chance and went for my car and got the hell out of there. No one stopped me."

"I have the way out of Gardner's blocked, at least for now. You'd love it. More fire. At any rate, that's why he's with me," Mike added. "C'mon, let's go find that portal and get it open. We're going to have a lot of visitors soon…visitors of all kinds. Can you feel it?" Mike said rubbing the chill from his arms as he led

The Diner

Lloyd inside the diner.

A strong cool breeze swirled around Dan, nearly knocking him off balance. He had become used to the feeling and stood there waiting to see which spirits would materialize, when a bolt of frigid energy sent him crashing against the diner door and to the ground.

Chapter 38

The Dumpster slid out to the end of the parking lot as the lids flew open and slammed shut. Trash sprung out of it as if someone was inside tossing it out to make room for more. As quick as the Dumpster reached one end of the parking lot, it raced back across and crashed into the back of the diner sending an awful crunching metal sound into the night.

"What the hell?" Dan yelled as he rubbed the back of his head after it had collided hard off the metal diner door. Finally able to focus, he looked up to see Milt and Bob Radke hovering over him with a handful of other spirits flying about and wreaking havoc. The spirits looked less lifelike than Milt and Bob. They were more like human energy forms with hollow, glowing eyes.

"What the hell, guys?" Dan asked. "I'm on your side."

"Sorry, kid, you just kind of got in their way," Milt said as the spirits seemed to be settling down and were now huddling around him, looking more like a person than a ghost. "They're all a bit charged up after what happened out at Gardner's. I don't have to tell you, but you need to open that portal sooner rather than later."

"We're trying. But why destroy the diner? That doesn't make sense."

"It's where it all started, and it's where it has to end."

The Diner

"Well, I'm working on it, but first things first. That son of a bitch Gardner will be here soon. I don't have time to deal with him and defend the diner from a bunch of renegade spirits."

"No, I guess you don't. Know this, he'll be here quicker than you think. Be careful."

"Fuck him. I've seen what he's capable of, how strong he thinks he is. I can handle it."

"Remember, kid, behind every strong man, there's an even stronger woman."

Another cool blast of air helped Dan clear his head as more spirits began to arrive.

"Why don't you and the others wait in the dining room and let me do what I have to do? I presume there's already a contingent of spirits in the diner, right?"

As soon as Dan said it, Milt nodded, and he and the spirits vanished, presumably into the dining room.

"What the heck were you doing out there?" Mike asked as Dan walked in. Christine rushed to his side. "Look at this place. As soon as we walked in, shit started flying everywhere. The place is trashed. Then it quickly stopped. Luckily none of it hit us."

Josh and Carlos were busy picking up pots, pans, and food items as the spirits continued to make their destructive intentions known. Not surprised to see his kitchen in shambles, Dan's attention was drawn to Lloyd who nervously paced back and forth with his eyes glued to the ground, seemingly uninterested in anything happening in the kitchen.

"Lloyd, what are you doing? Lloyd!" Dan asked as Lloyd ignored him initially.

"Huh? Yeah. Just thinking. Don't worry. I need to

think," Lloyd said, stepping over stainless steel serving trays.

"How about you?" Dan asked Christine. "Gees, they really did a number in here. They're pissed. We don't have much time."

"Yeah. What happened out there?" she asked.

"I was talking to Milt. The spirits went crazy out there too. Nearly killed me. They're all worked up after the display we put on at Gardner's. They're ready to either move on or destroy this town. I think in a way we're responsible for their new intensity. Because we basically burned Gardner's place to the ground, we've fueled their negative, destructive energy."

"What were we supposed to do? Let Gardner have his way? Bullshit," Mike replied.

"No. Hey, what's with Lloyd?"

"He'll be all right. So Josh, where's the portal?" Mike asked.

Josh repeated what he saw in the ceiling and how all of the framed newsprint displayed page thirty-five. When he saw the note on the refrigerator to maintain the thirty-five degree temperature, he knew it had to mean something.

"I still can't believe I missed that," Dan said. "That has to be it. Let's get this refrigerator moved…"

Just as Josh and Mike were about to wrap their arms around the refrigerator, two beams of intense bright light shot through the small twelve-inch-square windows in the swinging kitchen doors and reflected harshly off the polished stainless steel side of the refrigerator. The two men jumped back as if they were dodging a laser beam.

"What's going on out there?" Mike yelled out.

The Diner

Carlos was about to push open the doors when a loud, low-pitched electronic buzzing sound erupted from the dining room. The doors swung open, throwing Carlos against the wall. They continued to swing open and shut, though no one was coming in or out. Before Carlos could get up and approach the doors, he started rubbing his arms and the back of his neck. Within seconds, everyone followed suit as electricity filled the air.

"This is nuts," Carlos said turning to toward the group. "The dining room is humming. What is it? It sounds like that noise you hear around those high tension wires, all the buzzing and crackling."

"They're getting restless," Dan said.

"Who is?" Josh asked.

"The spirits," Mike replied, looking around the kitchen seeing spirits appear out of nowhere and then hover about.

"C'mon. Let's get this portal open," Dan said anxiously, feeling like the room was closing in on him.

"Danny!" Christine cried out. "That bitch Angela is here. I can feel her."

The entire diner shook and went completely black except for a faint yellow glow that seeped through the bottom of the swinging doors that were now closed and perfectly still. The spirits started to fly about madly. Once again, pots and pans began rattling and flying off the shelves and counters. Cabinet doors and drawers opened and closed. Mike and Josh swung their arms wildly trying to protect themselves from the flying kitchen utensils.

Christine's head flew back as she crashed into the refrigerator just as all the pots and pans began rattling

267

and flying off the shelves and counters. She continued to roll on the floor, banging into shelving units causing canned fruits and vegetables to hit the floor. No one could see her, but they could hear her moan as she battled Angela's spirit. Fighting off flying trays, Dan stumbled around looking and feeling for Christine.

"Angela, what's it going to take? I don't want you here," Dan commanded.

Christine continued to fly across the floor. Her arms and legs swung about wildly. With all the heavy, stationary kitchen equipment, Dan feared Christine was going to be severely hurt. A shove in the middle of his back pushed Dan against the refrigerator.

"Sorry, son, I got this. She's a nasty one," Bob Radke said joined by spirits on either side of him. They all had a pure white halo of light surrounding him that illuminated his features. "We have the power to contain her until you get the portal open. Just get it open, and we'll take her with us."

"Now you're gonna help?" Dan shot back reaching for Christine now that he was able to locate her from the light Bob and his friends cast.

"Always intended to. Just needed to make sure you weren't going to quit. Now step away," Bob said as he drifted closer to Christine.

"Where are you taking her? Tell me," Mike blurted out. No one answered. After a bright flash, Bob and the spirits vanished into Christine as she continued to thrash about on the kitchen floor. Dan had a hand on her leg, though it was difficult to maintain his grip as the electricity running through her body traveled through his arm and stung it with the pain of a thousand needles. Her body lifted about a foot off the ground and

The Diner

then fell hard to the floor. Dan caught her head before it hit the hard concrete floor. He knelt by her side. A flash of light flew out Christine, and her body went limp.

"Christine!"

"Who the hell was that?" Christine asked as she grabbed Dan's shoulder to pull herself up. "Some guys grabbed Angela and took off. Damn. How much more do I have to go through? I mean…"

"Damn, I need to know…" Mike started to say, but stopped.

"We're going to end this. Mike, see what you guys can do about moving the refrigerator and getting the portal open," Dan said, with his eyes wide open and shifting back and forth.

Before they could get a grip on the refrigerator, a huge boom echoed throughout the diner shaking it more violently than before. The lights flickered on and off like a strobe light. The faint yellow light in the dining room was gone. It was now as bright as during any lunch hour. The kitchen lights remained dim.

"What's happening?" Christine asked.

"It has to be Gardner. He's not going to let up," Dan replied.

Lloyd stopped pacing and looked toward the dining room. His back straightened, and his shoulders dropped.

"Lloyd, what is it?" Dan asked, sensing an air of calmness and confidence in Lloyd.

"Helen is out there. I'm going to her."

"I'm not sure that's a good idea. You ought to stay back."

"I don't think so, and I wouldn't try to stop me."

Dan realized there was no use arguing with Lloyd. Besides, he didn't have the time.

269

"Then let's go. Don't let anything stop you from getting that portal uncovered," Dan said as the guys wrapped their arms around the refrigerator. "I'm going out to the dining room."

"I'm going with you," Christine said.

"And I don't suppose I'll be able to talk you out of it?"

"Hardly."

Dan approached the kitchen doors cautiously like a gunfighter entering a saloon. After a deep breath and rolling his shoulders back to shake loose as much stress as possible, he stepped through the doors with Christine and Lloyd an arm's length behind him. Dan expected to see Gardner standing proudly and defiantly in the middle of the diner, like a dictator, commanding everyone and anyone within earshot. However, there were no human diner guests to rule at this hour, only spirits.

Standing like a statue, close to the entrance and under the light fixture, was the devil of Circle Lake draped in a long black cloak. His arms were positioned like those of a praying mantis, poised to dart out and destroy any prey within reach. His skin looked like dry, gray leather, and his eyes cycled from sickly yellow to fiery red and back again. His sparse white hair was long and stringy while his fingernails were long, black, and pointy. The veins in his neck, arms, and hands popped out from his pasty skin. Dan was certain it was venom coursing through Gardner's body, not blood.

Dan spotted Dorothy sitting at their usual table with Ansel and another man. She looked at her husband intently, studying him like he was a science project. Her lips moved as if she was whispering, but nothing

The Diner

audible could be heard. The men were shifted about in their seats looking out of place and uncomfortable.

Dan decided to acknowledge the spirits before saying anything to Gardner. It was his way of showing that he wasn't the least bit intimidated by Gardner; even if he was frightened by thoughts of the evil the man was capable of.

Dan recognized a few of the spirits and found it hard to believe that so many of his parent's friends and frequent guests of the diner were dead. Surprisingly absent was Milt and the other spirits that were so active at Lloyd's and Gardner's. Those in the diner all had a soft halo of white light that seemed to glow bright, then fade and become bright again. Dan thought he was seeing their heart beat; that is, if they even had one. Many of them were floating, while others sat or stood, but they were all in constant motion, even when seated. None of them approached within ten feet of Gardner. Dan wasn't sure if that was because Gardner's energy kept them at bay or if they were simply too afraid to be near him. One thing Dan was sure of was that they all had their eyes on the light above Gardner's head.

He's blocking an entrance to the portal.

Lloyd walked past Dan's right. He was about to grab his arm when he saw Helen's spirit sitting a few tables away from the entrance. Dan was expecting them to embrace, instead, they sat and stared at each other.

"What are they doing?" Dan whispered to Christine, who was now at his side.

"They're communicating. What are you going to do?"

"Wing it. We need the guys to get that portal open soon. And I need to get Gardner away from that light.

271

"Mr. Gardner," Dan said in a loud, booming voice. "You are no longer welcome in my diner. Please excuse yourself."

Gardner's head began to swivel from side to side. Dorothy reached up, took his hand, closed her eyes, and began to hum and chant.

What's she doing?

Only a few seconds had passed when Dorothy released his hand. Their eyes met. Dorothy nodded. Gardner turned his head and stared down everyone in the diner with glowing red eyes. Raising his arms, he let out a bone chilling bellow that shook the entire building. Cups and plates behind the counter crashed to the floor. Many of the spirits scattered like cockroaches, terrified but not scared enough to return to their vessels. Dan figured the allure of the portal and passage to the other side must have been too tempting.

Even though he was more scared than he had ever been in his life, Dan stood firm, determined not to let Gardner get the better of him. Christine took a step closer to Dan but kept her hands at her side.

"We can't let him frighten us," Dan whispered to Christine.

"No way. I'm through being afraid."

"I'm going to have to charge you for anything you break," Dan said to Gardner. "Tell you what, though. Leave now, and we'll forget the whole thing."

Gardner released another deep, guttural growl that shook the diner, once again sending the remaining coffee cups, saucers, and silverware crashing off the counter to the floor. He took a step toward Dan, still within reach of Dorothy, but now a pace or two from the entrance.

The Diner

"Perhaps another lesson from Diavolo will teach you some manners, son," Gardner said in a gravelly voice, void of any emotion. "This time I promise you will not forget my power. Since you're determined to take something of value from me, I will take someone of value to you. You have no idea of the lengths I will go to protect my enterprise and my town. If need be, I will destroy this place."

"I don't think so, Mr. Gardner. You need my diner. It's what keeps your enterprise alive or more precisely it did," Dan said as the light above the entrance shone brighter than any other time before. Gardner kept his eyes locked on Dan.

A pleasant harmonic tone resonated from the light and filled the dining room. All the spirits began vibrating and glowing. None of them could keep still. They looked at each other and then back at the light. Some started for the light, and then backed off.

This is perfect. He won't be able to stop them all.

"Everyone, you are now free to cross over," he announced.

Gardner took a few steps toward Dan and raised his hands. The diner went pitch black except for the portal ceiling light. A few of the spirits used that as their chance to make a break for it. Glowing orbs soared and zigzagged about the diner and then disappeared into the light. Realizing his mistake, Gardner lowered his arms and brought the diner lights back on.

"What the hell is going on out here?" Mike asked Dan.

"You tell me," Dan replied. "What did you do?"

"Once we moved the refrigerator we found a shiny, silver metal lid covering a hole in the floor; it easily

273

weighed seventy pounds. Once we lifted it, the whole kitchen started buzzing. A shaft of what I assume is pure energy blasted up. It looked like heat waves coming off a campfire. I assume the portal is open."

"Yeah, that had to be it. It's open. A couple of them crossed over," Dan said, pointing to the remaining spirits and talking only inches from Mike's ear. "We need to keep Gardner from blocking the entrance."

"The portal must be closed at once. Ansel!" Gardner ordered as he backed up toward the light.

Ansel and his sidekick got up and walked toward the kitchen doors.

"Scheffy, I'll take care of Ansel. You just slow up his buddy."

Dan didn't have time to reply, Gardner's men were on them in seconds. Mike dropped to his knees in front of Ansel.

"Please don't hurt us. I beg you. We'll do anything you ask." Mike screamed and pleaded. No one was more surprised than Dan.

The men stopped in their tracks. Ansel raised his fist to bring it down hard on Mike.

Christine screamed.

Dan didn't know what to do.

In the blink of an eye, Mike reached around to his back, pulled out the hunting knife, and plunged it deep into Ansel's thigh. Before Ansel crumbled to the floor, Mike finished him off by thrusting his knee squarely under Ansel's jaw.

Without thinking, Dan kicked the guy in front of him in the crotch. The man bent over. Dan copied Mike's move perfectly and kneed the guy in the jaw. Both men were out cold, limp on the floor.

The Diner

"Well, look at you, Scheffy. Nicely done," Mike said.

The temperature around Dan and Mike fell to near freezing. In seconds, both bodies slid along the floor and through the kitchen doors. With the bodies gone, the temperature returned to normal.

"Thanks, Milt," Dan said under his breath.

Feeling more confident, Dan walked out to the middle of the dining room with Mike and Christine following close behind. He noticed that Lloyd had pulled his eyes away from Helen. He was sitting on the edge of the booth seat, as if he was about to dash out of the diner, but his eyes were glued on Gardner.

Dan stopped near a table of spirits across from Lloyd and Helen. Christine took a step ahead of him, but Dan grabbed her arm and pulled her back by his side. Gardner opened his arms wide despite a firm tug on his arm and disapproving look from Dorothy.

"I need to end this," Gardner whispered to Dorothy.

"The answer is not always found in action," Dorothy said loud enough for the whole diner to hear.

"Grant me the power," Gardner pleaded. "There is no other way."

"There always is another way. Violence is available in measures…but you never learned that. So be it." Dorothy closed her eyes and began to chant.

He's asked her for permission…like she's fueling him somehow. Behind every strong man, there's an even stronger woman, Dan thought. "Milt was right," he said to no one.

"I've provided every chance for you to have the life everyone dreams of, to be with the love of your life forever. Perhaps you are incapable of such a love. Let the consequences of your actions be a burden you carry for eternity," Gardner growled out.

The diner began to shake and shudder as the lights sputtered off and on. Thunder boomed from every corner. It felt like the energy had been drained from the room, but the pressure increased. Dan's head pounded. The diner was no longer a happy, welcoming family restaurant but a place of sadness and despair. It crushed his soul knowing all that everything his parents put into it could be destroyed by Gardner. The spirits could feel it too as they all began to float and cling to the ceiling around the perimeter of the diner and as far away from Gardner as possible.

Gardner began to vibrate. His red, cavernous eyes were now three times their normal size and were locked on Christine. His whole body seemed to grow taller and wider. With bulging, rippling muscles that were nonexistent in his human form, he brought his hands together in prayer formation. Slowly he separated them as a glowing orange ball of energy materialized and grew. It resembled a small sun, complete with solar flares streaming from it.

"Death can never be avoided, but at times it arrives sooner than expected. Had you simply obeyed," Gardner growled, his words reverberated through the diner and into town. "Now death must make a visit, and it is at your hands, my son. Diavolo sees no other way."

Dan's heart was beating through his chest. The mad eyes of Diavolo stayed fixed on Christine, and that scared Dan more than his own death. He stepped out in front of Christine as he caught Lloyd rising slowly from the booth. He was looking at Helen's spirit who was

The Diner

inching her way toward the portal. Dan looked hard and didn't see any fear in Lloyd's eyes. What he saw was determination and resolve. Behind Gardner, Dorothy was chanting and swaying.

Behind every strong man…she has to be stopped.

"From this moment forward, you will obey the word of Diavolo," Gardner shouted, as he released the scorching ball of energy toward Christine.

"No," Dan shouted as Christine screamed.

Lloyd was in perfect position. Lloyd took one step and leaped in front of the fiery orb and caught it. It was absorbed inside of him immediately as his body collapsed on the floor. His body shook violently for a couple of seconds and smoldered on the floor and then went limp and lifeless.

"You son of a bitch!" Mike yelled as he raced to Lloyd's side. Christine was right behind him.

"It's time to end this," Dan said as he was already moving with his fists tightly clenched.

Gardner bellowed in anger and disbelief. The spirits started darting about, and then one by one they made a break for the portal. Gardner looked over at Dorothy, who was just beginning to come out her trance. Gardner quickly put his hands back together determined to unleash more punishment.

Dan saw no other way to stop him. Gardner and Dorothy were both Diavolo; he was sure of it.

There's no place for the devil in my diner.

Dan leaped around the tables and chairs. Never giving Gardner a glance, he flew by him and crashed into Dorothy sending her body into the corner of the wall. Her head hit the concrete with a massive thud. The sound of crunching bones was deafening.

277

Dorothy's eyes opened wide and stared deeply into Dan's as he lay on top of her. He froze in place not knowing if she was going to come to life with the strength of a hundred men and inflict an even harsher pain or just pass away. Instead a vengeful smile appeared on her face followed by a laugh. Dan would never forget the look or the sound. She closed her eyes as she exhaled her last breath.

Dan leaped off her and looked over at Gardner who let out an echoing, high pitched "No!" He took a step in Dan's direction and then collapsed to his knees. He no longer looked like Diavolo; he barely looked like the intimidating Ernest Gardner that conjured fear in everyone with his mere presence. He looked like a feeble old man.

The air around Dan grew colder as the spirits began to surround him. The appreciation on their faces was obvious.

"You're welcome. Now finish this and go," Dan said, still shaking.

Dan looked over at Lloyd lying on the floor. Helen was floating above him extending her hand. Christine and Mike stood and backed away. A white, smoky halo formed around Lloyd's body and then rose. Lloyd's spirit appeared with his hand in his wife's hand. They floated over to Dan and stared at him.

"Thank you, Lloyd," Dan said. "I'll tell your kids. I'm sure they'll be fine."

Lloyd nodded.

"Go. Cross over," Dan said.

Helen and Lloyd didn't move. Christine walked over to join Dan.

"Go!" Dan shouted, anxious to witness what he had

worked so hard to make happen.

"They want you to know that your parents are proud of you," Christine said.

"How do you know?" Dan asked.

"I just do."

Helen and Lloyd nodded and floated up to the portal and disappeared. The chill didn't leave the air.

"Hey kid, we're gonna clean up now," Milt said, surrounded by other the spirits. Just then a huge white orb, bigger than all the others, buzzed past and into the portal. "Angela will no longer be a problem."

"I never thought I'd be thrilled to see you all," Dan said, as Milt's spirit friends surrounded Gardner. They closed in so tightly around him that he was no longer visible. In seconds, the pod of spirits began buzzing while small white spirit orbs floated around them. They flew into the spirit ball around Gardner transforming it into one glowing orb. The floor around them began to vibrate. Dining tables and chairs began to shudder on the floor from the vibration. The sphere of spirits began to glow brighter and slowly rise. Spirits that were lining up for the portal pulled away to allow for the transport. As they approached the portal, the hum became deafening. Then a loud pop, followed by a brilliant flash occurred.

The sphere was gone.

Dan looked over at Milt.

"We couldn't do anything before, not while Dorothy was around," Milt said. "Her powers were too much for us."

"Where is she?" Dan said, looking back over at where Dorothy's body should have been.

"We don't know."

"But she was dead. I…I killed her."

"Sorry, kid, but you didn't. She's all spirit with the power to take a physical form. She didn't occupy a vessel. To kill her would require stopping her heart…a heart that's hard, calloused, and filled with hate. They say to kill her it takes a blade as old as her and delivered with as much hate. I don't know, kid," Milt said.

Dan stood in shock. He looked over at the booth and took a half step toward the seat when he heard a young woman's sinister laugh. He turned toward Christine, wondering if she had heard it, but she was busy talking with Mike and Milt. Josh and Carlos were talking about what they had just witnessed. No one seemed the least bit distracted by the sound of a cackling woman. He chalked it up to his imagination. Perhaps Dorothy's dying laugh was simply echoing in his head.

"What about all the vessels that are now without their spirits?" Christine asked.

"There's a good chance they may not remember much of their previous life. No one knows for sure, since it's never happened before. I guess a lot people are going to be surprised when they wake up. I know Mae will be," Milt said with a chuckle. "By the way, kid, not all the spirits are moving on. Many are staying with their vessels, so you need to keep the coffee going for them and of course keep the portal open."

"But Gardner supplied it, now with him gone…"

"Relax, Scheffy. I know where there's a warehouse full of it. I'll take care of it," Mike said. "Milt, tell me. What's it like on the other side? What's there?

Milt smiled and shook his head. "Thanks, kid. You

did good work. I'll tell Buck and Addy all about it. Take care of her too," Milt said pointing a Christine. "See ya, kid."

Milt floated up to toward the portal as a white halo engulfed him and compressed into a white translucent orb. As only Milt would do, he took a couple laps around the diner bringing smiles to everyone's face and then disappeared into the portal.

Chapter 39

"Do you want anything?" Dan asked, walking into the kitchen of his house. "I know it's late, but I'm still wired."

They finally left the diner around 1:30 a.m. Dan urged Christine and Carlos to take the day off, insisting that he would open the diner. Carlos wasn't having any of it; he'd be there to open at 5:30 a.m. as usual. He agreed to let Dan close, however. Dan then offered to take Christine home, but she didn't want to wake her family. They weren't expecting her home anyway.

"I'll grab a clean uniform from here and stay at your house and come in with you in the morning," she said matter-of-factly. After all they had been through, he knew there was no point in arguing with her.

"I could sure use a beer," Christine said, plopping herself down in the corner of the couch and kicking her shoes off. "With your head in the fridge, I thought for sure you were searching for another portal."

"That's funny," Dan said walking over with two bottles of beer. "I was going to say 'make yourself at home,' but I see you're well on your way. Nothing fancy here, so don't expect a glass."

"Don't need it," she said taking a long swallow. "That's just what the doctor ordered."

Dan sat in the opposite corner of the couch, letting out a heavy sigh as he sank into the cushions. They looked at each other and smiled and then stared straight ahead. He wasn't sure where to take the conversation after the ride home. As soon as they pulled away from the diner, he tried to apologize for all that Christine was put through. Christine wouldn't have any of it.

"This was all Gardner's doing," she insisted.

Dan knew she was right. Still he couldn't help feeling guilty.

"What could you have done differently?" Christine asked.

"Nothing really. It all happened so fast."

The last few miles home went by shrouded in silence. Their stares seemed to stretch well beyond the length of the road. When they pulled in front of the garage, they both let out a sigh.

"So what are we going to do with the horses?" Christine asked.

"Actually, I think we'll keep them. I'll make a couple calls tomorrow and have them boarded. What do you think?"

"I love the idea," Christine said looking up at the cloudy, but clearing sky. "They should be all right tonight. Won't you, Patches?" she said, patting him on the nose and then walking up to the house.

Christine nestled deeper into the couch, trying to get comfortable. Every time she moved even the slightest amount, it caught Dan's attention.

"What is it?" Dan asked.

"I was thinking how Gardner's operation lasted so long undetected."

"It wasn't totally undetected. I mean, I bet everyone in town knew about it. You hear about it all the time how small towns like this have their dark secrets. We just experienced Circle Lake's," Dan said, never thinking spirits taking over another's body would happen in his town. "It's crazy."

"What happens to the town now?" Christine asked, pulling her legs up underneath her and cradling the beer in both hands.

"I'm not sure. I guess we'll find out tomorrow. The next few months will really be the test. If the town can survive with Gardner, imagine what it can do without him."

"But was his operation the thing that kept this town together? I mean, sometimes people find strength and purpose in protecting a secret."

"I never thought of it that way. You might be right."

He took another swig of beer and laid his head back on the cushion of the couch and stared up at the ceiling, while Christine stared down at the floor. They stayed in that position for a few minutes, until Christine finally broke the silence. "Well, I've had it. I'm going to take a shower and go to bed."

"I'm going to do the same," Dan replied, fighting back a yawn. "I think the guest room has everything you need."

"Does it?" Christine said flashing a warm smile. She got up and walked straight to the guest room which was down the hall from the family room and directly across from the master bedroom.

"Goodnight," Dan said wondering if it had sounded as corny to Christine as it did to him. She didn't reply except for what he thought was a slight giggle. "Yeah, that sounded stupid," he said to himself.

He dragged himself off the couch and went into the

kitchen for another beer. Looking around the house and then out to the lake, he was more than relieved to finally experience a feeling of peace.

It's been a long time since this place felt like home.

He paused outside the guest room when he heard the shower. He laughed, a little surprised that after everything they'd been through that day, there he was standing in the hallway having intimate thoughts about Christine in the shower. He shook his head clear and realized that he had made for the master bedroom rather than his boyhood room upstairs. The new furnishings helped, though he'd eventually have those replaced to erase any lingering memories of Gardner and Angela. However for tonight it would be fine. He was too tired to think much about it anyway.

Nearly finishing the beer in one swallow, he took a couple heavy steps into the master bath to wash away as much of his past as possible with a hot shower. With one hand against the tiled wall to steady him from weight of exhaustion that was beginning to take its toll, he let the water cascade over him. He had no idea how long he was in the shower, but when he slid the shower doors open and stepped out; the bathroom was filled with steam. He flipped on the exhaust fan and wiped a clear patch on the mirror to shave and then decided he was even too tired to lift the razor.

As the fog cleared, he found a pair of running shorts to put on. He didn't expect Christine to still to be in the shower, but he turned off the exhaust fan so that he could hear if the water was still running. It wasn't. He walked out to the bedroom and found her in his bed wearing one his "Scheff's Restaurant" T-shirts and lying on her side facing away from him.

"Well, hello," Dan said, walking over what to he thought must be his side of the bed.

"No. It's good night," she said turning over and smiling. "You really didn't think that after all the crap we—I've—been through, I was going to sleep alone, do you?"

"Are you sure it's not this soon-to-be-in-shape swimmer's body that brought you here," he said, surprising himself at his own joke.

"Maybe some other time. Good night, Scheffy," Christine said and rolled back over on her side.

"Good night, Christine. You were amazing, by the way," Dan said turning off the light and then staring up at the ceiling.

"I was. You were too. Now go to sleep."

"Yes, dear."

As Dan's eyes adjusted to the darkness, he could see that the moon had won the war over the clouds and was now casting silver shadows across the bedroom. He looked over at Christine, who was lying perfect still. The shadowy silhouette of her body against the light coming in through the window was more than he could take. He wanted to put his hand on her and feel the warmth of her body but the words, "Now go to sleep," wouldn't fade from his mind. As exhausted as he was, there was an energy building inside him. It wasn't the shower. It was Christine lying next to him and the sound of her peaceful breathing, the smell of her skin, and the idea of her lying under the same blanket as him. He quietly turned over onto his back and counted the times the ceiling fan blades made one full rotation, thinking it would help him get to sleep. It didn't. After a couple deep sighs, he rolled onto his side, closed his eyes, and listened to Christine breathe. It was like listening to the soft sound of a lazy ocean's waves lapping the shore. Despite his desire to watch Christine sleep all night, Dan drifted off to sleep.

****

Dan began to stir as the birdsong blended well with the sound of the waves brushing against the seawall. He thought about his parents and how much they must have loved this place. He sure had loved growing up here. He couldn't think of a more peaceful sound to wake up to until he remembered listening to Christine sleep. Lying on his side facing Christine, he wrestled his eyelids open hoping to watch her wake up.

"Well, good morning, sleepyhead," Christine said, with her face only a few inches from Dan's.

"Hi. How long have you been awake?"

"Maybe ten minutes or so. It's so peaceful here. Charlie would…" Christine hesitated.

"Charlie would what?"

"Nothing. I need some coffee," Christine replied, rolling onto her back.

Dan pushed himself up on his elbows and looked down at her. "Charlie would love it here. That's what you were going to say, wasn't it?"

"Yeah. But I didn't want…you know. I didn't want make it sound like I was looking for something…something more from you."

Dan smiled. "I see. Do you want something more?"

"Do you?"

"Is that game we're going to play now?" he replied, unable to stop smiling.

"What are you smiling at?" Christine asked.

"You. You look amazing. And…and, yeah I think I

do want something more. Wait, before you say it. Let me be clear. I want someone."

They both smiled.

"Hmmm," Christine said under her breath.

"What?"

"Looks like we may want the same thing then."

"Well," Dan said, looking Christine up and down. "I can tell you one thing for sure. I'm going to definitely want my shirt back."

"You can have it now."

Christine crossed her arms, grabbed the bottom of the t-shirt and pulled it over her head and tossed it at Dan. The shirt draped over his face. Rather than rip the shirt away from his face, he delighted in the aroma of Christine in the shirt. After another deep inhalation, he tossed the shirt aside and was immediately held captive by the sight of Christine lying half naked in his bed. He couldn't move. They stared into each other's eyes. Christine's arms came up around his neck. The warmth of her touch set his body on fire. His chest slowly lowered on top of hers, their skin slowly fusing together inch by inch. Christine moaned in pleasure when Dan's chest covered her breasts. They kissed lightly at first, each expecting the other's doubts and fears to take over when the passion and desire that each had kept dormant in their lives came rushing to the surface.

Near exhaustion and with their arms and legs entwined like lace, they lay together trying to catch their breath.

"Damn, that was…" Dan started to say.

"Yeah, wasn't it? Damn," Christine interrupted.

After a couple minutes, they slowly started untangling themselves, but always managing to pause

The Diner

and hold the other, uncertain what the rest of their life was going to be like.

"You know," Dan said, staring into Christine's eyes. "I think you're right."

"About what?"

"Charlie has to see this place. We should get his opinion. What do you think?"

A few small tears quickly formed in her eyes and rolled down her cheek. She didn't say a word. Instead she wrapped her arms tightly around Dan's neck and pulled him so close he could barely breathe. He wanted to close his eyes and absorb every second with her, but his eyes darted about the room as soon as he heard a woman's laugh. It only lasted a second or two. It didn't come from outside but from inside the bedroom. No one was there, and he saw no spirit. And with Christine holding and continuing to stroke his back, he knew she didn't hear it. Dan would have blamed his imagination for what he heard except that it was the same laugh he heard last night. It made him shiver.

"Oh you poor thing, you're chilled," Christine said feeling the goose bumps on his arms. "Come here and let me warm you."

Chapter 40

Sitting at the kitchen table, they smiled at each other as much as they talked, behaving as though they had done this hundreds of times before. Conversation was made easy as Dan listed all the things Charlie could enjoy around the lake. Christine occasionally corrected him saying it was "something we could all enjoy." Dan didn't argue the point. As their coffee cups emptied for the second time, they reluctantly agreed it was time to get ready and head to the diner.

Dan slowed as he entered Circle Lake. Part of him was expecting to see people walking about with carefree smiles on their face, laughing and joking with each other as they celebrated their independence from Gardner's reign.

"Looks the same, doesn't it?" Dan said, clearly disappointed.

"Yeah, but it feels different. It feels lighter, less depressing. Maybe that's what the beginning of change feels like," Christine replied, waving her arm in the air outside the passenger side window.

"I hope you're right. The town has a fresh start. I hope it takes advantage of it."

"Maybe you should see that it does. That's something you can do."

Dan nodded in agreement. As he drove by the front of the diner, they both peered through the windows. He wasn't going to be surprised had it been empty. Then again, where else would they go for breakfast? It still was the only game in town. There were quite a few people inside even though it was approaching 11:00 a.m., past the breakfast rush and still too early for the lunch crowd. Dan shook his head in disbelief as he pulled into his parking space.

"No matter what happens in this town, they still show up. Amazing," he said.

"They need this place. Are you ready?" Christine asked.

"As I'm ever going to be," Dan replied taking Christine's hand and squeezing it lightly. "Let's go."

They walked in to see the kitchen looking like nothing had happened the night before and operating as usual. James was busy taking instruction from Ray, and the waitresses were busy preparing for the lunch crowd, though Rosie and Molly stopped for a moment to watch Christine as she walked so close to Dan.

Molly smiled and leaned closer to Rosie and whispered something. Rosie nodded in agreement.

"Good morning, Molly. Rosie. What's up?" Dan asked, playfully.

"So cute," Rosie replied, smiled and when back to work and continued to giggle like a schoolgirl with Molly.

"How's it going, Ray? How was this morning?" Dan asked, with an ear to ear smile. He and Christine stood perfectly still waiting for Ray to reply.

"Just like every other morning," Ray said, unemotionally, never looking up from the onions he was chopping.

"Well, that's good," Dan said more to Christine

than to Ray. "Can you believe how quickly normal returned. It's crazy. I'm going to go see how Carlos is doing. How are you?"

"Never been better," Christine said, flashing a reassuring smile that melted Dan. He wanted to pull her close and kiss her, but he was too self-conscious in front of his employees and was already in his "restaurant owner" character. He thought about the comment that Angela made that it was all about the food to him. Looking at Christine now, food was the furthest thing from his mind.

Christine walked over to join the other waitresses. Her eyes flashed wide open, followed by a huge grin when the ladies each put their arm around her and hugged her.

Dan smiled again and then walked into the dining room, nearly knocking Mike to the floor with the swinging door. Mike had had his back to the door holding a box.

"Couldn't stay away, huh?" Dan asked him. "What's in the box?"

"Sandwiches and drinks for the crew out at Gardner's. I have a couple of my employees and few guys from town out there doing their best to clean up the mess and doing what we can to bring some sense of order to the chaos. There's nothing left but the old man's house. Still creepy though. It's behind us, Scheff. All good. I'll catch up with you later. Are you going to be all right?"

Dan nodded and watched Mike all the way as he walked out the front entrance realizing how much he missed having a best friend back in his life. He knew Mike didn't want anything from him. All he wanted to do was help, "because that's what friends do," Mike would always say.

"So Carlos, how was it this morning?" Dan asked joining Carlos behind the cash register.

Dan scanned the dining room. Twelve of the twenty-four tables were occupied. Everyone looked familiar, though he still struggled with most of their names. Rob and Barbara Sanders were seated at the back corner booth against the front window. They waved and smiled at Dan. Dan couldn't recall the last time he saw anyone smile in the diner. He waved back.

"It's a little slower, but not by much. I mean I've only been here a few days, so maybe it's normal. And…" Carlos hesitated.

"What is it?"

"I know it's only been a few hours into the breakfast rush, but no one has sat at table one…you know, Gardner's booth. I've tried to seat few there, but no one would have any of it."

"Maybe they're still a little edgy. I wouldn't worry about it," Dan said, though he couldn't peel his eyes away from the booth nearest the entrance.

"Yeah, you're probably right. You know what's different though? The diner is noisier today. There's more conversation. People are talking."

"Hmm. You mean it is more alive," Dan replied.

"That's it. I have to admit it, I eavesdropped a little, and it seems like a few of the couples were on their first date. They were asking questions about the other's life. I guess it's not that strange given that some of them just 'woke up.' Still there were some who behaved like before, you know, long periods of silence."

"I could only imagine what you heard. Think about it. With the spirit gone, they're left with someone they barely know. And like Milt said, the vessel probably doesn't even remember who they were before."

"And by the way, the light by the entrance still flashes, just not as often, so that's good. So what do we do now?"

"I'm not sure we do anything other than what we always do, we run a restaurant. We'll figure it out over time. And now we have time."

"The Sanderses keep looking over here," Carlos said.

"I know. I should go talk with them."

"How about an iced coffee before you go?" Carlos said, smiling.

"Ha. I like your thinking."

Dan walked over to the Sanderses acknowledging the other guests with a "Hello" and "Have a nice day." Barbara slid over on the bench seat to make room for him. Dan reluctantly sat down. He didn't like having his back toward the entrance. He'd rather be able to look out over the diner.

"I guess you'll be putting that on the menu," Rob said seeing the iced coffee.

"This and few other items. How are you?"

"You did it," Barbara said before Rob could respond. "You opened the portal. More importantly, you saved the town."

"How did you know?" Dan asked.

"The whole town knows. Circle Lake isn't that big. New travels fast," Rob replied.

"So what exactly did you hear?"

"Everyone's saying that you and your friends

The Diner

destroyed Gardner's place. And somehow you stood up to him after you opened the portal. Don't worry, dear, some of the townspeople are already out at Gardner's cleaning up. No one is talking. How did you do manage to overpower him?" Barbara asked.

"We eliminated his source of power," Dan replied.

"What was that?"

"You don't know?" Dan asked, looking inquisitively as his eyes darted back and forth between Rob and Barbara. "It was Dorothy. She was his power. Let's just leave it at that," Dan added, still feeling weird that he may have killed her despite what Milt had said. "How is everybody doing? You know, those with vessels whose spirit has left."

"Not entirely sure," Rob added. "Some are here as you can see. I guess the vessel has nowhere else to go, so they're trying to work things out. Others? Who knows. I'm hoping the town will really come alive now."

Dan smiled at the unintended double entendre.

"What are you going to do?" Barbara asked.

"I'm going to stick around. I like being back home. Besides I have a few plans for the diner. New furniture, fresh paint, new menus…while keeping what my mom and dad built preserved. I'm also going to reach out to some people I know and see if we can bring more business to the town. We could sure use it. And like you said, it should help bring this town to life. What do you think?"

Rob didn't answer. He was looking past Dan toward the front. Barbara and Dan both turned around.

"She's just standing there," Barbara said, seeing Christine stare down at one of the benches of table one.

"Is she okay?"

"I'm sure she's fine," Dan said, doing his best to hide his concern. "I'll go check on her."

As he walked over, Dan didn't see anything in the booth, still Christine didn't move. She stood tilting her head to one side and leaning closer to the booth.

"Christine. What's up?" Dan asked to no reply. "Christine."

"I'm sorry. I'm fine. Don't worry. I don't hear it anymore," she said.

"Hear what?"

"I swear I heard a woman's voice talking over here. I mean, I'm certain I did."

"What did she say?"

"I'm not quite sure. I couldn't make it all out. But I swear I heard, 'It's not over, dear.' And then there was this woman's laugh. A creepy laugh."

"Damn," Dan said under his breath as he looked around the diner for a spirit. Everything looked normal.

Chapter 41

Six months later—Springtime in Circle Lake

"I can't believe how much progress they've made. It's interesting to see how much of the original architecture they kept. I love that the huge front windows are still there. Look at those massive copper vats. What is your friend calling it again?" Christine asked Dan as they drove slowly past the old Illinois Savings Bank building on their way to the diner.

"The Brewery Bank. It's what Ronny Paulson does; he names his restaurants after what it used to be or after the town it's in. We serve one of his beers at Scheff's downtown, Lyon's Lion Lager. It's from the first place he opened in Lyons, Illinois. I understand he's keeping the bank vault, complete with the heavy metal door and combination lock and using it as private tasting and dining room. I think this is his sixth microbrewery in the state. Knowing him like I do, he'll create some new beer recipe for the place. Probably call it something like Circle Lake Lager."

"The location is perfect, right on the lake. I hope he succeeds. The town can use it. Look at what the town has now. Besides the brewery, there's a bakery and a pizza place. This is great. Soon Mike will be opening one of his gyms too. I wonder how that will go over. I hope there will be more."

297

"There should be. Slowly but surely, the town is heading in the right direction. It turns out businesses were always interested, but with Gardner running the city council none of them stood a chance of getting a license."

Dan and Christine drove through the town proud of the changes they helped instigate. At first some people were hesitant, saying, "We've lived this way for so long, why change now?"

"Because it can be so much better for you and your family," Dan replied. It was Christine's passionate plea for change and to create a town "that you can show your kids and grand kids…a town you wanted to go to, not get away from." Dan and Christine never gave up, and the campaign brought them even closer together.

Their relationship blossomed quickly. She and Charlie moved into Dan's house shortly after the New Year. Christine didn't want to take Charlie away from her parents during the holidays. Still once a month, her parents took Charlie for the weekend or stayed at Dan's place which suited everyone just fine.

Dan's Scheff's Restaurants were in good hands as well. Once a month, he visited each location for a few days, while Christine stayed behind and managed the diner after Carlos' shift. Christine was a sponge learning all she could about the restaurant business and business in general. The staff preferred when Christine managed the diner; it left them with more tables and tips.

Carlos decided to stay on at the diner. He was fond of the slower and simpler pace. It allowed him to pursue one of his dreams of owning his own building and redesigning it into loft apartments. He bought an old building that last housed a few medical offices and an insurance agency. Being across from the old savings bank, the building had a perfect view of the lake. His goal was to have the rest of the units rented by the summer, and with the brewery going, he had a good chance of that. Now living within walking distance of the diner, it was easy for Carlos to open and sometimes close the diner in the same day. The diner began to get busier once it had been updated and renovated, so he was often needed at all hours which suited him just fine. He loved the place.

Diner renovations were the first project Dan put into motion. He had a few new appliances installed in the kitchen to replace those that simply couldn't be relied on. Next, the kitchen got a new coat of paint as did the entire diner. Gone was the white that had yellowed and tarnished with age. Now the diner was full of bright sunny colors. No matter how gloomy and gray it was outside, the diner always looked cheerful inside. He upgraded the floor, the ceiling tiles, tables, and chairs and updated the menu with a couple of healthy alternatives. The diner looked fresh, but it was still the same, especially at the counter. Dan kept all those colors the same, but with updated fixtures and seats that resembled the original ones. It was his commitment to the nostalgia and history of the diner. Some of the regulars would wait for a place at the counter even when there were tables and booths open.

Then there was the entrance. The three-foot-by-five-foot space remained completely unchanged from floor to ceiling, including the walls and especially the light fixture above the entrance. He didn't want to confuse any of the spirits that remained behind. He felt it necessary to preserve the portal gateway. Occasionally a spirit would cross over, leaving their spouse faced with a vessel looking like they had awoken from a decade-long nap. The intense energy burst and white light over the entrance was the signal for all diner guests to look around for the one person that looked lost. The vessel was never difficult to spot. Dan and the others were amazed how the town reacted to help assimilate the vessel back into the world. Still other spirits were content to stay behind with their spouse. No one knew exactly how many spirits had remained, but it was enough to keep the entrance flashing multiple times during the day.

As had been the habit every time Dan drove to the diner, he slowed as he passed to peer in and see if anyone was sitting at table one. No one who knew the history of the diner ever sat at that table. More often than not it was vacant, except when a new customer came in for a meal. Dan suggested that Christine and Carlos make it a point to check more frequently on the new guests particularly those at table one. Occasionally Carlos or Christine would tell Dan that they would catch the guest's head swiveling around and looking confused. They'd always return to their meal with a shoulder shrug. When asked, the guests would report that they had heard laughter coming from around them but never knew where or who it was coming from. Then about three months ago, the reports and the laughter stopped.

For weeks following, Christine and Dan would eat a meal or two at table one, but nothing ever happened. Christine and Carlos were convinced that the town was getting back to normal. Dan didn't believe it, though he

The Diner

never told them otherwise. He needed more proof, though he was relieved to see things had calmed down.

As Dan and Christine turned the corner on their way to the back parking lot, they were pleased to see Mike's truck parked on the street. They hadn't seen him in a few weeks. Mike had been busy at another one of his KickFits gym openings downstate, though he was happier to hang out at the diner and work on the equipment. He had become the default maintenance guy. Mike would only be too happy to tell Dan and Christine that he wasn't there to see them; he was there to see Charlie, who now called him "Uncle Mike."

Dan and Christine walked in through the back diner door, now comfortable in their couple routine. Mike was working on one the old deep fryers. Ray had mentioned that it wasn't maintaining the right temperature.

"Hey, kids," Mike said. "Where's my Chuckster?"

"My parents are dropping him off here soon. He and his grandpa went fishing this morning," Christine replied as she checked the kitchen and then went to talk with Carlos to see how things were going in the dining room.

"What's up with the fryer?" Dan asked.

"It's the thermostat. I can try to retrofit a new one on, but I think it's time for a whole new unit. I'll pick one up tomorrow. This one will make it through the day," Mike said, shutting the doors on the fryer.

"Are you sure? We can just have one delivered," Dan commented.

"I'd prefer that Mike picked it up, Scheff," Ray added. "That way we'll know we'll have it. It's my day off tomorrow and James will be flying solo, so…"

"Yeah, keep your nose out of it," Mike added with a big grin. "Go do what you do, whatever that is."

Dan laughed as he sat down at his father's desk, which looked the same as it did the day he found refuge at it during his parents' memorial service. Mike plopped down in the chair on the other side of the desk.

"So Carlos tells me it's been pretty quiet around here," Mike said referring to the laughter at table one. "What do you think?"

"Maybe we've finally turned a corner. I mean, the diner has never been busier. We have new folks coming in all the time now and with their kids. And with all the construction going on in town, workers stop by for lunch, along with visitors who are just passing through. Though I don't know, something still doesn't feel right. I can't put my finger on it," Dan said leaning back in the swivel chair as it squeaked.

"I have to fix that. It's annoying," Mike said. "And I'm with ya. I tell you, though, not a day goes by that I don't wonder what's on the other side. Don't you? What is the afterlife like? Is it heaven? You know?"

"No, I don't. I don't think about it at all. I figure sometime, and I hope it's a long time off, I'll find out."

The two of them nodded at each other and sat a few moments in silence.

"You know, I'm not ready to declare victory yet," Mike said. "You heard that there have been crews out at Gardner's place, right? Apparently, they installed an iron fence around the whole property. All sorts of construction traffic has been seen going in and out of the place. You must have seen the lights coming from his place at night. I mean, something's going on, but I can't tell what it is from the lake. And there's no way

I'm stepping back on his land."

"Yeah, I saw it. No one in town knows what's going on either, or at least they're not saying. No one seems bothered by it though. They seem to like the idea of Gardner's property being fenced in. Keep checking though, will you?"

Mike nodded. "I guess we just keep on keeping on. All good with Christine? How's my Chuckster doing? Any dates set yet?"

"What is this? Twenty questions? It's all good. Real good. Charlie loves the lake. He really likes it when his grandpa is with him. It's so damn cute to see the two of them together. And before you get jealous, he's anxious to see you. He asks about you all the time. Christine and I are good. We're adjusting well and that's just it; it's been an adjustment living together. We talk about marriage, but neither of us wants to screw up a good thing. We'll see."

"And you and Charlie, how's that going?"

"You know, it was rough at first. Christine was right, I was trying too hard. It's getting easier, except when I travel to one of the restaurants. When I'm gone more than a few days, we occasionally take a few steps backward. We'll get through it though."

"So what are you two talking about?" Christine said, walking over and sitting on the edge of the desk.

"I'm trying to convince Scheffy here to make an honest woman out of you. I'm in the mood for a wedding."

"I have to be married to be honest? What am I now?" Christine playfully snapped back.

Dan listened to them banter back and forth, feeling more contented than he had in a long time.

Maybe things really are getting back to normal.

They all chatted a while longer discussing other improvements they could make to the diner and what else they could do to attract more customers and businesses to town. They were interrupted when Christine's dad walked in through the kitchen doors.

"Hi, Daddy. Where's Mom and Charlie?" Christine asked as Mike got up to shake the man's hand.

"Charlie's sitting out there telling Carlos about the fish he caught. Your mother is waiting for me in the car. She wants me to take her to an Art Fair over in McHenry, so we'll be heading out."

"Want anything before you leave? Sandwich, cup of coffee?" Dan asked.

"Rosie is fixing me a coffee even though I don't want it."

"She's sweet on old Mr. Connor," Mike chided.

"Call me 'old Mr. Connor' again, and I'll knock you on your ass. My name's Al," Christine's dad said half joking.

"I haven't thrown hands in awhile. C'mon. Let's have this out once and for all," Mike shot back playfully.

"Quit picking on my daddy," Christine said. "Go out and see your Chuckster."

"I'll see you kids later. Can I go out that door? I'm parked back there," Al asked, pointing toward the back of the kitchen.

"Of course. See you later in the week," Dan replied, getting up to walk him out.

After a few minutes of conversation with the Connors, Dan walked in to see Christine looking out into the dining room through the window of the

The Diner

swinging kitchen door.

"Who are you spying on?" Dan asked.

"Mike and Charlie. They're really engaged in a deep conversation. I wonder what they're talking about."

"Why don't you go out there and find out?"

"I'm dying to, but this is good for the both of them. I'll find out later."

Seconds after she said that, Mike got up and walked over to Carlos and whispered something in his ear. Carlos's shoulders drooped, and his chin fell into his chest. After a pat on his arm from Mike, he looked over at Charlie and then nodded. He stared at Charlie for a few more seconds and then went back behind the cash register, all the time keeping his eyes on Charlie.

Christine backed away from the door as Mike walked in.

"What is it?" Christine asked seeing the worried look on Mike's face. Dan walked up beside her.

"Charlie's talking to a ghost. His words. He says they'll be here soon."

Chapter 42

"Who will be here soon? Who's he talking to?" Christine asked but didn't wait for Mike to answer. She dashed out into the dining room. Dan was right behind her. They approached Charlie slowly, not wanting to startle him and have him quickly think that something was wrong. He was sitting innocently at table one wearing the Cubs hat that Dan had bought for him, tilted to one side. His blonde hair was sticking out on all sides. His big blue eyes and little turned up nose always managed to coax an "Aww, he's so cute," from nearly every adult he came in contact with. Sitting with his legs tucked under him and pushing a toy pickup truck across the table, he looked like a typical four-year-old without a care in the world.

"Hey, Charlie, how was your morning with Grandpa?" Christine asked, sitting across from him.

Dan and Mike stood a few feet away deciding it best to let his mom get the conversation started, rather than pepper Charlie with a bunch of questions.

"Good," Charlie said. "This is like Uncle Mike's truck."

"It sure looks like it. Uncle Mike said you were talking to somebody before. Who was it?"

"I don't know," Charlie replied, never picking his eyes off the truck.

"He said it was a woman, but he never saw her

The Diner

before," Mike whispered to Dan.

"Is she still here?" Christine asked impatiently.

"Nope. I'm hungry. Can I have a grilled cheese?"

"Sure." Christine looked over at Dan, who looked back at Carlos. Carlos went into the kitchen. "What did the woman say?"

"She said I was cute. That I looked like you. And that they'll be here soon. She had a funny laugh."

"What do you mean a funny laugh?"

"Like a witch."

"Was she mean to you?" Christine asked, unable to hide the edge in her voice.

Dan and Mike approached the table.

Charlie shook his head. Then his eyes lit up as Mike sat down beside him.

"So are you telling your mom about that lady you were talking to? Can you remember what she looked like?"

"Yeah. Can I go play in your truck?"

"Maybe tomorrow. You can help me run a few errands if it's okay with your mom."

"Can I, Mom?"

"We'll see. Tell us what the woman looked like."

"She was old. Then she was young. She had a funny laugh. It was scary," Charlie said, never once pulling his eyes away from the toy truck.

Christine and Mike looked straight at Dan. He shrugged his shoulders and then raised his hand to pause them from launching a volley of questions at the youngster.

"Hey, Charlie. Tell me what made her look old and what made her look young?"

"Her hair. First it was white, then brown. And her

307

face looked pretty. I'm hungry."

"Carlos will be out in a minute with your grilled cheese. Do you remember anything else she said?"

"Nope."

"One super grilled cheese for our best customer. Here you go, pal," Carlos said, setting the plate down in front of Charlie.

"What do you say?" Christine said.

"Thank you," Charlie mumbled with his mouth full.

"Charlie, you eat your sandwich. I'm going to talk with Dan and Uncle Mike."

"Let's talk in the kitchen. The lunch crowd is starting to come in, and we don't need any of them hearing this. Carlos," Dan said, nodding his head at Charlie.

"I'll keep an eye on him. Everyone will," Carlos said smiling as people started walking in for lunch. All the regulars stopped to say hi to Charlie and coax a high-five from him.

"What do you think?" Christine asked.

"He definitely saw something," Dan replied. "Damn."

"But what?" Mike asked, as they all moved in closer together.

"I don't know. The laugh. We hadn't heard it in months. Now it's back. I think Charlie's right."

"About what, that she'll be here soon?" Mike interrupted.

"Yeah. And he said 'they'll' be here soon," Dan added.

"But when?" Christine said, looking around the kitchen at nothing particular, until her eyes fell on a

The Diner

bright light creeping out from behind the refrigerator that blocked the entrance to the path of the portal. She took a couple slow steps toward the light, not waiting for anyone to reply. Dan and Mike followed her with their eyes.

"What is that?" Dan asked.

"Can you feel it? It's getting damn cold around here and the door of the refrigerator is shut. Look at my arms. All the hair is standing up. It's energy."

"Not good energy. I've felt this before," Christine said. "Dan, this isn't good."

The refrigerator began to shake and shudder. The lights in the kitchen flickered then dimmed for a few seconds, then came back on. The three of them looked at each other and then around the kitchen. The other employees in the kitchen went about their business as if nothing happened.

"Don't they see it?" Mike asked. Dan shrugged his shoulders.

"Charlie," Christine shouted and made a dash for the swinging doors, with Dan and Mike on her heels.

The three of them stopped cold in their tracks when they looked over at Charlie sitting at table one. He wasn't alone. A young couple was sitting with Charlie and talking like they were long lost friends. Charlie giggled as he continued to gnaw at the grilled cheese in one hand and scooted his truck across the table with the other.

"Dan, it's her," Christine said as her voice cracked.

"Who?" Mike asked.

Dan didn't move. He kept his eyes focused on table one. "Stay here," he said sternly. "I'm going to go talk with them."

309

"But…," Christine started to say.

"No. You stay here. If it is her, we can't take any chance that she'll put you in some sort of trance. I'll send Charlie over to you," Dan said already walking toward the table. Mike put one arm around Christine's shoulders to hold her still and to comfort her. His other hand balled up into a fist.

"Hi, folks," Dan said, not yet looking into the couple's eyes. "Hey, Charlie, take your sandwich and truck over there to your mom and Uncle Mike. You can sit at the counter. Have Carlos make you his famous chocolate soda."

"Yay!" Charlie replied and ran over to his mom. Christine bent down immediately and wrapped her arms around him nearly knocking the sandwich and truck from his hands. Mike directed them toward the counter, further away from table one.

Dan stood at the edge of the table and looked down on the couple. The man was neatly dressed in what appeared to be a custom, finely tailored shirt with the initials "DEG" monogrammed on each cuff. Exquisite gold and diamond cuff links completed the look. He was clean shaven, with his hair looking recently cut. Everything about the man said money. Everything in his eyes said evil. The woman was equally elegantly put together and looked eerily familiar. Dan figured that they were both roughly the same age, possibly in their late twenties or early thirties. However there was something about the woman that made her look older and far more experienced. He wasn't sure what it was, her eyes, the occasional wrinkle that seemed to appear then fade, or the way she styled her brown hair.

Damn, it is her. The brown hair.

The Diner

"What's he doing? He's just standing there," Mike whispered to Christine who had one hand on Charlie while her eyes scoured the diner. Everything about the diner looked normal as the customers went about eating and ordering. The waitresses flitted about as they would on any normal Sunday.

"I don't know, but you know him. He manages to take control of every conversation," Christine replied, suddenly looking down at the ground. "Do you feel that?"

"The cold air? Yeah. It came in from the kitchen. What the hell is going on?"

"Who's that, Mommy?" Charlie asked. "Do they work here too?"

"Who honey?"

"The men behind you and Uncle Mike."

Mike and Christine looked behind them.

"Shit. What are you guys doing here?" Mike said.

"We're here for the kid. But we can't stay long," Milt replied, with Bob Radke standing by his side.

"Welcome to our diner. What can we get for you folks?" Dan asked the couple quite insincerely. The man never diverted his eyes from Christine and Charlie. The woman let out an all too familiar sound of laughter that sent Dan's stomach turning and his heart racing. Milt and Bob reacted to the sound of her laughter, floating higher above the floor, hovering like two Army helicopters ready to attack. The once carefree energy in the diner turned into palpable tension. Dan wasn't going to have it.

"Christine, whatever you do, do not leave Charlie's side. Keep your hand on him at all times. Milt and Bob, can you take a few more with you? Emil and Ansel

311

could use some friends," Mike said.

"Gladly," Bob replied. "We'll need to build a little more energy though. Do what you need to do, and we'll take it from there." He and Milt disappeared.

Mike moved slowly out from behind the counter. The eyes of the man at the table one never followed him, they stayed glued on Charlie. Mike continued moving out of view as the frigid air trailed behind him.

Dan sat down opposite of the couple, firmly staring them both down as his heart nearly beat through his chest. The moment felt odd and somewhat overdue. It was like he was prepared for it ever since he slammed Dorothy's body hard against the wall. She had never gone away. The occasional laughter that echoed from her empty soul and followed him and Christine around proved it. Where it had gone for the past six months was meaningless because she was now sitting across from him.

"I wish I could say it was good to see you again, Dorothy, but I can't. You're not welcome here," Dan said.

"Is that any way to do business, my friend," the young man said, sitting straight up in the booth, but with his eyes still fixed on Charlie.

"It's my business and I'll conduct it as I see fit. And I'm not your friend."

"Oh, but we will be, just like our ancestors were. Allow me to introduce myself. My name is David Ernest Gardner. Of course you know my wife, Dorothy. My father apparently had difficulty getting you to see his point of view. I can assure you Mr. Scheffelin that will not be a problem between you and me. You see my father's dark side is nothing compared to the hell I can

The Diner

create for you and your new family. Perhaps you'd like to see an example of that right now. Yes, I think that would prove most useful. That's a fine boy over there," David Gardner said as he raised his hand in the direction of Charlie. Dorothy closed her eyes and began to chant. The diner instantly grew darker and started vibrate as if hit by an earthquake.

"No!" Dan shouted.

Before he could leap up, Mike sprang over the next booth and slammed Gardner's head against the table. They wrestled and bounced off the window, nearly shattering it. Dorothy's eyes remained shut and her chanting grew louder. The pressure in the diner became intense as the energy seemed to drain from it and funnel into her. Dan looked around his refurbished diner, all sparkling and new, wishing he could turn back the clock to a simpler time, to the day his grandfather opened the place. The hatred for Gardner couldn't get any higher. What he did to his parents, the town, and the diner would never be forgotten. If he could, he'd change the course of the diner's history and the town. Looking down at the table he saw a piece of that history, a place setting as old, if not older than the diner itself. Hearing Charlie scream out in pain, the anger and hatred spewed out of every pore. He grabbed the tarnished steel knife off the table and lunged at Dorothy and with all his force, plunged the dull knife as deep as he could into her chest. They both fell to the ground in a heap.

"Dan!" Christine cried out, as she held onto Charlie.

"Milt...Bob...Now get us out of here," Mike shouted as felt his strength drain as Gardner began to gain control.

"You can't touch him," Milt shouted. "You need to break free."

"Fuck that. Take us both…Do it!" Mike screamed. "God damn…take this devil and me."

"No!" Christine shouted out.

"Mommy…my head," Charlie cried out.

Mike was losing the battle. The diner grew darker, even darker by the counter. Plates and cups began flying off the shelf pelting Christine and Carlos.

"Milt…What the hell are you waiting for? This is my fucking town… and these are…"

Bob moved first. Milt saw no other choice or the town would be back to where it was under Ernest Gardner. Milt and Bob swarmed around Mike and the young Gardner, collapsing around them. The diner began to lighten up. The huddled mass of spirits and bodies began to hum and form into a glowing, translucent sphere. The brighter it grew, the smaller it became. In seconds it was the size of a basketball, a glowing white hot vapor with a dark center. It hovered in the air for a few seconds, then shot up toward the light above the entrance and disappeared through the portal. The light and energy in the diner quickly returned to normal.

Christine picked up Charlie and ran over to Dan who was convulsing on the ground as he lay on top of Dorothy. Carlos was already at Dan's side, not sure what to do as guttural sounds spewed from the pair of bodies.

"Dan," Christine cried, kneeling down beside him. She was surrounded by everyone in the diner. Some were shaking their heads as if it was expected, others

The Diner

stood in shock. Christine pulled at Dan's shoulders trying to pull him off, but the electricity that ran through her arms was too much.

"We have to get him off her," Christine cried.

"C'mon, together…we can do it," Carlos said, hoping he was right.

"Mommy, is Dan sick? I don't like this. Can we go home?" Charlie cried.

Carlos and Christine put their hands under Dan's chest. They could feel the warmth of the blood that soaked his shirt. Their arms ached as it felt like they were being electrocuted. "Now!" Christine shouted out. With all their strength and determination, they pried Dan off Dorothy sending him rolling to the floor. He quit shaking, but Dorothy's body continued to convulse with a silver knife protruding from her heart. Then she let out a deep groan as her body began to age. She went from twenty-something to a frail hundred-year-old or more woman in seconds.

Christine rushed around to pull Dan's limp body to her chest. At that moment, Dorothy released a tired gasp and stopped moving. Her head fell lifeless to the side. Dan's eyes flashed open, as he pushed himself off the ground ready to fight whatever was before him.

"What the hell was that?" Dan said. Then he saw Dorothy's aged body on the ground. "Where's Gardner?"

Christine didn't say word. She wrapped her arms around Dan's neck. Charlie ran to them crying. Dan wrapped his arms around both of them and held on tight.

Carlos shook his arms out as the pain finally began to subside. "Damn, look at that," he said pointing to

315

Dorothy's body.

Her body had continued to age and then decay. In only a few minutes her body had turned to a pile of gray and black dust.

Everyone stood in silence. Carlos pulled a tablecloth off a table and laid it over the remains, attempting to restore some sense of order.

"Where's Gardner?" Dan asked again, looking around the diner. "And where's Mike?"

"Mommy, where's Uncle Mike?" Charlie asked again.

Christine fought back the tears. "Mike took Gardner…They're with Milt and Bob…I don't know…"

"No! Son of a…" Dan's head fell to his chest as the tears streamed down his face.

Dan stood dazed in the middle of the diner, like a statue. Christine took him and Charlie by the hand and led them back to the diner counter. She got Charlie some apple juice which seemed to soothe him. Dan collapsed on the stool, the same stool he had observed his parents' memorial service from. Christine threw an apron over his shirt to hide the blood stains. Looking out across the diner, emotionlessly he whispered under his breath, "God damn this diner and town. God damn."

As if nothing had happened, people continue to file in the diner for lunch. Carlos shook his head in amazement, as he and James, the busboy, cleaned up the diner, making it look like nothing more than a tray of dishes had been spilt. Rob Sanders and John McQueen walked in and headed straight for the diner counter.

"Hey there, Dan. How goes it?" John said. "The

The Diner

place looks great, but you look like crap. What were you doing, butchering a cow back there? Ha ha."

"Yeah," Rob added. "He's right; you do look awful. But you did it, Dan. There's something about this place and this town, especially today. It feels so alive. What are you going to have, John?"

"The usual. Right, Dan? Why change a good thing?"

Mourning the death of his good friend ate him up inside. He wanted to run. He wanted to be alone. At least he thought he did until he saw Charlie's sad face looking up at him.

"Are you still sick, Dan? Mommy, is Dan better?" Charlie asked placing his small hand on Dan's hand. The warmth and energy of the child's hand shot through Dan like nothing he had felt before.

"Yeah, kid," Dan said, thinking of Mike. "I'm good. What say you and I take Uncle Mike's truck back to our house and we go fishing?"

"Can I, Mom?"

Christine nodded, drying the tears that streamed down her face. Dan looked down at Charlie who now looked like the happiest four year-old in the world, seemingly forgetting what he just experienced.

Life through the eyes of an innocent child…amazing.

As he got up, he looked over at table one. It was now occupied by a couple and their young daughter who were laughing and thoroughly enjoying the diner as they pointed at various items on the menu, discussing what they'd have. The diner was alive and full of conversation. Laughter seemed to dominate every conversation. People waved across the tables, got up, and joined others at their table. If they looked up and saw Dan, they waved and smiled.

Dan lifted his body off the stool and looked through the windows of the diner. For the first time that he could remember, traffic was backing up in Circle Lake. The town was coming alive.

Thanks, Mike.

It took all of Dan's strength to stem the flow of tears.

"So Dan, are you going to get our lunch or have Ray mess it up?" John joked.

"I got it. A couple of special grilled cheese sandwiches coming right up."

A word about the author…

From a very young age, Dean Michael Zadak has experienced paranormal phenomena from ghostly encounters to eerie psychic connections. Never intimidated, he's channeled these experiences into dynamic, page turning stories. He's often sought out by family and friends to see if he can "make a connection" with a loved one who has passed on. These experiences have provided the inspiration for his debut novel, *Painted From Memory* and *The Diner*.

Dean spends his days in the corporate world as a Sales Director, released his first novel in 2014, and has been published in various magazines sharing a humorous viewpoint on life, music, and Crossfit. As an avid Crossfit athlete who qualifies for the Master's age bracket, he's seen enough to know that life can always use more laughter, plus it's required for a lifetime Chicago Cubs fan. Dean lives in Hawthorn Woods, Illinois, with his wife, Kathy.

http://www.deanmichaelzadak.com

Thank you for purchasing
this publication of The Wild Rose Press, Inc.

If you enjoyed the story, we would appreciate your
letting others know by leaving a review.

For other wonderful stories,
please visit our on-line bookstore at
www.thewildrosepress.com.

For questions or more information
contact us at
info@thewildrosepress.com.

The Wild Rose Press, Inc.
www.thewildrosepress.com

Stay current with The Wild Rose Press, Inc.

Like us on Facebook

https://www.facebook.com/TheWildRosePress

And Follow us on Twitter
https://twitter.com/WildRosePress

Made in the USA
Lexington, KY
12 August 2016